Ventura could not think what to do next. If it was discovered that Lord Lynke's page was a girl disguised as a boy, it would discredit him at court and make him an outcast.

She could not even admit to her true feelings for the haughty Englishman. Their stations in life were too far apart. Dona Alcira had wealth and position to offer him, but what had she ... except her love?

And if Dona Alcira should make another attempt to dispose of her, how could she protect herself? She must make a decision. There was no time to be lost.

Also in Pyramid Books

by

BARBARA CARTLAND

DESIRE OF THE HEART
A HAZARD OF HEARTS
THE COIN OF LOVE
LOVE IN HIDING
THE ENCHANTING EVIL
THE UNPREDICTABLE BRIDE
THE SECRET HEART
A DUEL OF HEARTS
LOVE IS THE ENEMY
THE HIDDEN HEART
LOVE TO THE RESCUE
LOVE HOLDS THE CARDS
LOVE LOST
LOVE IS CONTRABAND
LOVE ME FOREVER
THE INNOCENT HEIRESS
DEBT OF HONOR

SWEET ADVENTURE

Barbara Cartland

▲ PYRAMID BOOKS • NEW YORK

To my son Ian

Who showed me some of the beauty
and history of Spain

SWEET ADVENTURE

A PYRAMID BOOK

Pyramid edition published November 1970

© Barbara Cartland 1957

Printed in the United States of America

PYRAMID BOOKS are published by Pyramid Publications
A Division of The Walter Reade Organization, Inc.
444 Madison Avenue, New York, New York 10022, U.S.A.

1

Lord Lynke was in a vile temper as he stepped ashore at San Sebastian. Irritably he waved aside the suggestion of the captain that he should hire a coach until his own was disembarked and strode off alone in search of the inn, which he was already convinced in his mind would be quite insupportable.

The ground seemed to be heaving and rocking beneath his feet, which was not surprising after the tempest they had encountered in the Bay of Biscay. Lord Lynke himself had not been unduly perturbed by the storm. He was an excellent sailor and believed firmly that the most queasy stomach could be settled by a glass of the best cognac. This belief was, however, of little comfort to his staff, who either were not able to obtain the best cognac or found the remedy singularly inefficacious.

They had been prostrated one by one, while Lord Lynke cursed them for their weakness and even found a certain exciting exhilaration in the fact that the captain prophesied that another twenty-four hours of such weather would result in the ship being split in two.

Three days late, but they had reached San Sebastian safely. Safely, that was, as far as the ship and Lord Lynke were concerned. But there were several casualties. Two men had been lost overboard in the storm, one of them his personal servant. His secretary, whom he also counted as a friend, had broken his leg.

To complete the catastrophes, the very day before they sighted the coast of Spain, Lord Lynke's page had an accident. He had been an incredible nuisance during the whole voyage and he had fallen from the rigging, which he had been forbidden to climb, and fractured his skull. He was lying now in a darkened cabin, and arrangements were being made to carry him, with his lordship's secretary, back on the return journey.

'The devil take the lot of them!' Lord Lynke muttered as he strode down the roughly cobbled street, ignoring the glances of admiration and astonishment with which he was watched by the native population.

There was no doubt that he was an exceedingly fine figure of a man in his full-skirted velvet coat and long gold-threaded brocade waistcoat. His lace cravat and powdered hair caught back with a black ribbon were in pleasing contrast to his handsome sunburnt face. His sword hilt, appearing through the side pleats of his coat, glittered golden in the sunshine.

A woman leaning from a window shouted a word of greeting and when he did not answer her, cried aloud that her heart was broken. There was a little ripple of laughter from the passers-by. Hugo Lynke hardly heard them. He was deep in his own thoughts and blinded by rage at the circumstances that had made things so difficult for him.

It was bad enough, he thought, to be in this accursed country, let alone without the comforts and companionship to which he was entitled.

He strode away from the quay up a long, narrow street which led towards the town. The spring sun, warm and golden, seemed to bring out the colour of the old bricks, the mellowed roofs, the gay glimpses of colour that could be seen through the barred windows. The sky above was blue. Even the puddles in the street seemed to take on something of the hue of the Madonna's Robe.

The road was still heaving a little beneath Lord Lynke's feet. The sea had been worse than he had ever remembered it in the whole of his life, and yet there was some satisfaction in knowing that he had experienced it and survived unscathed.

He remembered the accident which had deprived him of Anthony Clayton, his secretary, and cursed. The journey was going to be a dead bore without anyone in whom he could confide. What was more, he was going to cut a pretty poor figure at the Court of Madrid, arriving unattended save for his coachmen, grooms and only a partially trained valet. He had thought to cut a dash with his coach, his horses, his secretary acting the part of an aide-de-camp, and his titled page.

He cursed again at the thought of it. Little Roderick Lane was a baronet besides being an extremely intelligent boy. It had been, Lord Lynke thought, a stroke of genius to bring him on this trip.

It had been difficult to persuade his mother to permit Roderick to leave Eton, where he had already gained a name for himself as being exceptionally clever. Lord Lynke had had several talks with him and decided he was just the type of lad he wanted for a page, but there was more to it than that. Roderick could speak Spanish.

Lord Lynke had confided his ideas only to Anthony Clayton.

'You and I can speak the lingo passably well, Tony,' he had said. 'That is to be expected. And anyhow, everyone will be very careful in front of us. But a page is someone they will take at face value—an unintelligent English boy, chosen for his parentage. They will never for a moment suspect that he understands their language. At any rate, the servants will talk freely in front of him.'

'You are taking this whole project quite seriously,' Anthony Clayton had said with a smile.

Lord Lynke had shrugged his shoulders petulantly.

'What else can I do?' he asked.

No, indeed, he thought now as he walked scowling in the sunlight. There was nothing else for him to do but accept the unavoidable.

An old donkey, heavily laden, came unexpectedly round a corner. Its burden was so large that Lord Lynke was forced to step from the roadway on to the narrow stone pavement. As he did so, from the other corner of the street a small figure collided with him with all the force of a cannon-ball. Though the culprit was small the impact was violent and quite painful.

'Socorro, señor! Socorro!' a shrill, frightened voice cried. For a moment two dirty hands clung to his blue velvet coat, and then, with incredible speed, the boy—for Lord Lynke could see now it was a small, dirty boy—stepped behind him as if for protection, as round the corner there appeared an angry man brandishing a stick.

'Come here, you spawn of the devil,' the man cried in Spanish. 'Don't think you can escape me this time. I swear I'll give you a beating that will break every bone in your demon-infested body.'

The man spoke with a vehemence which seemed to make every word infinitely menacing. He was an ugly customer and there was no doubt from the way he brandished his stick that he meant every word he said.

Lord Lynke felt two hands tugging at his coat-tails.

'Socorro, señor! Socorro!'

He was about to shake himself free, thinking that this was none of his business and he did not in the least wish

7

to be implicated in a local brawl, when the man brandishing the stick said impatiently:

'Out of my way, *señor*.'

This was an insult which Lord Lynke was not prepared to tolerate.

'Are you speaking to me, my good man?' he said in somewhat scholarly Spanish.

'Who else, *señor*?' the man inquired insolently. 'That there accursed urchin sheltering behind you deserves a thrashing and, Mother of God, he's going to have it.'

He advanced a step nearer while Lord Lynke stood looking at him. They were of the same height and their eyes met, one pair dark and smouldering with anger, the other cool, grey, unexpectedly steel-like.

The silence was broken by the Spaniard.

'The boy is a thief and a liar,' he said. 'I pay him money to clean the back of my shop. He wastes his time and steals from me.'

'It is not true,' a little voice said from behind Lord Lynke. 'I stole nothing. I only ate an apple that he had thrown away. It was too rotten to sell.'

'Pah! He spews up lies,' the Spaniard said disgustedly. 'He would twist the Gospels themselves. My stick will teach him the truth.'

He made a movement as if to dive behind Lord Lynke and snatch the boy sheltering there, but a quick twist of his lordship's body prevented him.

Hugo Lynke did not know why he had become the champion of the dirty child clinging to his coat. He only knew that he disliked the attitude of the blustering man facing him. He had always detested bullies and the Spaniard was undoubtedly nothing more or less than a bully of the first water.

He put his hand in his pocket.

'*Aguarde un momento*,' he said. 'This has gone far enough. I will pay for what the boy has stolen. How much is it?'

The man's eyes glinted greedily at the sight of the coins.

'At least five *pesetas*' worth of goods, *señor*. But the time he has wasted come to far more.'

'I will pay you merely for the goods that he has stolen,' Lord Lynke said slowly. 'And you are not to beat him— not today at any rate.'

He selected a coin carefully from those that lay on his palm. The Spaniard watched him curiously.

8

'And why should you do this, *señor*? What should it matter to you if the boy is beaten today or tomorrow?'

'It does not matter, I suppose,' Lord Lynke answered. 'Say that I am English and I do not care for cruelty either to children or animals.'

He flicked a five *peseta* piece into the air as he spoke. It spun for a moment in the sunshine and fell into the gutter. The man bent down to grovel for it.

Lord Lynke walked on. He had gone quite a number of steps before he heard a voice behind him say:

'Thank you, sir! Thank you very much!'

He spun round in astonishment. The words had been spoken in English.

He found himself looking at the small, incredibly dirty boy. His feet were bare, his clothes were nothing but rags, his hands and face appeared to be black with soot.

'I am exceedingly grateful, sir!' the boy said in a quiet, cultured voice.

His face was thin almost to emaciation, the bones standing out sharp and clear as if the skin was stretched taut across them. It was difficult to see his features for dirt. But one thing at any rate was astonishing. The eyes looking up at Lord Lynke were blue, deep blue, as blue as the sea he had just left behind.

'Who are you?'

'My name, sir, is . . . Venturo.'

'Then how do you speak English?'

'My father was a Scotsman.'

'Was?' Lord Lynke queried. 'He is dead?'

'Yes, sir, he is dead.'

'And your mother, I suppose, was Spanish?'

'That is right, sir.'

'A nice combination. It is understandable now why you should speak two languages.'

Lord Lynke felt in his pocket again and produced a slightly larger coin than the one he had given to the bullying Spaniard.

'Here, boy. Buy yourself something to eat,' he said. 'And next time you steal don't get caught.'

He held out the coin and a thin, incredibly slender hand came out to take it. Lord Lynke, who was just about to turn away, put yet another question.

'Your father, he was a seafaring man I suppose?'

He had visions as he spoke of the smiles on the sailors' faces as the ship had finally reached the port. He knew

9

they were thinking of what they would find ashore. Wine and women—and after a long voyage the latter were inevitably the most important.

He wondered if this wretched boy was the result of some gay evening ashore. Then he heard the boy's answer.

'No, sir, my father was a gentleman.'

It was such a surprising reply that Hugo Lynke found himself staring at the boy, not only in astonishment but with curiosity. The child, for he was nothing more, put up his hand, wiped his face and brushed back the hair that was flopping over his forehead, still damp from the urgency of his dash for safety.

Yes, Lord Lynke thought, the boy was probably telling the truth. There was, indeed, evidence of breeding in that well-shaped brow as well as in the long, thin fingers and the proud carriage of his head.

'Who was your father?' he asked.

The boy's eyes flickered and looked away from him.

'He was a follower of England's rightful king, sir.'

'A Jacobite!' Lord Lynke ejaculated.

This, of course, accounted for it. The man would have been one of the followers of the Old Pretender; one of the many Scots who were exiled eighteen years ago after the attempted rebellion of 1719, when the Spanish ships landed three hundred soldiers near Kintail in Ross-shire. He remembered hearing about it when he was a boy, and people still talked of how the Spaniards had brought arms for two thousand and captured Doran Castle.

This child's father would have been just about the right age to have taken part in that ill-fated attempt to put James Stuart on the throne.

'You say your father is dead?' he said aloud.

'Yes, sir. He died three years ago.'

'Your mother?'

'She is also dead. Six months ago she was knocked down by a coach and died from the injuries she received.'

The deep blue eyes clouded and just for a moment there was a suspicion of tears in them. Then with an effort, as if the boy told himself he must be a man and not show his emotion, his chin went up and he said:

'Now they are together in heaven.'

'Let us hope so,' Lord Lynke said solemnly. 'And what are you doing?

'I am looking after myself,' the boy replied.

'Not very successfully it seems,' Lord Lynke said. He

glanced down the road where the Spaniard had disappeared from sight. 'If you take my advice, you will look for another job.'

'I shall do that, sir,' the boy replied.

'Well, the best of luck to you,' Lord Lynke smiled.

He felt in his waistcoat pocket for a gold piece. It was the least he could do, he thought, for the son of a countryman. And even as he took it from his pocket a sudden thought came to him. It was such an outrageous idea that for a moment he could hardly bring himself to put it into words. Yet the more he thought about it, the more it made sense.

Here was a boy who could speak both Spanish and English. His Spanish was certainly better than that of poor Roderick Lane, lying aboard the *Sea Hawk*, while his English, and doubtless his manners, would be very inferior. Yet the result was about equal, and the most important thing was that he was in need of a page.

He put the gold piece back in his pocket.

'Listen,' he said. 'I believe I could offer you a job. Would you come with me to Madrid?'

'What as?'

The question was asked coolly and contemplatively, with none of the excitement or enthusiasm which Lord Lynke had expected from such a suggestion.

Deliberately he pretended to be in doubt. He made a little gesture with his hand.

'I have no idea,' he said. 'Perhaps as scullion to my chef, when I engage one; perhaps as a stable boy. Would either of those situations appeal to you?'

There was irony in his voice, thinking, as he spoke, there was something amusing in the fact that he should be offering a position to this ragged urchin and that the boy apparently wished it clearly defined before he accepted.

There was a little bow from the dark head, then Venturo's chin went up even higher than before.

'I thank you, sir, for your kind suggestion, but I do not wait on servants.'

It was said with so much pride and so much dignity that instinctively, but with difficulty, Lord Lynke repressed the laughter which rose to his lips.

'I understand,' he said courteously. 'And I regret I made such a mistake. The position I am offering you is that of my page.'

Even as he said it he thought he must be mad. And yet

11

quickly came the thought to his mind that if the boy was hopeless he could sack him long before he got to Madrid.

'Your personal page?'

The small, insistent voice intruded on his thoughts.

'My personal page,' he repeated.

'In which case, sir, I am delighted to accept your offer.'

Lord Lynke stared down at the child, and then he said abruptly:

'Your duties commence immediately. Show me the way to the best inn. There is one I suppose?'

El Gallo de Ora is the best, sir, and you will find it just at the end of the street. Before I come to you, will you permit me to make my farewells to my friends and to ... tidy myself?'

' "Clean" is the right word,' Lord Lynke corrected.

'I know, sir. The man for whom I worked insisted that I should scrape out his furnaces every morning. It was dirty work, but, although you may not believe it, I did what he told me.'

'You certainly look as if you tried,' Lord Lynke said. 'Very well. Cut along and make your farewells. You can meet me at the inn in an hour's time.'

He turned to go, but again he was delayed.

'I regret to trouble you, sir. But there are two things I must say. First, as your page I shall need suitable clothes. Secondly, may I know your name?'

Lord Lynke smiled.

'Intensely practical I see. We should deal well together. With regard to clothes, you can instruct the best tailor in the town to attend me at the inn at the same time as you yourself meet me there. But so that you shall not be ashamed, buy yourself something to wear until he can fit you up.'

Two gold coins passed from hand to hand.

'And now, as regards my name,' he went on. 'It is Lynke—Lord Lynke of Hatharton Castle in Sussex.'

The boy bowed.

'I thank you, my lord. I will attend you in an hour's time.'

There was a flash as if a piece of quicksilver sped across the street, and then Lord Lynke found himself alone except for the curious eyes of passers-by and those who were eternally watching from behind the window-panes.

He stood for a moment irresolute and then shrugged his shoulders.

12

'Either I have lost a couple of the best,' he said to himself, 'or I have found myself a new page.'

The boy was obviously of gentle birth. He would be undoubtedly in need of training, but what an opportunity to find out things which otherwise would remain secret! If he was clever enough to act the part of an English boy, to conceal from everyone the fact that he could speak Spanish, there was so much that might be learned, so much that might be discovered.

At the same time, there was always the chance that having received two gold pieces he would never be seen again. Yet somehow Lord Lynke thought he would keep his word.

'My father was a gentleman.' There had been both pride and a kind of arrogance in his voice as he had said it, and in his 'I do not wait on servants.'

What cheek! And yet somehow he liked the little devil for having the guts to say it. It was hard to be choosy when one was hungry, and Lord Lynke was quite certain that Venturo had been very hungry on many occasions. He had seen that particular look before and there was no mistaking it.

It was not far to *El Gallo de Oro* and Lord Lynke entered to find that if it was not luxurious, it was at least clean and welcoming. A private room was put at his disposal and the landlord undertook at once to send porters to the ship to tell the sailors where to bring his lordship's trunks. The stables at the back of the inn were quite passable; and though Lord Lynke knew his coachman would look at them askance, he anticipated that his horses would experience worse accommodation before they reached Madrid.

He ordered dinner and then commanded that a bottle of wine should be sent to his stting-room immediately.

'*Pronto, Excellency! Pronto!*' the proprietor said, bowing and scraping and well pleased with the thought that such a distinguished guest with well-lined pockets should patronise his inn.

'A boy will be asking for me in an hour's time,' Lord Lynke said. 'See that he is shown in here.'

'*Si, si, Excellency!*'

'He may also be accompanied by a tailor and I wish to see him as well.'

'*Si, si, Excellency!*'

If the landlord was surprised, he did not show it. He

13

was used to the vagaries and peculiarities of the aristocracy. He hurried away with suggestions for the chef and to get the key of the cellars, which lay deep beneath the building.

Lord Lynke stretched his legs out in front of the log fire. How boring this was, he thought. He was already filled with foreboding of how uncomfortable, how incredibly dull the journey to Madrid was to be. And even when he reached the capital there was not much to look forward to.

He muttered a sudden oath, and then told himself it was no use kicking against the pricks. He had brought it on his own head, although that was poor consolation.

He could see his uncle now—the Duke of Newcastle, Secretary of State for Foreign Affairs—saying in his prim, precise voice:

'I am ashamed of you, Hugo.'

'I cannot see why,' he had answered, wondering as he spoke how much the old boy knew and having a nasty, uneasy foreboding of what was to come.

'I am both ashamed and distressed,' the Duke repeated.

'Perhaps you will enlighten me as to the reason for such disturbance, my lord.'

'I think you know the reason as well as I do,' the Duke had replied. 'I sent for you immediately after an interview with Lord Rustington.'

The blow had fallen! Lord Lynke knew that he had expected it. He hoped, however, that he did not betray, by even a flicker of an eyelid, what the name meant to him.

'Lord Rustington,' the Duke went on impressively, 'has discovered all.'

'I hope not!'

The reply was irrepressible and it had the effect of making the Duke look even more pious and even more precise.

'Hugo! You are the son of my favourite sister. I have done my best for you. I have endeavoured, since your poor father's death, to guide and help you. I have failed lamentably. That is obvious both by your way of living and by the shocking, indeed, horrifying, revelations that Lord Rustington made this day.'

'I am grieved if my behaviour distresses you,' Lord Lynke said. 'But I would remind you, Uncle, that I am no longer a boy. In fact I am very nearly a middle-aged man, and as such I consider that I am entitled to behave as I wish.'

The Duke of Newcastle sighed.

'At twenty-nine years of age, my dear Hugo, you are making the same mistake that many other foolish people have made. We are none of us permitted to do as we wish. We have our responsibilities, not only to other people but also to our country.'

'Our country, sir?'

'Yes, Hugo, our country. A scandal at this moment would do a great deal of harm to the Monarchy.'

'I had not thought of that,' Lord Lynke said involuntarily.

'That is what I imagined,' the Duke said drily. 'But unfortunately Lady Rustington is a Lady of the Bedchamber to Her Majesty. It was in that consideration and for that reason only that Lord Rustington came to see me rather than settling the matter himself, either by a duel or by divorce.'

'Divorce!'

Lord Lynke looked startled.

'Yes, divorce. It would require an Act of Parliament, but a man whose wife behaved as Lady Rustington has done might well consider that such an irrevocable action was essential.'

'Poor Charlotte!' Lord Lynke murmured. 'But I would, of course, stand by her.'

The Duke of Newcastle looked slightly incredulous.

'You will perhaps forgive me if I remind you, my dear Hugo, that you have not stood by the other ladies whom you involved in similar and most distasteful scandals. There was, if I remember right, Lady Winslow, that pretty Mrs. Fitzgerald, Lady Margaret . . .'

Lord Lynke held out his hand.

'All right, Uncle. Spare me, I beg of you, the list of my indiscretions. But Lady Rustington is different. I . . . I love her.'

The Duke permitted himself a pained smile.

'Love is a word which has many meanings. I have always been quite convinced, Hugo, that you love nobody except yourself. I would also remind you that Lady Rustington is ten years older than you; and, what is more, she is not, as you appear confidently to expect, anxious to spend the rest of her life in your company. She has, in fact, begged her husband, on her knees, to forgive her.'

15

Lord Lynke's face darkened.

'He must have driven her to it then. Charlotte would, I am convinced, rather die than kotow to that stuck-up, whited sepulchre who calls himself her husband.'

'Nevertheless she has done so,' the Duke said sharply, 'and the position is that Lord Rustington, most generously I must say, has agreed to forget this very reprehensible episode on one condition.'

'He wants his pound of flesh, of course,' Lord Lynke said. 'Edward Rustington is a nefarious, grasping . . .'

The Duke of Newcastle raised his hand.

'Thank you, Hugo. Your opinion of Lord Rustington is quite unnecessary. He has, in this matter, behaved extremely well.'

'But his condition is . . . ?' Lord Lynke prompted.

'That you should go abroad immediately.'

'And that I refuse,' Lord Lynke said. 'I am engaged at Newmarket next week. I have two horses running and some very high stakes are involved. If Rustington thinks he is going to drive me away, he is very much mistaken.'

'I am afraid you have no choice in the matter,' the Duke said drily. 'I have already accepted Lord Rustington's conditions on your behalf.'

'The devil you have!' Lord Lynke exclaimed.

'Yes, Hugo, I have,' the Duke answered. 'I have worked all my life for one thing, for the preservation of England's greatness abroad and for the preservation of peace at home. At this moment we cannot afford a scandal in Court circles. The Young Pretender Prince Charles Stuart, is just across the Channel awaiting his opportunity. The people are restless, the King is worried.'

'Not without reason,' Lord Lynke murmured. 'A lot of people wish that Charles Stuart was on the throne.'

The Duke ignored him.

'Lord Rustington's conditions are therefore something which concerns not only you and his wife, but the whole British constitution.'

'You make me sound damned important,' Lord Lynke said.

'You are important only so far as I cannot allow you to make a disturbance at this particular moment. I have therefore arranged for you to go to Spain.'

'To Spain!' Lord Lynke ejaculated. 'Now, why Spain? A country of which I know nothing although you made me learn the curst language when I was at school.'

'A very wise precaution,' the Duke said. 'I believed that foreign languages would prove useful at some time in your life. I see I was not mistaken.'

The Duke crossed the room to his desk and picked up some papers.

'There are two reasons why you are to go to Spain,' he went on. 'First, because the Queen of Spain, Elizabeth Farnese, made the suggestion a short while ago that a marriage between the King's ward, Doña Alcira, and an Englishman might be to the advantage of both countries. The suggestion was ignored at the time simply because no one quite understood her motive for making such a suggestion. And, also because there was no one particularly suitable whom we could suggest as a bridegroom.'

'And now you think that I am suitable?' Lord Lynke asked.

'On the contrary, I think you are most unsuitable,' the Duke said coldly. 'But if you go to Spain as an aspirant for Doña Alcira's hand, it will certainly give you the *entrée* into Royal and diplomatic circles.'

'As a reluctant bridegroom!' Lord Lynke said drily. 'Not a very attractive mission; and surely the punishment exceeds the crime?'

'The punishment, as you put it, may not be so very arduous as you imagine,' the Duke answered. 'Doña Alcira is the daughter of the late Duke of Carcastillo. She was married when she was very young to the Count of Talavera. He was killed shortly after their marriage when he was out hunting. Doña Alcira has inherited not only his estates, which were quite considerable, but also those of her father. She is one of the wealthiest women in Spain, and reputedly one of the most beautiful.'

'And you really think that I would marry a woman not loving her?' Lord Lynke inquired.

The Duke of Newcastle brought his hand down with what was almost a blow of violence on his desk.

'Love! Love! You keep on harping on love, Hugo. How many women have you loved in the past year? In the past five years? In the past ten years since you left Eton? I dare swear that you will have difficulty in remembering half of them. Do you call that love? You lust after a woman for a short while. You imagine you are giving her your heart.'

The Duke sniffed derisively——

'When you see Doña Alcira, you will doubtless imagine

17

that you love her. Anyway, you will pretend to love her so that you can control the vast estates of the Dukes of Carcastillo in Spain as well as your own very considerable estates here in England. That is an order, not only from me but from His Majesty.'

'From His Majesty? From the King?'

Lord Lynke looked astonished.

'From the King. I have discussed the matter with him and with the Prime Minister. They both give their approval.'

'So it has gone as far as that?'

'Most certainly.'

'But can Spain really want this?'

'That, Hugo, is the most intelligent question you have asked so far,' his uncle said. 'We have no real idea as to why Elizabeth Farnese made the suggestion in the first place, unless it was yet another bid for Gibraltar. We have always got to remember what is at the back of her mind—the return of Gibraltar to Spain. We will never relinquish it—never!'

Again the Duke brought down his clenched fist on the desk——

'And another thing. The Spanish Government has struggled incessantly since the peace of Utrecht to evade the performance of their commercial engagements. They have employed every artifice to obstruct our trade in America. We find that wherever there are Spaniards there are troubles in the West Indian ports and officers who obstruct our lawful business.'

'Well, what am I supposed to do about that?' Lord Lynke asked.

'Quite a lot,' the Duke replied. 'Sir Benjamin Keene, our Minister in Madrid, has written frequently asking for help, begging me to send out men whom he would trust to assist him in finding out what is going on beneath the veneer of pleasantry and peace. He is quite sure that something is afoot, but in his position it is very difficult to discover what it is.

'That can be your job, Hugo. A little clever espionage, which will be easy because no one will suspect you as being in the least interested in anything except love.'

The Duke spoke sarcastically. Lord Lynke threw back his head and laughed.

'Really Uncle! I have never heard such a preposterous school-boyish plot in the whole of my life,' he said. 'If you

18

imagine for one moment I shall be of the slightest use to you in such exploits, you must be demented. And if you imagine that I am likely to marry this swarthy-skinned heiress, you are also very much mistaken.'

The Duke rose to his feet. His eyes were cold; his long, thin nose seemed to register disapproval.

'I am afraid, Hugo,' he said slowly, 'you have no alternative. One of our trading ships, the *Sea Hawk*, will be waiting for you in Southampton Harbour a week from today. You can take with you what servants you wish. You will be treated with every courtesy, offered every facility while travelling abroad. You will be a distinguished visitor to a friendly country with introductions from myself as the Secretary of State, and from Mr. Walpole as Prime Minister.'

'It sounds very attractive,' Lord Lynke said mockingly. 'But . . .'

'There is no "but",' the Duke of Newcastle interrupted. 'If you do not agree, you will be shanghaied; and when you recover consciousness with an extremely aching head, you will find yourself aboard a ship heading for Canada.'

'You really mean that?' Lord Lynke asked incredulously.

'I really mean it,' the Duke of Newcastle repeated. 'You see, Hugo, it is a choice between you and England—and I have chosen England.'

Staring into the flames of the log fire in front of him, Hugo Lynke could see his uncle's face as he said the last words.

'I have chosen England.'

The Duke was not very imaginative. He would never really be a great man. History would doubtless forget him and make small mention of his talents. And yet to him his country meant everything. More than wife and children and family; more even than himself.

For the first time in his life Hugo Lynke felt a kind of affection for the man who had tried to play the very difficult part of guardian over his wildness and irresponsibility.

'Dammit!' he said aloud. 'A dark-eyed heiress who will doubtless hate me as much as I hate her.'

His head sank forward a little despondently on his chest as he thought of his horses at Newmarket, his friends

19

gathered round the gaming tables, the pretty women who would miss him in all the gay spots of St. James's.

He felt a sudden sinking of his spirits. Spain, dark-eyed *señoritas*, castanets and bullfights. He hated the lot of them already.

He had a sudden vision of Charlotte, her fair hair streaming over her shoulders as she put her arms around his neck. He could see her red lips quivering, the sudden tumultuous rise and fall of her breasts.

Was it love that he felt for her? He asked himself the question and had a sudden nostalgia for England, for the world that he knew, for his friends, their conversation and laughter, for soft, tender moments with women like Charlotte who were so much a part of his life.

He knew he was as homesick as any schoolboy; and then through the darkness of his thoughts came a proud little voice saying:

'I do not wait on servants.'

He chuckled unexpectedly. Even Spain might have its lighter moments.

2

Señor Padilla bowed his customer to the door and turned towards the over-crowded counter. The floor was dirty, the beamed ceiling grey with cobwebs, but the *delicatessen* which was piled high in every corner of the tiny shop was of good quality.

Señor Padilla was fat and lazy, but he could select a sausage or purchase a ham with a keen eye which saw through the outer skin of the article into its very heart. He could detect a flavour where his competitors least expected it. He could persuade the farmers to bring him butter made of the choicest cream, and eggs which had really been laid that morning.

He waddled across the shop now, wiping his hands on his apron and contemplating with a faint sense of satisfaction that it was near his dinner time.

The door of the inner room opened. A small, rather dirty face peered into the shop.

'Señor Padilla,' a voice said in an excited whisper.

'Is that you, Venturo?' he asked loudly.

'Quick, *señor*, I must speak to you.'

Señor Padilla advanced to where his thin, disagreeable wife sat adding up the accounts.

'I will not be a moment, my dear,' he said mildly.

His wife did not even acknowledge that he had spoken to her, but the end of her thin nose quivered a little as if in anger.

Señor Padilla coaxed his large stomach through the gap in the counter, edged his way sideways along the narrow space behind it and pushed open the door of the inner room.

In the centre of the room a small figure appeared to be dancing with excitement.

'*Señor, señor!* What do you think has happened?'

'What, indeed?' Señor Padilla inquired.

In answer an open palm was extended to him on which reposed two gold coins. Señor Padilla stared at them as if he could hardly believe his eyes.

'Mother of God!' he ejaculated at last. 'Where did you get them? You have not . . . you have not . . .'

'No I have not stolen them,' he was interrupted. 'I am ashamed of you, *señor*, for having such suspicions of me.'

'Then where, where could you have got them?' the *señor* inquired. 'You have not. . . . No, you cannot have . . .'

He stammered over the word and in answer he received a little laugh of sheer, unbridled amusement.

'No, *señor*.'

'I do not believe it,' Señor Padilla thundered. 'What would your sainted mother, God rest her soul, have said? And your father, may he be free from purgatory. It is hard to be poor, but it is a sin to save the body at the expense of the soul.'

There was sincerity in the *señor*'s dark eyes peering between the bags of flesh, and in his voice, which seemed to come from the depths of his great wobbling body.

The ragged boy put out a hand and laid it on his arm.

'I promise you, *señor*, that I have done nothing that I would be ashamed for my father or my mother to know. But I will not tease you any longer. I have a job, a new job. This money was given me by my employer, an English milord who has just arrived in the town.'

'But how will you serve him?' the *señor* asked.

21

The boy bowed from the waist, dark hair flopping untidily around the small, smiling face.

'Behold his lordship's page.'

'Page! Page! What is this?' Señor Padilla asked. 'Do you imagine for one moment that he will not discover? That he will not guess? Stupid child! You may deceive the ordinary people for whom you work, the beggars you pass in the street, the customers who come to my shop and who are not interested in ragged, dirty boys. But if you are to be a page to a gentleman who is perceptive, who has some knowledge of the world, he will not be deceived for even one moment. Bah! It is ridiculous to think of it.'

As he spoke, his voice booming round the tiny, untidy room where the packing cases were kept, it seemed as if all the joy and elation steadily drained away from the small figure in front of him. And yet, when he had finished, the dark head was turned away from him and a voice said, with something suspiciously like a sob:

'You are wrong, quite wrong. He will not discover.'

'He is bound to,' Señor Padilla insisted. 'Venturo ... no ... Señorita Ventura, listen to me. I love you. I have tried to help you, though indeed there was little I could do. I have known you since you were a little baby, since your mother brought you here first in her arms to buy some special delicacy with which to tempt your father.'

He wiped his eyes, and there was a sob in his voice as he continued:

' "Look at my little Ventura," she said to me then. "I have given her that name because she will bring us good luck! Do you not think so, *señor*?" I can see her face now, so soft, so eager that I should reassure her. "Yes, she will be very lucky, *señora*," I answered.'

'That was untrue. I did not bring them luck,' a small voice said. There was no doubt now that it was broken with tears.

'That is a lie,' Señor Padilla said heavily. 'You brought them happiness, great happiness because they had you. It was not your fault that your father's cough got worse, that he could not stand the cold of the winter. It was not your fault that your mother, God bless her, should have been taken into the arms of Heaven many years before her time.'

The small figure suddenly straightened itself.

'But this chance is lucky for me,' she said defiantly. 'I know it. And why should the English lord discover about

22

me? He will not be very interested in his page. I shall be in attendance upon him and because a gentleman's page is of noble birth I shall not have to sleep with the servants.'

'And if he discovers, what then?' Señor Padilla inquired. There was a smile once again on Ventura's face.

'By then,' she said lightly, 'I shall be in Madrid. It was where my mother told me to go. Perhaps once I am there I shall find out why.'

'It is a risk,' Señor Padilla said doubtfully.

'A risk of what?' Ventura inquired. 'If I remain here, I must go on working for that swine of a fruiterer. Today he tried to beat me. That was how I met the English lord. I ran to him for protection and he saved me.'

'Tried to beat you, indeed. By the Rope of Mary, I will beat him if he lays so much as a finger upon you.'

Ventura put out her hand and laid it on his arm.

'No, no,' she said. 'You must not quarrel on my behalf. Besides, why should you interfere between a badly behaved boy and his master?'

'You should not have gone there in the first place,' Señor Padilla cried. 'Ah, *señorita*! I have failed bitterly in the task I set myself of looking after you.'

Ventura smiled.

'You are not to blame yourself,' she said gently. 'You saved me from the orphanage where your wife would have sent me. You have allowed me to creep into your warehouse at night and you have given me food when no one was looking. No one could have done more. I am eternally in your debt.'

'No, no! I should have stood up to Maria. I should have told her that I was taking you into our house. But . . .' the *señor* shrugged his shoulders. 'She would not have understood. If you had really been a boy, it would have been different. But a girl, and a very pretty girl, no, Maria would not countenance it.'

'I can understand her feelings, *señor*. Such a good husband as you does not grow on every orange tree.'

Ventura spoke solemnly, but there was a twinkle in her blue eyes, a twitch of her lips. Then she was serious again.

'But, *señor*, we must not stand here talking. I have so much to do. This money is to purchase clothes for me to wear when I attend milord at *El Gallo de Oro*. I am to take with me also the best tailor in San Sebastian.'

Ventura pressed the two gold coins in Señor Padilla's fat hand.

'Hurry, *señor*,' she said. 'Go to Pedro across the street and ask him to give you the velvet suit he has made for the younger son of the Marqués de Gamilla.'

'Do you think that Pedro will let me have it?' Señor Padilla asked.

'If you show him the money, he will beg you to take it,' Ventura answered. 'The *Marqués*, has not paid his bill for nearly two years. Pedro grudges every stitch that he puts into the suit. He can make another for the Marqués, but today the gold can be his.'

'I will go and ask him,' Señor promised obediently.

'I dare not go myself,' Ventura said. 'If I show him the coins, he will imagine I have stolen them. But wait! Tell him I also want for the money the shoes of the son of Don Ferdinand on which he was sewing velvet bows. They fit me and, though I would prefer shoes with silver buckles, I must, for the moment take what I can get.'

'Anything else your lordship requires?' Señor Padilla asked ironically.

'Yes, a pair of stockings. Pedro has some in the shop. Tell him to give you a pair.'

'I am but a servant to obey your commands,' Señor Padilla said and waddled away.

Ventura laughed and ran through the door at the back of the outer room into the yard outside. Here there was a pump, and standing under it in the sunshine she pumped the water over her hair and face, gasping a little from the coldness of it, rubbing herself clean regardless of the fact that her ragged clothes were soaked.

She washed herself for several minutes, and then, diving through the door of the warehouse beyond, she climbed up a rickety ladder to an attic which was the only place she had to call her home.

There was a straw palliasse covered with two blankets, and a rug. There was also some furniture—a broken and cracked chest-of-drawers, a cheap unpolished *prie-dieu* arranged before a small crucifix which hung on the rough, unplastered wall. These were Ventura's sole possessions.

She pulled off her sodden rags and picking up a towel dried herself. Then she looked in a drawer for clean underclothes, choosing the plainest and least feminine of those she possessed.

She heard a whistle from below and looking down the ladder saw that Señor Padilla had just come in through the warehouse door.

'You have them?' she asked excitedly.

'I have them,' he answered. 'He did not wish to part with the suit, but the sight of the money was too much for him. Besides, I lied and said it was for a good patron who would patronise him in the future and would always pay cash.'

'Poor Pedro,' Ventura laughed. 'I knew he would be unable to resist such blandishments; his rent falls due at the end of the week.'

'You know too much,' Señor Padilla murmured beneath his breath, but aloud he said: 'The clothes are here. What shall I do with them?'

Ventura kneeled down on the floor and reached her hand down the ladder. Señor Padilla had only to mount two steps so that she could take from him the parcel he held in his hands.

'Thank you, *señor*,' she smiled. 'Now wait for me in the inner room.'

He had reached the door before she called him back.

'We have forgotten something,' she said. 'I cannot take Pedro with me to the English milord. He will be suspicious. I shall have to take Minito. He is a better tailor, but not such a nice man.'

'You wish me to run half-way across the town to Minito's shop?' Señor Padilla demanded.

'No, no,' Ventura answered. 'There is sure to be a boy hanging about the street who will wish to earn two *pesetas*. Send him running for Minito and one day I will pay you back.'

'One day!'

Señor Padilla laughed scornfully, but he went away as if he intended to do Ventura's bidding.

She scrambled to her feet and opened the parcel. The suit of deep blue velvet had been finished. The silver buttons were in place; the waistcoat of paler blue satin was a dream of elegance.

It took Ventura only a few minutes to dress herself. As she had anticipated, the suit, made for a boy of eleven, fitted her almost exactly. The shoes, which she had tried on once when Pedro had set her the task of cleaning out his shop, felt heavy, but were otherwise comfortable. The stockings which encased her thin legs were, she considered, too coarse, but that could be remedied later.

There was a small looking glass on top of the chest-of-drawers. She looked in it and then brushed her hair back

25

from her forehead. She wished now she had not cut it so short. Her long hair had reached her waist and been much admired. She was dark, as her mother had been, and yet there was some hint of her father's red head in that there were fiery lights beneath the sombre darkness. One was not always aware of them and then a sudden turn of the head, a glint of sunshine or a flicker of the flames from the fire, and they were very apparent.

From her drawer Ventura selected a ribbon. She tied the short ends of her hair back with a bow at the nape of her neck. Now she was ready.

She looked round at her belongings—the straw palliasse on which she had slept for the past six months; the *prie-dieu* at which she had prayed incessantly. Her prayers had been answered. She was to escape from the life of misery, from the hunger, from the loneliness. It might not be for long. If she were discovered, she would have to come back again. But at least she would have a few days, perhaps weeks, of escape.

She dropped for a moment on her knees, crossed herself and prayed. Then she picked up a box which lay on the top of the chest-of-drawers. It was an elaborate box, carved and inlaid with mother-of-pearl and with a monogram set in seed pearls. There was a heavy lock and the key was of gold.

It was something which would have fetched quite a considerable sum of money in the town. But it had belonged to Ventura's mother.

'You must never part with this, Ventura,' she had said more than once. 'You understand? This must be kept whatever else must go.'

She had said that after Ventura's father had died and they had been forced to sell up the little house in which they had lived and move into one room in a shabby, dirty street. But some of their possessions had gone with them.

And then after her mother's death Ventura had sold everything but the chest-of-drawers and the *prie-dieu* for which no one would make an offer. More than once she had been tempted to part with the jewel-case. Sometimes at night when hunger kept her awake and her body ached with the labour she had been forced to do during the day, she would wonder whether she was not being silly to cling to a useless *objet d'art* which would have belonged to some leisured, luxurious young woman.

And then her mother's words would come back to her

26

and she would know that, however much she wanted the money, she would not sell. Everything else had gone bit by bit; even her mother's clothes had fetched a few coins. But still the jewel-case remained.

Ventura looked down at it. She would take it with her to Madrid. Perhaps it would bring her luck just to have it with her. Perhaps there she would discover what her mother had meant by her dying words.

Even as she thought of them Ventura could see again that terrible moment in the market-place when the Conte d'Ardisa's horses had got out of control and galloped wildly through the stalls, overturning the tables, scattering everything in every direction.

No one knew what had frightened them. One moment all was peace and the busy chatter of voices bargaining, coaxing and tempting the passers-by. The next minute pandemonium broke forth. A man was knocked down first; and then, as people scattered in all directions, Ventura, who had been looking at some books in the pedlar's tray, saw the horses bearing down upon her mother.

She had no time to shriek, hardly time to breathe, before the hoofs struck her mother on the back as she turned to flee, and flung her to the ground. The wheels of the carriage passed over her.

Ventura had to fight her way through a crowd to reach her mother's side. Only as she knelt to lift her head did her mother open her eyes and her pale lips moved with difficulty.

'Go . . . to . . . Madrid,' she murmured in a voice so low and broken that Ventura could hardly catch the words. 'Take . . . the letters . . . to . . .'

She gave a little convulsive shiver and then suddenly her head fell back and she was still. Her lips were still parted as if the word that she had been about to say had actually died with her.

At first Ventura had been too dazed with grief to think of anything but that her mother was gone and that she was utterly alone. And then she had pulled herself together and begun to look for the letters.

What letters? And where could her mother have hidden them? She searched everywhere in the room. They were not to be found.

What then had her mother meant? Ventura had no idea. Her mother had never spoken of Madrid, except

27

sometimes to tell her gay stories of the *fiestas* that she had seen when she was young.

It was only when she was alone that Ventura began to realise how very little she knew about her mother. With the unquestioning faith of a child she had accepted her parents without curiosity, without asking about their past. She had known that her father was a rebel and he had talked incessantly of his home in Scotland and of his devotion to the Stuart cause.

Of her mother's past she knew nothing. She did not even know what had been her maiden name.

On an impulse Ventura crossed the room and took down the crucifix from the battered wall. She slipped it into the jewel-case. That, she told herself, was a more valuable jewel than anything it had ever carried before. And yet, woman-like, she wished for a necklace of diamonds, for sparkling rings and bracelets set with precious stones.

She gave a little shrug of her shoulders as she remembered that these things were never likely to be hers; and then, proceeding carefully so as not to spoil the spendour of her velvet suit, she climbed down the rickety ladder on to the floor of the warehouse.

Señor Padilla was waiting for her in the inner room. He gave a great shout of exclamation as she appeared, clapping his fat hands together.

'It is magnificent!' he said. 'Stupendous! Indeed, you look the perfect gentleman. I should not have known you, *señorita.*'

Ventura put up a finger and laid on his lips.

'Hush!' she said. 'No one must know. News travels fast in this town. There would be someone only too willing to tell milord or his servants that I am not what I appear. What did you do about Minito?'

'I told the boy that there was an important commission for him at *El Gallo de Oro*. I told him that if he wanted to make clothes for a nobleman as important as the King himself, he was to be there in twenty minutes' time.' Señor Padilla chuckled. 'Minito is a greedy man. He will be there.'

'That was clever of you,' Ventura smiled. 'I thought after I had said it, it was a mistake for him to come here or for him to see me with you. He must not connect us in any way.'

'Do not trouble your little head,' Señor Padilla said.

28

'Minito will think only of the gold. He is a man whose head is permanently in his cash-box.'

Ventura laughed and then was solemn again as she said:

'And now, *señor*, I must say good-bye.'

'God go with you, my child,' he answered. 'I shall think of you often. Perhaps one day you will return.'

'I will write to you,' Ventura promised. 'I know you cannot read, but take my letters to the priest, not to anyone else, it might not be safe.'

'I will pray for you, too,' Señor Padilla said, and now there were tears in his eyes and one trickled over his fat cheeks. 'Good-bye, little Ventura! I have not done for you all that I might have done because I am such a cowardly man. Yes, I am afraid of my wife. I, who am big and strong, am afraid of that skinny little woman with the long nose. Had it not been so, you would have been brought up as my own child. You would not have had to demean yourself as you have done.'

'You have done all it was possible for you to do,' Ventura said quietly.

She took his hand in hers and laid her soft cheek against it.

'Bless you, *señor*, for being a kind man,' she said. 'I shall never forget you. Guard my little treasures well. One day I will come back for them.'

She straightened herself and once again there was a twinkle in her eye.

'Perhaps sooner than either of us anticipate,' she said, and added: 'If I am discovered, I may not even leave San Sebastian.'

'Why should they discover you?' Señor Padilla asked. 'You look a very fine figure of a man.'

'That is what I tell myself,' Ventura replied. '*Adiós, señor.*'

'*Adiós*, Señor Venturo,' was the reply. 'The saints guide your feet.'

Holding her jewel-box under her arm, Ventura slipped out of the large double doors which led into the court-yard. She looked quickly up and down the street to see if there was anyone in sight and then walked with a swagger down the narrow lanes which led into the main street. Here she walked quickly along, taking no notice of the curious glances of the passers-by and ignoring one or two ribald remarks that were called after her by some cheeky children.

She reached the inn and only then did she feel a sudden apprehension and fear within herself. She was starting off on a new life. It was exciting, but she was not such a fool as to underestimate the danger of what she did.

She knew nothing about her new employer save what he had told her. And yet she had liked the look of him. It was not only his handsome, rather dissolute looks, it was not only the swagger and gallantry of him, it was something else—something which she had often found sadly lacking in her own countrymen.

Was it determination? Was it belief in his own importance? She was not sure. But as man to man she felt she could trust him. As a woman she could not be so sure.

'Today I am a man,' Ventura told herself; and tucking her jewel-box a little more securely under her arm, she opened the door of the inn and walked in.

She hesitated for a moment as to which way to go. She had never been inside *El Gallo de Oro* before and she was not quite certain what to expect.

There were a certain number of men sitting about at small tables, drinking. There was an atmosphere of tobacco smoke mixed with the aroma of cooking coming through an open door beyond the fireplace.

As Ventura stood irresolute, a man who she realised must be the proprietor hurried forward.

'You require a seat, *señor?*'

'I am here at the order of Lord Lynke,' she replied. 'I understand he is a guest in your establishment.'

'Milord is in a private room,' the proprietor said. 'If you will come this way.'

Ventura followed him, but not before she had heard one of the men at the table make some bawdy remark about boys being too pretty nowadays.

It gave her a sense of satisfaction to realise that she was being accepted entirely at her face value; and swaggering a little, she followed the proprietor down the dark passage. He flung open the door of a small room.

Lord Lynke was sitting with his feet out in front of the fire. He looked up lazily as Ventura entered. Then he stared at her blankly until she said hesitantly:

'I have . . . come, m'lord, as you commanded.'

'Good God! I didn't recognise you.'

Lord Lynke sat up in the chair and stared at her.

'Are you really the ragamuffin I encountered on the street a short time ago? I'd almost forgotten about you, and I certainly should not have recognised you.'

'Clothes make a great difference, m'lord.'

'So that's how you spent my money! Well, it's certainly a success.'

'The tailor is here, Excellency,' the proprietor said from the door. 'He told me that he had a message to attend an illustrious patron at my inn. When he said that, I was certain it was Your Excellency who had commanded his presence here.'

'Tell him to come in,' Lord Lynke said.

'At once, Excellency.'

The proprietor shut the door behind him. Lord Lynke continued to stare at Ventura.

'I could not have believed it possible,' he said. 'Well, you will certainly play the part well—at least, I hope so.'

'What part, m'lord?'

'I will tell you after we have seen the tailor,' Lord Lynke said. 'Damnation! Must I bother with the chap? You can tell him what you require.'

Ventura hesitated.

'I am not quite certain, m'lord, what sort of dress your page should wear for more formal occasions.'

'No, of course you wouldn't know that. Why should you?' Lord Lynke said.

The door opened and the proprietor said:

'The tailor, Excellency,'

Minito came into the room. He was a small, ferrety little man with shifty eyes and an unpleasant habit of swallowing his words. He invariably smarmed over those who could afford to pay and was insolent to those who could not. At the same time, he was a good tailor and he grasped in a few seconds what was expected of him.

'I shall be here for two days, two days only. Do you understand?' Lord Lynke said. 'If the suits are not ready by then, they will be left behind and not paid for.'

'I understand. It is my privilege to obey Your Excellency's commands. I promise you that they shall be fulfilled.'

'Very good. That will be all.'

Lord Lynke dismissed him with an airy wave of the hand. Ventura, who had been standing in the centre of the room while she was being measured, came nearer the fire.

'You can sit down,' Lord Lynke said.

'Thank you, m'lord. I am afraid there are many things

you will have to tell me,' Ventura said. 'When I sit without your invitation; when I remain in your company and when I leave. I will try to remember everything you tell me, but at first it will not be easy.'

As she spoke the last words, she felt her voice going faint. To her horror she felt the room receding from her. She shut her eyes to open them again with a tremendous effort. Everything seemed to be swimming round her.

'I am . . . sorry, m'lord,' she said faintly. 'Perhaps . . . it is the heat . . . of the room.'

Lord Lynke got to his feet and poured out a glass of wine from the flagon that stood beside him and held it to her lips.

'Drink this,' he said.

Ventura felt the wine burn down her throat and the faintness recede.

'I am . . . sorry, m'lord,' she stammered.

'It is all right,' Lord Lynke answered. 'When did you last eat?'

'I . . . I had some . . . breakfast,' Ventura answered.

'And not much I bargain,' he said.

He reached out his hand and pulled the bell. They could hear it echoing away somewhere in the depths of the inn. The proprietor came running.

'Food,' his lordship commanded. 'Beef, ham, eggs, anything you have ready at this moment. My page is hungry and so am I.'

'Your dinner, Excellency, cannot be ready for another half-hour at least.'

'Am I talking about dinner?' Lord Lynke inquired. 'I said food, any sort of food; whatever you have ready. Cold or hot, it does not matter.'

The proprietor hurried away.

'I am sorry,' Ventura said again.

Lord Lynke stood looking down at her peaked face, the skin so pale that it was in almost violent contrast to the deep blue of her coat. He noticed, too, the blue veins of her hands, now spotlessly clean, but unnaturally thin, the long fingers seeming little more than bones covered with skin.

'Until we arrive in Madrid you will eat with me,' he said. 'I shall see if we cannot put some colour into your face, some flesh on your bones. A boy of your age ought to be able to play games, but I doubt if you would stand anything strenuous. How old are you, by the way?'

32

'Fifteen,' Ventura said quickly.

She decided that that was about the right age. Anything younger would seem irresponsible and it would be impossible for him to believe that she was older.

'I am very small for my age,' she added apologetically.

I should think you are. Young Roderick, who was coming with me, was double your size and he is about the same age.'

'I am strong, though,' Ventura said.

'I hope so. I have the greatest dislike of illness, especially in those who serve me.'

Lord Lynke spoke indifferently. Ventura, glancing up at him, thought that he could be hard, almost brutal, at times. She watched his face. It was the face of a man who had not found life particularly satisfying, she thought, and wondered in what form his particular disillusionment lay.

She had seen the same expression on her father's face at times; and whenever it appeared, she had known that he was yearning for the land that he had left, for his friends, for his kith and kin, for the cause for which he had sacrificed his freedom.

'Will you tell me now the part I have to play?' she asked.

'I have been thinking about it, wondering how I could best explain to you,' Lord Lynke replied.

He hesitated and looked down at the fire.

'I wonder, with your mixed ancestry, to whom you feel you owe allegiance. To Spain, because your mother was a Spaniard? To Britain, because your father was British?'

'He thought of himself only as a Scot,' Ventura corrected.

'And yet if I am not mistaken he thought that everyone outside the British Isles was a foreigner,' Lord Lynke said.

Ventura laughed.

'That is true. How did you know? When he was angry with anyone, he used to say: "What is the use of trying to make these foreigners understand?" '

'I was sure that he would say that,' Lord Lynke said. 'Well, you will answer my question.'

'I do not know,' Ventura said. 'All the people I have known have been Spaniards with the exception of my father. It is here that I have always lived, here I have felt that I belonged.'

'And yet in reality you are British,' Lord Lynke said.

33

'You could have a British passport; you are your father's child, you bear his name.'

'I have often thought of Scotland,' Ventura said in a quiet voice. 'My father talked of it so much that sometimes I feel as if I had been there. I think, as you say, my allegiance should be with Britain, even though it exiled my father to a foreign land.'

She smiled as she spoke, yet at the same time there was something wistful in her words.

Lord Lynke said:

'I am not asking you to fight against the Spaniards. I am only asking you to act a role which it should not be hard for you to play.'

'What is it?' Ventura inquired.

'I want you to pretend that as my page you can speak only English. You speak so well and so fluently that it will not be at all difficult for people to believe that I brought you, as I brought Roderick Lane, from England.'

Lord Lynke paused, then continued slowly as if he was choosing his words with care:

'I want you to pretend that you know no word of Spanish whatsoever. That means that you have got to think in English, that you have got to be ready even at the most unexpected moments, when you are startled, surprised, astonished, to ejaculate or to exclaim only in English. Your Spanish must be forgotten. But I wish you to listen to what is going on; and when I am not there, when people say things which you think are important, to tell me what they have said. Is that clear?'

'Quite clear,' Ventura said. 'Except how should I know whether the things that they say are important to you or not?'

Lord Lynke glanced at her as if he approved her shrewdness.

'That, of course, is something I must explain,' he replied. 'And what I am saying to you is obviously only in confidence.'

'But of course!' Ventura said.

They were interrupted at this moment by the proprietor returning to the room with a tray laden with cold meats, with freshly cooked lobster, with crisp bread fresh from the oven, and a huge pat of yellow butter. He set the food out on a table by the fire and despite her resolution to behave with the utmost propriety Ventura could not help her eyes going towards the dishes. It was years since she had seen such a spread. In fact she wondered if she had ever seen so much food in one place before.

'Eat!' Lord Lynke commanded.

She tried to walk slowly towards the chair which had been set at the table. Despite every resolution her feet hurried. She tried to cut the bread deliberately, to spread the butter as if she had all the time in the world. But she found herself thrusting the buttered bread into her mouth, her teeth crunching on it ravenously.

Then, with a sense of horror, she remembered her manners.

'But you, m'lord,' she said. 'What will you have?'

She felt the blood rushing into her cheeks at the thought that she had been so gauche, so ill-mannered, as not to remember him first.

'Go on, boy,' Lord Lynke replied kindly. 'I shall wait for my dinner. I am not in the least hungry.'

'It was unpardonable of me to start without asking you your choice,' Ventura said humbly.

'I can understand it,' Lord Lynke replied. 'I have been hungry once or twice in my life, but never starving to the point of exhaustion. Eat and we can talk afterwards.'

It was a quarter of an hour later before Ventura found that she could eat no more. The ham, the cold chicken, the lobster had all tasted like ambrosia. She had drunk, too, a little of the wine which Lord Lynke had poured out for her, and now at his command she took the glass in her hand and joined him again nearer the fire.

'I feel I shall never be hungry again,' she told him.

He laughed at that.

'You will,' he said. 'Boys have an insatiable appetite for food. I remember when I was at Eton thinking it was a pity there ever had to be an interval between meals. Yet now I have to be tempted to eat and even the most excellent dish will find me curiously indifferent to it.'

'Please go on with what you were saying, m'lord. You were telling me why you require a page who can act as a spy.'

Lord Lynke looked at her sharply.

'I did not say a spy,' he said.

'But that is what you meant, wasn't it?' Ventura asked.

It might have been the wine or may be the food which had given her the courage to say what she thought. She was no longer so afraid of doing the wrong thing.

'All right, if you prefer to use harsh words,' Lord Lynke

said. 'You are to spy for me. It will be of great assistance in the very delicate mission I have to perform in Madrid.'

'Which is?' Ventura asked.

Lord Lynke hesitated.

'To betroth myself to the prettiest and richest woman in Spain,' he said lightly.

Ventura felt curiously disappointed. Somehow she had expected something else, something which vitally concerned either Britain or Spain. She wondered if Lord Lynke was telling her the truth, and then decided that such a statement was one which could easily be verified and must therefore undoubtedly be the truth.

'Do you know the lady already, m'lord?'

'I have never set eyes on her,' Lord Lynke replied, and yawned as if the subject bored him.

'That is enough for the moment,' he said, rising to his feet. 'We can talk of such things as we journey along.'

He walked across to the table and poured himself out another glass of wine.

'Is there anything to see in this accursed town?'

'There is a bullfight tomorrow,' Ventura replied.

'I am not interested in bullfights.'

'There is a fair outside the town—performing animals, clowns.'

'They would certainly not amuse me,' Lord Lynke sneered.

Ventura cudgelled her brains.

'There is Juanita at the theatre.'

'Juanita?' Lord Lynke queried.

'She is a dancer. She is very famous in this part of the world.'

'That sounds more interesting,' Lord Lynke said. 'Is she pretty?'

'They say that a man who has looked at Juanita is blind to all other women for life,' Ventura answered. 'But I do not think that it is true.'

'I am quite sure it isn't,' Lord Lynke said with a slight twist of the lips. 'Nevertheless, we will go and see her. Beautiful women are an international currency which no one should refuse to handle.'

He tugged at the bell rope.

'Where is my dinner?' he commanded. 'I want it immediately. I am off to see Juanita and I cannot be kept waiting.'

'Ah, Juanita!' The proprietor threw up his hands in

ecstasy. 'She is wonderful! She is beautiful! Milord will be delighted! He will find her so alluring, so beautiful, that ever afterwards he will be blind . . .'

'I know, I know,' Lord Lynke interrupted. 'Get the dinner, and quickly.'

'*Pronto, pronto!*' the proprietor said and hurried from the room.

Lord Lynke looked at Ventura and his eyes were twinkling.

'Tonight, my boy,' he said, 'we will start your education. On a subject which is always important to a man—that of women!'

3

Ventura kept herself awake with an effort. The warmth of the room, the food and the wine that she had drunk made her feel almost uncontrollably sleepy.

She felt it was very long since she had known such contentment—the contentment of being well fed, of not knowing the sharp, uncomfortable pains of hunger, of not feeling cold and alone.

As if in a dream she heard Lord Lynke call for more wine, and thought with a childlike satisfaction of the meal she had just eaten. The *Sopa de Cangrejos* made with the crabs which had been brought alive to the kitchen only an hour before they were eaten; the *Arroz a la Valenciana* which was her favourite dish—chicken mixed with rice, fish, lobster, sausage, pimento, artichoke and green peas.

Ventura told herself with a faint smile that she had made a pig of herself. She did not realise that from the long months of starvation her stomach had shrunk and that actually, to anyone watching her, she had merely pecked at a few mouthfuls and left far more on her plate than she ate.

It had been a satisfaction to realise that she could enjoy her food and not trouble about the other guests at Lord Lynke's table. They had certainly paid no attention to her. For one thing they did not speak English and they had no idea that she spoke their language. For another, they had more important things to think about than a young boy.

Ventura looked to the top of the table where Lord Lynke, a glass of wine in one hand, had his other arm round Juanita's waist. She was leaning her head against his shoulder, staring up passionately into his face, her red lips very close to his.

Something she said made him laugh. He threw back his head, his square chin sharply etched against the dark panelling of the wall behind him.

Ventura felt her lip curl a little. She knew all about Juanita. No one who had lived in San Sebastian had any illusions about the dancer's morals; they had known her too long.

It was popularly supposed that her father had been a gipsy while her mother had been a famous ballerina. The child had been farmed out with foster parents. As soon as she was old enough to stand, she began to dance and there was no question what her future would be.

She had danced at the fair grounds, in inns, at any place where men gathered together and were ready to chuck her a few coins for entertaining them. And then, as she grew older and more beautiful, the manager of the theatre allowed her a short turn at the beginning of the performance before most people had arrived.

She had an instantaneous success and a nobleman who had heard of her fame came to watch her one evening and took her away with him. He was the first of many who were to assist Juanita in her travels.

She danced in Seville, Toledo and Madrid. But always once a year she came back to San Sebastian. Perhaps it was for partly sentimental reasons, but far more likely it was because she had better audiences and collected more money in her home town than anywhere else in Spain.

Ventura had once been to the theatre to watch Juanita dance. She had been impressed, not so much by the actual dancing, but by the extraordinary allure and enticement that Juanita managed to exude from her slim, sensuous body. Child though she was at the time, Ventura had understood why the men in the audience sat with glazed, protruding eyes, moist lips and sweating foreheads as they watched Juanita.

Now, seeing her at close quarters at the end of the table, Ventura thought that the dancer was wearing badly. She was still in her twenties, but the exotic life she led was already taking its toll. There were dark lines under her eyes, an unnatural thinness about her neck, a nervous tension in the incessant gesture of her hands.

It was not that she danced too long or too often, it was because Juanita always turned night into day. There were too many parties in her life, too much wine and far too many lovers. She was greedy, too, greedy for adulation, for money, for the applause which she now believed was her right, however little she did for it.

The other members of the company were obviously in awe of her. Lord Lynke had asked half a dozen of them to supper and now they were sprawling in their chairs, satiated with food and drink and looking for some stimulus to excite their senses.

As if he could bear inaction no longer, a young man with dark hair greased until it shone and a full, petulant red mouth that looked as if it were painted, suddenly sprang to his feet and began to dance. He danced well, clicking with his heels on the wooden floor, imitating the gestures and actions of a bull-fighter, and yet all the time speaking eloquently with his eyes to the pretty, immature girl who was Juanita's understudy.

It was clear to Ventura that the girl was frightened of the attention he was paying her because it might incur the wrath of Juanita. She glanced uneasily over her shoulder, but the dancer was too engrossed with Lord Lynke to pay attention to anything else.

Another man rose a little unsteadily, dragging his dinner partner to her feet, trying to make her perform with him for the amusement of the others.

'We will show them the *flamenco*,' he said; but she pushed him away with a loud, drunken laugh and sat down again at the table.

Ventura rested her chin on her hand and wondered why men and women seemed so stupid when they had had too much to drink. There was something absurd about their unsteadiness, their loose mouths, their befuddled speech. She felt herself yawning and wished she could go to bed.

This was the second night that she had been forced to sit up to the early hours of the morning. The night before when she had taken Lord Lynke to the theatre he had told her that he intended to turn in early.

'We won't be late,' he had said. 'What is the use? There will be little, I anticipate, to keep me awake.'

But after he had seen Juanita he had changed his mind.

He had invited her out to supper and they had sat drinking and making love to each other until it was almost dawn.

Lord Lynke had slept late the next morning, but Ventura had woken early. She was used to being abroad before the rest of the people in the town, and when the sun had come through the window to rest its warm, golden fingers on her face, she had found herself instantly awake.

But now after a long day she longed for her bed. Every muscle in her body seemed to be aching.

'I must grow used to late nights,' she told herself.

She had already gathered from Lord Lynke's conversation that he thought an evening passed without a party was an evening wasted.

'If I were in London tonight,' he had said just before they went to the theatre, 'I should be getting ready for a dinner party at the Duke of Devonshire's. He is giving a ball tonight and I was to dine with his Grace. I should have told myself while I was dressing that it was certain to be a dead bore. I should protest that I had much better make my excuses and go out to some night haunts of my own. But in the end I should go, if only to see all the most beautiful women in England.'

'Are they very beautiful?' Ventura asked.

'Many of them are breath-taking,' Lord Lynke replied solemnly, and then he gave a little angry laugh. 'But what is the point of thinking about them? It is Spanish women we have got to concentrate on now.'

'They, too, can be beautiful,' Ventura said quietly.

'Yesterday I should have argued with you,' Lord Lynke replied. 'But now I have seen Juanita I am inclined to agree there is something in what you say.'

Ventura did not consider Juanita, with her sensuous, serpentine, over-painted and very obvious attractions, was at all a typical Spanish beauty. But she realised instinctively that it was no use saying that to Lord Lynke. So she let the matter drop.

'Cannot he see,' she asked herself now, 'how false she is with her honeyed flattery and her obviously professional arts of enticement?'

She felt a slight pang of disgust as Juanita put her arm round Lord Lynke's neck and drew his head down to hers.

'You are so strong, so handsome,' she was murmuring

in her deep, caressing voice. 'I did not know Englishmen were so attractive.'

'I expect she says that to every man she meets,' Ventura thought sourly. She yawned and felt her eyelids falling over her cheeks.

It was no use. She knew it was impossible for her to keep awake. Hoping no one would notice she crept away from the table and settled herself in a corner of the chimney-piece. The warmth of the fire made her feel even more drowsy and it was a long time before she awoke.

It must have been a log falling in the fire which startled her out of her dreams. Her eyes blinked and opened. She looked across the room to see that everyone had left save Lord Lynke and Juanita. They were both drinking, still sitting closely entwined together; but as Ventura grew more awake she realised that Juanita was arguing with his lordship and for once she was not getting her own way.

'Come,' she said with her eyes half closed. 'We have had enough. It is almost morning. Let us go upstairs. I love you. I love you so much.'

'We'll have another drink first,' Lord Lynke answered and he shouted for the waiter. 'Hi, waiter,' he ordered when the man appeared, 'bring some more wine. What is the use of empty bottles?'

As he spoke he gave the bottle on the table in front of him a push. It fell over, rolled across the table and then crashed to the floor where it shattered into a thousand pieces. Lord Lynke laughed.

'We have had enough,' Juanita said. 'We do not want any more.'

'I want a drink,' Lord Lynke insisted.

'Look at me,' she whispered.

He looked down at her, although for a moment it seemed difficult for him to focus his eyes.

'You are very beautiful,' he said. 'Very beautiful. I want to drink to your beauty.'

'No, no,' Juanita said. 'You do not want to drink. You want to love me. Kiss me. Let me show you what I feel for you.'

Her lips were on his. She pressed herself closer still, her arms entwined around his neck, her head thrown back, her eyes glinting a little as her body moved against him.

'Come. Do not let us stay here any longer.'

'You are very enticing,' he said. 'I wonder what you really feel about me or about any other man. Do they mean anything in your life or are they just something to be bewitched and beguiled by your beauty and then thrown away as soon as you know that they are your slaves?'

'You are different, quite different,' Juanita answered. 'Other men—what do they matter to me? It is you who count, and we are alone here.'

Perhaps it was the word 'alone' which made Ventura make an uncalculated movement, or perhaps it was just an instinctive feeling that she was eavesdropping which led her to make her presence noticed. Whatever it was, the sound she made focused the attention of both Juanita and Lord Lynke upon her. Juanita gave a little cry.

'That child! He should have been in bed long ago.'

'Why yes. I should have thought of it myself,' Lord Lynke ejaculated.

He looked at Ventura and said kindly:

'Go to bed.'

White faced with tiredness, Ventura answered:

'I am ready to attend your lordship should you still need me.'

Lord Lynke smiled.

'I do not need you, you stupid boy. Can you not see that I have other matters on hand?'

He spoke in English and now he added:

'Well, have you learned a little about women? She is beautiful, isn't she? And very desirable.'

'I cannot agree, m'lord.'

Lord Lynke's eyebrows went up.

'What? You disagree with me? On what account? That she is not beautiful or not desirable?'

'It all depends on one's personal taste, I suppose, m'lord,' Ventura replied.

'Then I can assure you,' Lord Lynke said, 'she is very much to my taste. Besides, what else is there in this benighted hole? And for that matter I think I shall ask her to accompany us to Madrid. She will at least lessen the tediousness of the journey.'

Ventura smiled scornfully.

'I am afraid, m'lord, you are already too late. She is leaving at dawn with her company for France, and she has arranged with her lover, a gentleman who was supping at this table tonight, to bundle most of your clothes out of the window to him as soon as you are asleep.'

Lord Lynke stared at Ventura.

'The devil take you, but that's a lie!' he exclaimed.

'Why else is she so anxious to go upstairs?' Ventura inquired.

Juanita put up her hand to touch Lord Lynke's cheek and turned his head towards her.

'Why must you talk with this English boy?' she asked. 'Talk to me. I love you. Let us retire and I will tell you more, much more, of my love.'

'Are you speaking the truth?' Lord Lynke asked Ventura.

'Look at me,' Juanita said, holding back her head. 'Cannot you see the love in my eyes? Cannot you feel it on my lips?'

Lord Lynke looked down at her then raised his head to glance at Ventura.

'Go to bed,' he commanded. 'You are talking nonsense.'

'Certainly, m'lord,' Ventura replied. 'You will find your cravat pin in a little silk purse she wears inside the garter on her right leg.'

Lord Lynke's hand went instinctively to where the diamond and sapphire pin had rested before supper. It was not there and he brought his fist down heavily on the table, making the glasses jump.

'Hell and damnation!' he shouted. 'It is impossible to enjoy anything when you are about.'

Ventura slipped from the room. She was smiling as she went upstairs to her bedchamber. She had not heard Juanita tell her lover that she would throw Lord Lynke's clothes out of the window to him, but she had done that on a former occasion in Seville. The story of how an infatuated nobleman had found himself bereft of everything save his nightshirt had been a piece of gossip that had kept San Sebastian laughing all through one cold winter.

She had, however, seen Juanita slip the diamond pin from Lord Lynke's cravat as she placed her arms around his neck. It had been done cleverly and he had not suspected the movement nor had he noticed when she bent down to adjust her garter.

'What fools men are,' Ventura thought.

She remembered her mother saying once, when her father had been more than usually depressed and homesick:

'Men are like children, Ventura. They never grow up however old they become. They long always for what they cannot get and get bored with what they have. They talk

43

of freedom and are afraid, always, of loneliness. They crave for a home and yet say that marriage puts them in chains. They are children, just children, and more than anything they need us to be constantly in attendance on them.'

Ventura sat down on her narrow bed and wondered if her mother would have considered Lord Lynke a child. He seemed so sure of himself, so arrogant, so impetuous when he wanted something, so disagreeable if anyone stood in his way.

Ventura found the answer to her question. Yes, undoubtedly he was a child, and a very spoilt one.

She wondered what was happening downstairs now she had left. Knowing Lord Lynke, she was quite certain that he would not allow Juanita to steal his cravat pin. He was generous enough when he pleased; but it was obvious to Ventura already that he could be hard and even cruel to anyone who tried to cheat him.

Life with him, she thought, was not going to be easy. At the same time, it was certainly not going to be dull.

She undressed, putting her velvet suit carefully over a chair. Then she undid the ribbon at the back of her neck and let her hair fall softly around her face. She hoped it would soon grow. She felt somehow naked without her long hair which had at one time fallen below her waist.

'I have no time for vanity,' she told her reflection severely in the small, cracked mirror which hung on the wall. 'I am a boy and I have got to think like one.' And yet, womanlike, when she got into bed she could not sleep, tired though she was, for wondering what was happening downstairs.

She thought suddenly that she hated Juanita. There was something about that type of woman which degraded the very sex they represented. Their only use for a man was what they could get out of him. They sold their bodies with charm and beguilement simply because it paid them.

Juanita's deep voice saying, 'I love you,' seemed to echo in Ventura's ears. She felt herself shudder and made a little sound of disgust into her pillow. What did the dancer know of love, real love? Love that meant sacrifice, the giving of oneself rather than just taking and stealing.

There was a sound outside. Ventura held her breath. Someone was coming upstairs. She listened. The footsteps were heavy; there was not even the suspicion of lighter feet accompanying them. Someone walked heavily across the landing. Lord Lynke went into his bedroom and slammed the door.

Ventura gave a little gurgle into the darkness. Juanita would go to France empty handed. It was what she deserved. Ventura chuckled again and then her eyes closed and she fell asleep.

She dreamed strange dreams. She dreamed that she was dancing madly and crazily on a stage made of gold coins, while Lord Lynke seated on a barrel of wine applauded her in time to the music. She danced and danced until she felt herself falling, and then as she fell she awoke.

She opened her eyes to find the sun shining in strongly through the open window. She heard the church bells in the distance and realised it must be nine o'clock. She hurried out of bed with a sense of dismay. In an hour's time they were due to start their journey to Madrid. What would his lordship think of her if she were late?

She poured a jug of cold water into the basin and washed hastily. Then she dressed herself neatly and was just ready when there came a knock on the door.

'The tailor is here,' a voice said outside.

Ventura flung open the door and saw Simon, his lordship's valet, standing there with Minito. The tailor carried the two suits which Lord Lynke had ordered for her.

'*Buenos dias, señor*,' Minito said.

'Good morning,' Ventura replied in English. Then, politeness forgotten, she gave a little cry of delight. 'The suits!' she said to Simon. 'How beautiful they are!'

Minito understood her expression if not her words.

'I am glad you are pleased, *señor*,' he said. 'My brother and I have worked without ceasing but for one hour's sleep a night which we allowed ourselves. But they are finished. Regard the satin vest. Is it not elegant?'

He showed off the waistcoat.

'It is lovely!' Ventura exclaimed. She touched the things on his arm. 'And you have brought the shoes? Shoes?' She touched her feet. 'Stockings?' She touched her legs.

'*Si, si*. Shoes and stockings,' Minito replied. 'But the buckles were expensive. Solid silver. I am afraid lest His Excellency will think them too expensive.'

'I do not understand,' Ventura said. 'How much? The bill, you understand?' She wrote with her finger on her hand.

Minito named a figure which made Ventura's head reel.

45

Then she remembered the money that had been spent on the parties for Juanita. In comparison it seemed quite small.

'Wait here,' she said.

She crossed the landing to rap on Lord Lynke's door.

'Who is it?' he inquired.

'It is I, m'lord,' she answered in English.

'Come in.'

She opened the door and found him partially dressed and seated at a table in the window enjoying his breakfast. He was eating a thick steak with a heartiness which surprised her.

'Good morning, Venturo,' he said. 'Have you breakfasted?'

'Not yet, m'lord. I am afraid I overslept.'

He looked at her darkly.

'The sleep of the just, I suppose,' he said sarcastically.

'I was tired, m'lord.'

'Well, I will spare you any recriminations,' Lord Lynke said. 'But you undoubtedly spoilt my evening.'

Ventura could not help looking towards the dressing-table. There, lying beside a watch and gold signet ring, was the cravat pin, its diamonds sparkling in the sunshine.

'Oh, yes! She had it all right,' Lord Lynke said, following Ventura's eyes. Then suddenly he laughed. 'Dammit! I have been hoist with my own petard. I asked you to spy and you have obeyed my instructions. I cannot blame you, even though last night I was infuriated to find you were speaking the truth.'

'What happened to Juanita?' Ventura asked.

Lord Lynke grinned.

'I sent her off with a flea in her ear. She told me a few home truths before she left. I undoubtedly disappointed her in more ways than one.'

Ventura gave a little giggle and then suddenly they were both laughing.

'Lord, but you should have seen her face when I told her that I knew what she had planned,' Lord Lynke exclaimed. 'And she screamed like a scalded cat when I took the cravat pin from her. If she had carried a stiletto I would undoubtedly have received it in the chest.'

'You will not, I am afraid, have received a very good impression of Spanish women,' Ventura said demurely.

Lord Lynke looked at her sharply.

'If you are being impudent, which I suspect,' he said,

'you will get a very different impression of Englishmen than you have at the moment.'

It was a threat which could not be misunderstood and Ventura said quickly and humbly:

'I am sorry, m'lord.'

'I accept your apology,' Lord Lynke said. 'Better go downstairs and get your breakfast. We shall be leaving shortly.'

'Minito is here, m'lord. He has finished the suits and brought everything that you ordered.'

'And now he wishes to be paid I suppose?' Lord Lynke inquired. 'Well, how much is it?'

Ventura told him and to her relief he made no comment, merely handing her his purse.

'Pay him,' he ordered.

Ventura went to the door. She counted out the gold pieces into Minito's hand, listened to his expression of delight and gratitude; then, shutting the purse, she took it back to Lord Lynke. He took it from her, chucked it on the table, saying as he did so:

'And how much did you keep for yourself?'

Ventura did not understand for a moment. When she did so, her eyes darkened. She drew herself up proudly.

'I do not steal, m'lord.'

'So you have told me before.'

Ventura felt herself tremble.

'If you do not trust me,' she said in a low voice, 'then I would rather not come with you. I have told you that I am not a thief. I have never stolen anything in the whole of my life, even when I was hungry; and after all you have done for me I would not take anything of yours even if it was to save my life.'

There was a sudden passion in her voice, and then, quite unexpectedly, she found herself near to tears.

Lord Lynke said nothing. Blindly, with a kind of desperation which made her want to run away, Ventura turned towards the door. Only as she reached it did his voice arrest her.

'I was but joking,' he said.

She stood irresolute and he added, after a glance at her white face:

'If I have upset you, forget it. Dammit all! It is the outside of enough if I have to kotow to my own page.'

Ventura said nothing and after a moment Lord Lynke asked:

'Well, aren't you satisfied? What are you waiting for now?'

'I only wanted to tell you,' Ventura inquired a little unsteadily. 'that you can trust me. As long as I remain with you, I will serve you whole-heartedly and to the very best of my ability.'

Again she felt as if her tears must fall, and so before Lord Lynke could say any more she slipped from the door and went into her own room where the suits Minito had made for her were lying on the bed.

One was in black velvet. An evening suit, she supposed; it had a waistcoat of silver and red brocade and a pair of black shoes to go with it with red heels. The other was in pale blue brocade with buttons of red enamel and a waistcoat in which all the colours of the spring flowers seemed to be intermingled.

Ventura packed them hastily but with care in a trunk she had procured the day before from a shop in the town. It was a leather trunk. It had been well used by its previous owner and it was stamped with a coronet and the initials 'P.J.'. She wondered if P.J., whoever he might be, had ever been as thrilled as she was with the lovely garments that his box contained.

She had a sudden wish that they could be the clothes that she ought to wear. A dress of silk billowing over a stiffened petticoat, the open sleeves trimmed with lace, the low-cut *décolletage* filled with lace to match.

Then with a wistful smile Ventura thought how awful she would look at the moment were she to wear women's dress. She was far too thin. The bones at the base of her neck stuck out prominently; her breasts were hardly noticeable and her whole figure was more like a boy's than a girl's.

No. she did not look attractive, expecially since she had cut off her hair. It was absurd to have regrets. Besides, were she not a boy she would not be setting off on this great adventure.

The clothes were all in the trunk. Now, before she closed it, she put in the jewel-case that had been her mother's. It sat easily on the top, and then the trunk was closed and strapped.

She heard steps on the stairs and looked out to see Simon coming up the stairs. He was a shy, rather pleasant-faced young man, who had taken the post simply for the chance of getting abroad.

'I have always wanted to travel,' he told Ventura, and she agreed with him that he had been wise to take the opportunity.

Lord Lynke had told his servants that Ventura was the son of an old friend whom he had happened to meet in San Sebastian immediately on arrival, and who had suggested that his son took the place of the incapacitated Roderick Lane.

'We shall have to find a name for you,' he had said to Ventura when they discussed what to say after she had been measured for her clothes by Minito.

'I would prefer to use my father's name,' she said. 'He was christened Euan.'

'You have not yet told me the surname,' Lord Lynke said.

In answer Ventura had dropped her eyes and looked embarrassed.

'You must forgive me,' she answered, 'but I cannot mention that. There are reasons why I cannot use it or talk about him.'

Lord Lynke had looked surprised, but he had said:

'That, of course, is entirely your business. But if we call you Euan, we shall still have to have another name. What would you choose?"

Ventura hesitated for a moment and then she said:

'My father had a friend of whom he often spoke called Cameron.'

'Euan Cameron,' Lord Lynke exclaimed. 'An excellent choice. I shall explain to my servants, of course, that you have lived nearly all your life in Spain. That is why to them you will not sound particularly English.'

'Do you mean that my English is not good enough for me to pass as an English boy?' Ventura inquired.

'Your English is perfect,' Lord Lynke said. 'But occasionally the intonation is at fault. To a Spaniard it would be quite imperceptible, but to an Englishman—well, he might question your identity.'

'I understand,' Ventura said. 'But if I am continually with you, m'lord. I feel sure my accent and intonation will improve.'

'It is one of the many things I must teach you,' Lord Lynke had said carelessly. . . .

Simon looked round the small bedchamber.

'Have you got everything packed, Mr. Cameron?' he asked.

'Yes, I am ready,' Ventura answered. 'What about his lordship?'

'It won't take me more than five minutes to finish his things,' Simon said.

'I had better take my box downstairs,' Ventura said, grasping the handle of the trunk.

'Here, let me do that,' Simon said kindly. 'You look as if a puff of wind would blow you away. You want to feed yourself up. Have you been ill?'

'Yes, I was ill during the winter,' Ventura said quickly, thinking that such an explanation would excuse her thinness and pallor.

'That accounts for it, then,' Simon said. 'Don't you worry about your things, Mr. Cameron. I'll see to them. You slip downstairs and have your breakfast. I saw it ready in the sitting-room as I came by.'

'Thank you, Simon. You are very kind to me,' Ventura said.

She wondered if it was because unconsciously they sensed that she was not a robust boy that all Lord Lynke's servants went out of the way to save her from unnecessary exertion. Then, as she caught a glimpse of herself in a mirror, she realised there was every reason for their solicitude.

Her small, peaked face, with the skin taut over the bones, looked as if she had emerged from a very long illness. The velvet suit, which had been made for a boy six or seven years her junior, hung on her loosely and she was conscious of how many inches had to be taken in at the waist of the breeches before she could keep them up.

'I must try to look better than this,' she told herself, and remembered how well she had looked when her father was alive. Once she had heard her father and mother talking when they had not known that she was listening.

'That child is going to be a beauty,' her father said.

'She had a sweet nature which is far more important,' her mother answered.

'Important to whom?' her father inquired. 'In the eyes of men she will be a delight. That, in a woman, is a very important thing.'

'All men think about is beauty,' her mother said a little sharply.

'The first time I saw you I thought you were the most beautiful thing I had ever seen in my life,' he answered.

'Oh, Euan!'

Her hands had gone out towards him and Ventura had crept away lest she should disturb them.

She made a little grimace at herself in the mirror.

'Nobody would think you were anything but a freak,' she said rudely, and went down to the sitting-room to the loaded breakfast table.

She felt her heart leap at the sight of so much food; and yet, when she started to eat, she found she could not manage it. After a moment she thrust her loaded plate aside and contented herself with sipping the cup of hot chocolate which she told the waiter that she much preferred to wine.

'Chocolate is a woman's drink,' he said disgustedly. 'Give me a glass of grape on which to start the day. I feel as strong as an ox. Wine is what you need, little *señor*; wine to make you grow into a big man.'

Ventura smiled a little sadly. The movement of her mouth showed the deep lines running from nose to chin and the little fretwork of lines around her eyes.

'Every day I must eat a little more,' she told herself. 'One cannot start suddenly to eat a lot when one has lived on dry crusts and rotten fruit that has been thrown away. Last week I was thankful if I had one meal a day. Now I am offered three and sometimes four, but it is no use being in a hurry. If I am sensible, my body will adjust itself. If I force too much upon it, I shall only be sick.'

She finished up the chocolate just as she heard Lord Lynke come downstairs. He was dressed in riding clothes with high boots reaching to the thigh, his coat was grey as the English skies and the huge turned-back cuffs were trimmed with crimson velvet to match his waistcoat.

He set his tricorn hat down on the table.

'Finish your breakfast, boy,' he said as Ventura rose.

'I have finished, m'lord.'

'Then as soon as the luggage is on the coach we can start. I will ride the first part of the journey.'

Ventura felt a sense of disappointment that he would not be sitting beside her in the coach. As if he sensed what she was feeling, Lord Lynke said kindly:

'I may join you after the midday meal. The proprietor tells me there is an inn about three hours' journey from here. There we will eat and then push on as quickly as we can. I do not want this journey to take a month.'

'The roads are good for the first part, I am told,' Ventura said.

'Then my horses will make short work of the road,' Lord Lynke assured her.

They walked outside the inn and Ventura saw that he had not boasted. He horses were magnificent. Six of them were pulling a coach with painted panels emblazoned with his coat of arms. Four more were ridden by grooms as outriders, or Lord Lynke would ride one himself when he felt so inclined. The luggage was piled, some on top of the coach and the rest in the basket.

Simon came hurrying out of the inn to climb up the side of the coach. Lord Lynke paid the proprietor. There were bows and scrapings and expressions of gratitude which he cut short as he swung himself into the saddle of a magnificent black stallion which pranced and reared about as if impatient to be off.

The door of the coach was held open for Ventura. She stepped in, conscious of the comfortable padded seats, the cushions and the footwarmer on the floor. Yet at the same time she felt small and insignificant and lonely. The adventure was beginning. Would she be strong enough to see it through?

'Adios, Your Excellency! A safe journey and God go with you,' the proprietor cried.

'Adiós!' Lord Lynke replied, and the coach moved off.

The whole cavalcade kept together as they went down the long, cobbled streets which led out of the town. And then, as the houses were left behind, Lord Lynke spurred his horse forward. He galloped away, man and beast seemingly in perfect unison with one another; and Ventura, watching him from the window of the coach, saw him gradually vanish out of sight.

It was only then, when she could no longer see her employer, that she turned to look back at the town she had left behind. The sun was shining on the roofs; beyond, vividly blue, she could see the sea.

She looked at all the landmarks she knew so well, the roof of *El Gallo de Oro*, the lighthouse at the harbour, the high tower of the church beneath which lay the graves of her father and mother.

She was leaving yesterday behind, she thought suddenly. This coach was the present and ahead lay the future.

What did it hold? She felt a sudden panic sweep over her, a fear of what she would find, a terror of the unfamiliar and the unknown.

Then, as she sat trembling, the wheels of the coach seeming to carry her inexorably forward to a new life, she looked and saw down the road ahead that Lord Lynke was coming back towards them. She could see the skirts of his coat flying out with the speed with which he was travelling. She could see the horse straining itself to go faster. And then she saw the delight on the rider's face, the smile of sheer, unbridled joy.

It was the expression of a man who finds life utterly delightful, utterly absorbing, and quite unexpectedly she found herself respond to the happiness she was watching.

Life was not only going to be an adventure, it was going to be a delight. She felt herself tingle with the realisation of it even as Lord Lynke turned a smiling face towards her as he passed the coach and saluted her with his whip.

4

The coach came to a standstill and Ventura realised that it was at a signal from Lord Lynke. It had started to rain and as he swung himself from the saddle to the ground he took off his tricorn hat and shook the water from it. Then he climbed into the coach.

He seated himself comfortably against the cushions, and Ventura, as she felt would be expected of her, moved to the seat facing him with her back to the horses.

'We are in for a wet night,' he said as the coach started forward again.

'What time do you expect us to reach the inn, m'lord?' Ventura inquired.

'In another two hours,' he answered. He stretched his legs out in front of him. 'By Jupiter, but I'm stiff. 'Tis over a month since I have been on a horse and I feel as if all my limbs were made of wood.'

Ventura was not surprised that he felt stiff. He had been in the saddle, except for a short break for their midday meal, ever since they left San Sebastian. Seven hours' riding when one was out of practice would try the stamina of any man.

But she was beginning to realise that Lord Lynke was exceedingly strong. His appearance of being elegant and at times almost languid was very deceptive. He had a wiry strength which was not noticeable until one saw him spring into the saddle or control a prancing horse.

'Bored?' Lord Lynke asked suddenly, looking at Ventura on the other side of the carriage.

She shook her head.

'I have been looking out of the windows at the country. It has been a long day, but I have enjoyed every moment of it.'

'You are easily pleased,' Lord Lynke said shortly. 'This wild, uncultivated country is not to my taste.'

A look of depression came over his face and Ventura, to change the trend of his thoughts, said quickly:

'You will find Madrid very gay, m'lord, and there will be many things to amuse you.'

'Including Doña Alcira, I suppose,' Lord Lynke said sarcastically.

'If she is as beautiful as reports tell, m'lord will find his task a pleasant one.'

'And if she is not?' Lord Lynke parried. 'There is nothing I can do about it. No, you are a good boy, Venturo, but you won't puff my spirits up that way. Still, doubtless there will be compensations. Juanita spoke very highly of the flamenço dancers.'

'I should not imagine Juanita is a very good judge,' Ventura said coldly.

'On the contrary, she can speak with experience,' Lord Lynke contradicted. 'So we will go and see them. Who knows? We may find another Juanita to amuse us, and one who is not so light-fingered as the last.'

Ventura felt her heart sink.

'There are other things to see in Madrid,' she said. 'At the Court . . .'

'A fig for the Court!' Lord Lynke interrupted. 'All Courts are a dead bore, filled with pompous, self-important individuals scheming and manoeuvring to gain the attention of the Royal ear. No, no! We shall find warmer entertainment than that, you'll see.'

Ventura gave a little sigh but said nothing, and after a moment Lord Lynke went on:

'But I dare say you will find your own amusements. And that reminds me. You will need money. I must pay you a proper wage for your services to me.'

'A w . . . wage?' Ventura questioned.

'You sound surprised,' Lord Lynke smiled. 'Isn't there something in the Bible which says "a workman is worthy of his hire"?'

Ventura felt herself stiffen.

'Did . . . your former . . . page, Sir Roderick Lane, receive a wage? she asked.

'Roderick was different,' Lord Lynke replied. 'He had money of his own!'

'I have taken Sir Roderick's place,' Ventura said. 'I shall not need anything more than you have given me already, m'lord.'

'Gammon! Lord Lynke said brusquely. 'You must have money to spend on whatever takes your fancy. I shall give you a couple of guineas a week—whatever that is translated into Spanish currency.'

'I thank you, m'lord, but I do not want it.'

'Then you are damned well going to have it,' Lord Lynke answered.

'My apologies, m'lord, but I refuse.'

Lord Lynke sat up suddenly.

'Now what's all this about? You want money—everyone wants money. You cannot walk about Madrid without a *peseta* in your pocket. You will take what I give you and no argument about it.'

Ventura's blue eyes met his grey ones and sparks seemed to radiate across the carriage.

'I won't take your money,' Ventura stormed. 'I am your page, m'lord, not a scullion or a stable-hand.'

Lord Lynke threw back his head and laughed.

'So that still rankles! The devil take it, but you are as touchy as a woman.'

His laughter ceased and the smile faded from his lips.

'Make no mistake about it,' he said. 'I shall have my way. Two guineas a week starting from now.'

He put his hand deep in his pocket.

'If you give me the coins, m'lord,' Ventura said between clenched teeth, 'I shall throw them out of the window.'

'Oh, you will, will you?'

Lord Lynke stared at her, frowning, his eyebrows almost meeting across his nose.

'Now, let us get this quite clear, my lad. I have no use

for recreant pages. If you throw that money out of the window, you will go after it. Or, if you prefer, I can stop the coach and you can walk back to San Sebastian. You can take your choice.'

There was a long silence. Blue eyes met grey ... then Ventura's eyes fell before his.

'Very well, m'lord,' she said in a voice that was hardly above a whisper. 'You force me to take the money.'

'Good!'

Lord Lynke threw two coins across the carriage on to the seat beside her.

'I can understand why your past employer wished to beat you. Kindly remember in future that I intend to be obeyed.'

'Yes ... m'lord.'

The voice was unsteady. Ventura picked up the coins as if they were red-hot coals and placed them in the pocket of her coat. Then she turned her head away to stare out of the window at the darkening landscape.

Lord Lynke seemed engrossed in his own thoughts, and then after a long time turned his eyes to look at her. Her profile was etched against the windows. The oval forehead, the straight, aristocratic little nose, the wistful lips and straight, proud line of her shapely neck.

There was no doubt at all that the boy had breeding, and Lord Lynke wondered once again who his father might have been. And then impatiently he deliberately switched his thoughts to other matters. It was ridiculous to be so engrossed by the moods and vagaries of a boy who ought to be at school.

He tried to think of Charlotte, but somehow it was difficult to conjure up a vivid picture of her pink and white beauty. England seemed very far away. He put his feet up on the opposite seat beside Ventura, tipped his hat over his eyes and tried to sleep.

Ventura was arguing with herself. It was her pride, she thought, that had caused her to make an unnecessary scene. Lord Lynke was right, she must have some money in her purse. And yet it went against the grain to take it from him.

It had been different when she was disguised as a ragged urchin, when she had been content to scrape a *peseta* here, a *peseta* there, if only to keep herself from starving. But she and Lord Lynke were of the same class, and she rebelled against receiving a wage for what was an honourable position.

It was somehow different that he should pay for her clothes, that he should feed and house her. But in the exchange of coins she felt that her position was no different from the post of scullion or stableboy which he had offered her originally.

'I am being nonsensical,' she told herself. And yet she felt the tears of offended pride prick her eyes.

They travelled in silence until, as dusk was falling and the tired horses were getting slower and slower, they pulled up at an inn.

They had been moving uphill for a long time—a thickly wooded hill with a rough, uneven road that was very different from that on which they had journeyed when they first left San Sebastian.

As the coach drew to a standstill Lord Lynke started into wakefulness, and as soon as the coach door was opened and the steps lifted up he descended without a word to Ventura, who followed him.

The inn was not particularly prepossessing. It was a low, roughly built building which was obviously badly in need of repair. The proprietor, who came hurrying to the doorway wiping his hands on his apron, was a dark, shifty-eyed individual who told them that he had but one bedroom for hire, but that it was furnished with '*una cama de matrimonio*'.

The man spoke with a strange accent that made it difficult for Lord Lynke to understand him.

He looked inquiringly at Ventura and she knew that he wanted her to translate.

'He says he has only one room,' she said in English, 'but that it has a large bed.'

'Well, we shall have to put up with what we can get,' Lord Lynke said. 'The horses can go no farther tonight. Let me see the stables.'

He strode away to look at the stalls where his horses could be rubbed down and fed, and at the hay lofts above, where the coachman and outriders could sleep.

Ventura felt her heart beating in a frightened manner. Where was she to sleep? She almost disobeyed Lord Lynke's orders and spoke to the proprietor in Spanish; but she resisted the temptation, and when Lord Lynke came back to say that the stables were dirty, but they would have to make the best of them, she said timidly:

57

'Could you ask the man if there is not a small room that I can have?'

Lord Lynke put his hand on her shoulder.

'What are you worrying about?' he said. 'We shall not sleep much in this flea-infested place, and I dare say you will find I am not too bad a bed companion. Those who have shared my couch in the past assure me that I do not snore.'

He still had his hand on Ventura's shoulder and they walked into the inn where the landlord produced some coarse, strong wine and promised that dinner would be ready as quickly as possible.

'I'll wager it's uneatable when it comes,' Lord Lynke said to Ventura. 'Come and warm yourself by the fire, boy. You look half frozen.'

That was not far from the truth. Ventura had felt herself growing colder and colder during the last part of the journey. She supposed that lack of food had thinned her blood and when the sun was not shining she found it hard not to shiver. The raw wine, however, brought a flush to her cheeks, and the warmth of the fire was conforting.

Lord Lynke kicked a log with the toe of his boot to make the blaze higher.

'What a hellish country!' he ejaculated.

For once Ventura felt inclined to agree with him. The dinner was excruciatingly bad, and the bedroom, which they were shown before dinner, was small and dark. The four-poster bed was hung with dirty curtains and covered with torn blankets.

Simon, however, carried in rugs from the coach, and cushions which he covered with fine linen pillow-cases. He also brushed out the room, lit a fire, and brought hot water for Lord Lynke to wash his hands.

'I will wash downstairs,' Ventura said and slipped from the room as Lord Lynke started to take off his coat.

'Where are you sleeping, Simon?' she asked as the valet came after her to show her the way to the sink.

'In the loft with the other men,' he answered. 'It won't be too uncomfortable. At least the hay is clean.'

'You're fortunate,' Ventura said, and she wondered all through dinner whether she could say that she, too, preferred the hay to the room upstairs.

If Lord Lynke discovered that she was a woman, she thought desperately, he would undoubtedly send her back to San Sebastian. Whatever happened she must get to Madrid. It was what her mother had wanted.

She could hear her now, her voice broken and so faint as to be hardly discernible as she lay in the roadway after the wheels of the carriage had passed over her.

'Go . . . to . . . Madrid. Give . . . the . . . letters. . . .'

She tried to say more, but the blood from her broken body had suddenly filled her mouth and choked her. Her eyes closed and Ventura knew that she was dead.

'Go to Madrid.' Why had she said that? There had never been any talk of her visiting Madrid. And what letters had she meant?

Ventura had searched the room they had shared together from floor to ceiling. She had looked in the books, under the mattress, in her mother's clothing, in every drawer—but there had been no sign of any letters.

What could her mother have meant? Only one thing was clear. She was to go to Madrid. It had seemed an impossible aspiration a week ago, yet now she was on her way. Nothing and nobody must prevent her getting there.

It was late before they finished dinner, and, yawning, Lord Lynke announced that he intended to retire to bed.

'We will leave as soon as it is light in the morning,' he said. 'We do not want to spend longer than can be helped in this filthy hole.' He rose to his feet and Ventura jumped up from the table.

'I will follow you as soon as I have told Simon you are ready for him, m'lord,' she said.

She had suddenly thought of a plan.

She called Simon and then hurried up the stairs ahead of him. Lord Lynke was standing in the centre of the bedroom, unbuckling his sword. He seemed too big for the low-ceilinged room.

'The proprietor has just spoken to me, m'lord,' Ventura said breathlessly. 'He tells me there is another chamber available. The man who had engaged it has left the inn unexpectedly.'

'And I don't blame him,' Lord Lynke retorted. 'Well, cut along to your bed and I hope it's comfortable.'

'Thank you, m'lord. Good night.'

Ventura hurried down the stairs, passing Simon, who was bringing up a can of hot water, without speaking to him. She did not wish him to ask any questions as to where she was going.

Downstairs, the room where they had dined was empty.

It was the only room on the ground floor of the inn with the exception of the kitchens. She could hear voices and laughter and guessed that the proprietor was entertaining the coachmen.

She looked round the room. There was depressingly little furniture—a few high-backed, wooden chairs; a roughly polished table; an ancient sideboard. But in the far corner there was an alcove, which she had noticed during dinner, curtained off with a dirty bit of faded brocade.

She pulled the curtain aside and saw that it served as a storage place for things that were no longer in use. Several broken chairs, upturned one against the other, a stool with only two legs, and several pans and brushes were jumbled together. But there were also some piled-up straw mattresses which Ventura guessed were pulled into the sitting-room when the inn was full and were slept on by travellers who were glad of any sort of night's shelter so long as it was under cover.

She climbed on top of the mattresses and found that she could be comparatively comfortable there. She suspected that they were dirty and also that there was every likelihood of her suffering from cramp before the night was out, but at least it was better than having to share a bed with Lord Lynke.

She pushed and pummelled the mattresses into some sort of shape, slipped off her shoes and then took off her coat and covered herself with it. She was so tired that she felt herself drop immediately into a half sleep where dreams meet reality.

She was letting herself drift away, feeling her body relax, when suddenly she heard the outer door open and footsteps come into the room. She knew it was unlikely that she would be discovered, and whoever it was she resented their presence only because they had awoken her.

Then almost despite herself she found herself listening. For new guests they were behaving in a very strange way. There were two of them. They shut the door quickly with the utmost caution, then she heard them whispering together. They were tiptoeing across the room. She could not see them, but she could imagine that they were fairly heavy men so that to walk silently was a considerable effort to them.

They came near to the fire and now Ventura could hear what they were saying.

'That's his coach all right.'

'You're sure of it?'

'Quite sure. The coat of arms with the crowned eagle. That was what we were told to look for.'

'What do you suggest we do?'

'Wait an hour or so. Even if he's gone to bed, he won't be asleep yet.'

'And the landlord? Shall we say we're here?'

'Not unless he comes and finds us. If nobody notices our arrival, it's all the better.'

'What shall we do then?'

'Just sit ourselves down by the fire and wait.'

'I could do with a drink. I need something to give me courage.'

'The gold in your pocket should do that. But perhaps there's some wine left on the table.'

Ventura heard footsteps going towards the table. There was the sound of wine being poured into two glasses. Then the footsteps went back towards the fire.

'Ah! That's better.'

'Now, listen. In about an hour's time we will creep up the stairs. We will open the door as quietly as possible, but quickly. Then I will stab him while you deal with anyone else who's in the room.'

'And if there's no one else?'

'Then hurry downstairs and get the outer door open. The landlord may have bolted it before then.'

'Supposing I can't get it open?'

'Then I'll be down to help you. You know where the horses are. If anyone does hear us, we'll be away long before they can sound an alarm.'

'Supposing his door is locked?'

'Supposing! Supposing! Is that all you can say? It won't be. I've known this inn for ten years. There's never been anything working in it yet. Even if there is a lock, there won't be a key in it. The people who usually stay here haven't got anything worth stealing.'

'It sounds all right.'

'It is all right. Stop being chicken-hearted. Remember the gold we're to get for it.'

'I should think so. Murder ought to be expensive. It isn't particularly nice.'

'Nice! What an expression!'

The man smothered his laughter and then said almost kindly:

61

'You're too young for the job. When you've done as many killings as I have, you'll get used to it. Now, sit down and take a rest. We've got a long way to go tomorrow.'

There was the sound of two people lowering themselves into the chairs by the fireplace. Ventura held her breath. There was no doubt at all why these men had come, what they intended to do, and whom they meant to murder.

The crowned eagle! She had been looking at it only that morning while she was waiting for Lord Lynke to come out of *El Gallo de Oro* and start their journey. She had thought how beautifully the outstretched golden wings contrasted with the deep blue of the coach.

The crowned eagle! And these men had been told to kill the man whose arms bore that sign.

She looked round the little alcove. There was no window, no possible exit save through the room where the two men were sitting.

Very, very cautiously she stirred on the mattresses and peeped through a crack in the curtains. She could see the men now, dark, swarthy creatures with heavy travelling cloaks over their shoulders. She knew by their speech that they came from the south. Their accent was unmistakable.

The candles on the table were guttering low. The light came mostly from the fire. Soon, she thought, the candles would go out; then the rest of the room would be in darkness. She looked at the candles again. How long would they last? she wondered.

From the kitchen she could still hear laughter and voices. If she screamed, she thought, she could perhaps attract the attention of the coachman and Simon. But supposing she did not get the chance to tell them why she had screamed. The men by the fire would reach her quickly and she could be effectively silenced before the others entered the room.

The moment she raised her voice they would know she had overheard what they had said. They would not risk her betrayal and Lord Lynke would still be at their mercy. No, she had got to be cleverer than that.

She looked again at the candles. She must creep past the men and up the stairs without their seeing her. It was all a question of time. They were prepared to wait an hour. Would the candles last as long as that?

Even as she wondered, one flickered, sizzled against a pool of grease and slowly, very slowly, was extinguished.

This left only two—but one was still nearly three inches high.

The younger man spoke suddenly.

'Supposing the landlord comes in? What explanation shall we make for not having called him? Travellers arriving at this time of night would ask for rooms.'

'Oh, stop fussing,' the elder man answered sharply. 'Ten to one he won't appear. And if he does, he may be too drunk to see us. Blow out the candles. He would be too lazy to light them again.'

'That's a good idea,' the younger man said.

He got to his feet and going to the table blew out the two remaining candles.

Ventura felt as if the deep breath of relief she drew must be audible. The older man yawned.

'Now perhaps you're satisfied,' he said. 'If you take my advice you'll get a bit of sleep.'

He drew his cloak more closely round him as he spoke and let his head drop forward on to his chest. The younger man made an attempt to seat himself more comfortably. Ventura was quite certain that he was too frightened and too tense to sleep.

She waited five minutes, ten, and then, feeling more afraid than she had ever been in her life before, she slipped silently down from the mattresses on to the floor of the alcove. She was thankful that she had taken off her shoes, but afraid that she might stumble against them in the dark.

Slowly she crept forward and then dropping down on her knees slipped beneath the curtain into the room. The light of the fire was just enough for her to see across the room. There was nothing in her way. She must creep behind the seated men, past the sideboard, round the table, and once she had reached the stairs where they came down into the room she would be hidden from anyone sitting by the fire-place. Her greatest danger was now!

The young man had his back to her, but his nerves would make him susceptible to the slightest sound. The boards on the floor were rough. She could feel them splintering against her knees. They hurt her hands, too, as she moved along, slowly, very slowly, resisting her impulse to hurry because she was so afraid.

A log fell in the fire. She was instantly still, hardly daring to breathe. She realised suddenly that there was no sound from the kitchen. The coachmen must have gone to bed. There would be no help from that quarter. Even if she screamed now, the men would not hear her once they were in the lofts above the stables.

She crept on again—one foot ... two feet. ... It seemed to her that she had been crawling for an eternity of time. Her knees were hurting almost unbearably. She thought to herself that it would have been better if she had been plumper, and then wondered how at this moment she could think of anything but danger.

One of the men stirred in his chair, the wood cracked and once again Ventura kept utterly still and wondered if they would hear the beating of her heart.

On, on. The room seemed endless until at last she reached the foot of the stairs. There was one moment of danger when she must rise from the floor to crawl up the first two steps. The men by the fire never stirred, and suddenly she was out of their sight.

She straightened herself and stood for a moment holding on to the banisters, feeling faint now that she had reached her goal. Then with an effort she realised that she must go on. There was no time to be lost.

She reached the top of the stairs and lifted the latch of the door. It was extraordinary how silently it could open. The door creaked a little, but very little, not enough to arouse Lord Lynke. The fire was still burning brightly and she could see the outline of the bed quite clearly and his head upon the pillow.

She shut the door behind her and tiptoed across the room. She put her hand out and touched his shoulder.

'M'lord.'

He awoke instantly, every sense alert, like a man who has been used to danger all his life.

'Venturo! What is it . . . ?' he began.

She put her fingers hastily to his lips.

'Hush!' she whispered. 'Do not let them hear you.'

'Let who hear me?' he asked. 'What is it?'

He sat up in bed, but he spoke in a whisper.

'There are two men downstairs. They have been sent here to kill you. They did not say your name, but they said they had been told to look for the coach with the crowned eagle on it.'

'Two men you said?' Lord Lynke asked.

'The older man will stab you,' Ventura answered. 'The other is to engage anyone else who is in the room.'

64

Lord Lynke threw back the rugs which covered him and Ventura saw that he had not undressed but had lain down on the bed in his shirt and breeches. He wore no shoes and he made no sound as he leapt on to the floor.

His sword was lying on a chair at the bottom of the bed. He drew it now and holding it in his hand turned to Ventura.

'You are sure of this?' he asked. 'Why should anyone want to kill me?'

'I do not know,' Ventura answered. 'But that is what they said they had come to do.'

'I will be ready for them,' Lord Lynke said grimly.

He went across to the fire and threw another log on it. Then he looked round the room as if checking points of vantage from its very emptiness.

'Go into that corner,' he commanded Ventura. 'And do not come out. Put a chair in front of you and keep out of the way. I do not want you hurt.'

'What are you going to do?' Ventura inquired.

'You will see,' Lord Lynke answered.

She did as he told her, getting into the corner and quietly pulling a high-backed chair in front of her.

Lord Lynke stood behind the door. Even as he did so there was a faint sound on the stairs. It was very faint and yet Ventura heard it; and even as she looked at Lord Lynke in a sudden alarm, she realised that he had heard it, too.

He bent his head a little to listen and then there was another sound, very faint, nothing more than the creaking of a board, and any other time it would have passed unnoticed. It would certainly not have woken a man who was fast asleep in bed.

The latch of the door was lifted almost silently. The door opened very slowly and then suddenly the two men were in the room. The first one received a prick on the arm which brought a gasp from his throat and sent the blood pouring over his hand. It was the younger man and in sheer, unbridled terror he ran from the room and down the stairs. A second later Ventura could hear him fumbling with the outer door.

The older man was of sterner stuff and turned to face Lord Lynke. Ventura saw then that he carried a sharp dagger in one hand and in the other a drawn sword. It was but the work of a moment for him to transfer the

65

weapons so that the sword was in his right hand almost before Lord Lynke had finished wounding the younger man.

There was a clash of steel, their swords flashing and glittering in the firelight. It was obvious to Ventura that the older man was no mean swordsman. But he was handicapped by his heavy riding boots and enveloping cloak. Lord Lynke, shoeless and coatless, had every advantage, and it was also soon obvious that he was the better swordsman.

It was all over in a matter of seconds. With a brilliant thrust Lord Lynke evaded the other's guard, and the point of his sword entered the man's throat just below the chin. He staggered and fell to the ground. Lord Lynke withdrew his sword and the blood started to flow from the man's throat in an ugly red flood which spread over his shirt and coat.

'Who sent you to kill me?'

Lord Lynke was down on one knee beside his fallen opponent.

The man's eyes were already closing.

'Tell me who sent you?' Lord Lynke commanded.

It was the voice of authority, and somehow it forced an answer from the man's failing senses.

'Don . . . Carlos . . .' he said as his eyes closed.

Lord Lynke rose to his feet.

'Don Carlos,' he repeated. 'I wonder who he can be?'

Ventura came from behind her barricade.

'Is he dead?' she asked in a frightened voice.

'Quite dead,' Lord Lynke answered.

'What are you going to do about him? What are you going to say?' Ventura asked.

Lord Lynke considered for a moment.

'Is the landlord in on this?'

Ventura shook her head.

'No. He does not know they are here. He was in the kitchen when they arrived and they crept into the inn so that he should not see them.'

'That makes it easier,' Lord Lynke said.

He looked round the room. In one corner was a built-in cupboard. He walked across, opened the door and looked inside. There was room for a man to lie on the floor. He dragged the dead swordsman across the floor and put him in the cupboard. Then he threw after him the sword and

66

the dagger which lay on the floor where they had fallen, and closed the cupboard door.

'Are you going to leave him there?' Ventura asked with wide eyes.

'Someone will find him,' Lord Lynke said. 'But judging by the general cleanliness of this inn, it will not be for some time.'

'And now what are you going to do?' Ventura inquired.

Lord Lynke smiled.

'Now I am going to put that chair and the dressing-table across the door and then go back to bed. I doubt if we shall have any more visitors tonight. If we do, they will wake us up trying to open the door.'

Ventura stood irresolute.

'You had best stay with me,' Lord Lynke said. 'You refused my company earlier this evening, but now perhaps you will be glad of it.'

He had seen how frightened she was, Ventura thought. Now that it was all over, she was trembling and she knew that she had not enough courage to go downstairs again. There was always a chance that the other man might return. Besides, she had a sudden horror of the room downstairs through which she had crawled.

She remembered now that her coat and her shoes were downstairs. They must wait for the daylight before she dared to go in search of them.

'You are quite sure I shall not disturb you, m'lord?' she asked.

'Not more than you have done already,' he replied.

As he spoke he laid himself on the bed and pulled the rugs over him. Tentatively Ventura lay down on the very edge of the mattress. She felt inexpressibly shy and her heart was beating almost suffocatingly. And yet because Lord Lynke was beside her she felt safe.

Now it was over, the full horror of what had taken place began to creep over her. She wondered who Don Carlos was. Why did he want to take Lord Lynke's life? And would he be satisfied when he learned that the attempt was a failure? Would there not be another attempt and perhaps yet another?

She felt herself shiver. Lord Lynke turned over on his pillow.

'I ought to thank you, Venturo, for saving my life,' he said. 'I thought I was looking after you—it seems you're looking after me.'

'If I had not heard what they were planning, they might have killed you,' Ventura said in a low voice.

She thought how terrible it would have been if she had come into this room and found Lord Lynke dead. Supposing he was lying dead like the man in the cupboard, the blood oozing out of him. She shivered again, and as if he guessed what she was thinking, Lord Lynke said:

'Forget it, and thank you. I am in your debt.'

His words made her glow with happiness. They were almost square, she thought. He had done so much for her; now she had been able to do something for him.

5

'Still sulking?' Doña Alcira asked in her soft, sensuous voice.

There was no reply for the moment from the man standing in front of the mirror. He was admiring his broad shoulders and narrow hips, his small waist and dark, clear-cut features which, as well as his skill, had made him Miajado the Magnificent, the most admired and acclaimed matador in all Spain.

Doña Alcira shrugged her shoulders. Her body was like carved ivory against the exquisitely embroidered cushions and covers of the low couch. Then she threw her arms behind her dark head with a little derisive laugh.

'So you are enangered with me?'

Miajado turned round.

'Angry? Of course I am angry. What did you expect? Am I just a plaything to be used and tossed aside? Who is this Englishman of whom everyone is talking? Why should he aspire to your hand while I may only possess your body?'

You are jealous, my love!'

Doña Alcira held out her arms invitingly, seductively.

Her lips were parted, her eyes half closed. She was so beautiful in her abandonment that it was hard to believe that any man could resist her. But Miajado stood still and made no movement to go to her.

'I want to know,' he repeated, looking rather like a

68

spoilt, cross child, with his full lips pouted, a frown disturbing the serenity of his square brow.

Doña Alcira dropped her arms.

'You are being a bore!' she said. 'What can it matter to you? This Englishman will not disturb us or what we mean to each other.'

'He will be your husband!'

Doña Alcira made a gesture with her hands that expressed uncertainty.

'That depends,' she said. 'I have not yet accepted him.'

'You will not dare refuse any arrangement made by the Queen,' Miajado scoffed.

'How do you know what I will refuse or accept?' Doña Alcira replied provocatively. She gave another little low laugh.

'Smile at me,' she coaxed. 'We have had so much happiness here, within the secrecy of these four walls. What does it matter to us what happens outside? The Englishman is but a puppet to be used by the Queen for her own interests.'

'What interests?' inquired Miajado darkly. 'One can be sure that they are not Spanish interests. The Queen is Italian. It is only of Italy that she thinks. It is only Italians whom she favours. I am a Spaniard. I do not care what goes on beyond the borders of my own country.'

Doña Alcira gave a little smile. She knew all too well that Miajado was saying in words what all Spain thought. The Queen's Italian sympathies were causing resentment everywhere. It was true that Italian interests, Italian ways of life, and Italian officials were infiltrating into the country, into every profession and every branch of the Government. But Doña Alcira was not concerned with anything which did not affect herself.

'Perhaps, in this matter,' she said aloud, 'the Queen is right. I must have a husband, and therefore why not an Englishman who will bring some benefits with him?'

Miajado stamped his feet.

'Husband!' he said, and spat on the floor; then, towering above her, he stormed: 'How can I listen to you saying those words? How can I bear to think of you giving yourself to another man? You have had lovers in the past, many lovers, but never one like me. Why cannot I marry you? Why cannot I possess you so that no other man shall own you, no other man touch what is mine!'

He threw himself down on the couch beside Doña

69

Alcira and took her in his arms. He rained fierce, violent, passionate kisses on her mouth, her eyes, her neck and her breasts. He felt her go limp beneath him. His passion kindled a flame in her until they were linked together by a fire which consumed them both, burning fiercely in heart pressed against heart, until everything was forgotten but the need one for the other. ....

A long time later Doña Alcira, wearing a wrap of blood-red velvet, walked across the room to her dressing-table. She stared at her face reflected in the gilt-framed mirror ornamented with flying cupids and entwined love-knots. Her beauty was all the more vivid because it was blurred by exhaustion. Her dark eyes, faintly shadowed, seemed to blaze out of her oval face with its magnolia skin and small classical features, her lips warm and still pulsating from her lover's kisses, parted to reveal her perfect teeth.

She swept her hair back from her forehead, then turned to look over her shoulder at the matador who was watching her from the coach.

'We have got to be sensible,' she said, and suddenly there was a hard note in her voice.

'What do you mean by that?'

'I mean that we must be careful. No one must suspect that you come here. There are enemies who would only be too pleased to inform the Englishman that my affections are already engaged! Besides, the English expect their wives to be virtuous.'

'So do the Spaniards,' Miajado retorted.

He rose to his feet, and walking across the room, passed into the dressing-room.

'Do you suppose,' he said through the open door, 'that any man wants a woman who has learnt of love except from himself? A man should be not only the master, but the teacher.'

Doña Alcira laughed.

'You are old-fashioned, Miajado, or should I say provincial?'

She was being deliberately cruel, knowing that Miajado resented more than anything else the gulf between them that existed because of their different positions in life.

She was the ward of the King, daughter of the Duke of Carcastillo, owner of vast estates, and, after the Queen, one of the most important women in Spain.

He was a man of the people, son of a shopkeeper in an obscure country town—a provincial bull-fighter, a man who had become a hero only because of his skill.

Despite the fact that Philip V and his Queen, Elizabeth Farnese, frowned upon bullfights and had made every effort to discourage them, the people of Spain were not prepared to forgo their national sport.

Among the noble families, too, there was much dissatisfaction at the Royal attitude, everyone attributing it solely to the Queen's foreign nationality and the fact that she made no effort to adjust herself to Spanish ways. Bullfights, therefore, took place as they had always done; but they were not talked about at Court although the majority of the courtiers attended them.

Doña Alcira had been sitting in the Royal Box in the Plaza Mayor when she first saw Miajado. He had come to Madrid with a great reputation. He had been acclaimed in all the towns of the south. Madrid had expected something good, but even the most critical audience in the country had realised that here was someone exceptional, a man who was not only a natural genius at the sport, but also an artist to his finger-tips.

'Olé! Olé! Olé!'

The crowd had gone mad as Miajado killed his bull accurately and cleanly. Flowers and hats, mantillas and gloves, came showering into the arena. Doña Alcira had sat without moving, only her eyes narrowing a little as she watched him.

She had commanded that he be brought to the box; and when he stood there close beside her and bowed over her hand, she had known at the touch of him that she had never wanted a man so much before.

Miajado was, in many ways, a simple character. Because of his good looks women had made a fuss of him ever since he had been a child. Because, too, he had that indefinable aura of masculinity, he had the power to draw women as aniseed can draw cats.

But his love affairs to date had been simple and uncomplicated. He slept with women when he wished to, but he accepted their adulation and their gifts as a tribute not to himself as a man, but to his skill in the bullring.

He had been surprised at Doña Alcira's invitation to supper. It had also flattered and intrigued him. He had never before met a woman of such noble birth at close quarters.

Noblemen patronised him, of course. He had been invited to drink with them, to express his views on the quality of the bulls. They even slapped him on the back, told him he was a good chap and that he was without equal in the whole country. But their wives and daughters remained at a distance.

He would see them, beautiful, proud and aloof, watching him from the balconies round the plaza. He would see them hurry past as their male escorts stopped to talk with him. A slight inclination of the head, a very faint twist of the lips, such as they might give to a shopkeeper or a servant, was all they accorded him.

But now he had been asked to supper with the most beautiful woman in Spain. He had heard her praises sung even as far south as Seville. He had seen her for that moment on the balcony, and he knew that the tales of her were not exaggerated. What she wanted of him he did not know, but he had gone to her palace with a quickly beating heart, to find that he was to have supper alone with her in her boudoir. That was nearly a year ago.

Invitations had come to Miajado from all over Spain bringing promises of money which exceeded, by vast amounts, all that he was receiving in Madrid, but he could not tear himself away. Doña Alcira was in Madrid, and that was where he must remain.

He came back into the room now, dressed in the tight, resplendent clothes that he wore almost as a uniform because they ensured that, wherever he went, he was recognised.

As he walked towards her, Doña Alcira felt again the almost feline grace. It was like watching a black leopard; there was something in him as beautiful and yet as dangerous.

She was sitting on a low stool and looked up at him, her long hair streaming over the blood-red wrap, her eyes dark and mysterious above the crimson lips.

'You will come tomorrow night,' she said. It was a command rather than a request.

'Unless the Englishman is here,' he replied bitterly.

'If he is, you would not expect him to be with me at this hour!' Doña Alcira smiled.

Miajado put his hands on her shoulders and almost brutally turned her round to face him.

'I think I will kill you!' he said hoarsely. 'Then no other

man can ever look at you. Then you will remain mine for all time.'

His hands moved to her neck. They were slim hands and they moved delicately to enfold the warm column which held her head so proudly. Slowly, almost imperceptibly, his fingers tightened. Doña Alcira did not move—she only looked up at him.

'And would a dead woman give you what I can give?' she asked softly. 'Would a dead woman have lips that long for yours? Would a dead woman have arms to hold you close, and would a dead woman ache for you as I shall ache until tomorrow night?'

His eyes looked into her eyes, and for a moment it seemed as if he could not resist the invitation which he saw there— For a moment his lips quivered and his breath came quickly; and then, roughly, he flung her away from him. She would have fallen to the floor had she not reached out her hand to steady herself.

'Curse you!' he said. 'You have bewitched me. You are in my blood and I cannot keep away. I am humiliated. I am insulted, and yet, because of what you do to me, I must crawl back asking for more. I am your slave, your serf. I hate you, and yet I love you until I can think of nothing else. One day I shall kill you, if only so that I can be free.'

Miajado turned towards the door even while the whole room seemed to echo with the passion of his words; and then, as he reached it, Doña Alcira was beside him, her arms reaching up towards him, her body strained against him.

'My sweet, my beloved, my lover!' she said. 'Do not go away from me in anger. You know that I love you. I am yours. Haven't I proved it again and again?'

She drew her head down to his. Her lips sought his mouth as he would have withheld it from her, and then they were fused together in a kiss which, once again, seemed to ignite them both with a desire that was a raging fire.

Only when Miajado was holding her so close that she was almost unable to breathe, only when he was kissing her with a fierceness and a passion that bruised her mouth, did Doña Alcira withdraw herself from his arms.

'You must go,' she said, and, even as he moved towards her, his face alight with desire, she touched the gold bell which stood on an adjacent table. It tinkled faintly, but the door opened almost immediately and an elderly maid

73

stood there holding a long dark cloak in her hands. Without a word she slipped it over Miajado's shoulders. He swept it round him, flinging it in a great high fold over his left shoulder so that his face was half obscured.

'Be careful there is no one about,' Doña Alcira said to the maid. She looked again at Miajado.

'*Adiós*,' she said softly.

'*Adiós*,' he replied.

The door shut behind him. Doña Alcira stood for a moment looking at it with a faint smile on her lips; then she went back to the dressing-table, looked at her reflection once again in the mirror, and gave a little laugh of satisfaction. It was a laugh of a woman who knows her own power and is convinced that she is invincible.

For some time Doña Alcira sat staring at herself, then the door opened and the maid came back into the room.

'It was all right?' Doña Alcira asked.

The maid nodded.

'There was no one about, m'lady'.

Doña Alcira stretched her arms above her head.

'The night is still young; I am not tired. What shall I do, Joanna?'

'Have you forgotten that Don Carlos asked you to supper tonight, m'lady?' the maid replied. 'He has a party, I believe.'

'Don Carlos! I am tired of him.'

Doña Alcira made a little grimace of distaste; then, changing her mind, she said:

'But it would be better than being alone. Bring me my new gown of coral satin, and with it I will wear the necklace of emeralds that have just been reset. Send a message to tell Frivolo that he shall accompany me. You have kept him shut up?'

'He has been locked in all the evening, m'lady.'

'You must always be sure of that,' Doña Alcira said. 'He loves me, I am sure of it; yet his tongue is so mischievous that one can never be certain that he will not repeat what he has seen and heard.'

'Frivolo has no idea that anyone visits m'lady while she is resting.'

'I am glad of that,' Doña Alcira replied.

In a very short time, with Joanna's skilful help, Doña Alcira was ready. The dress of coral satin stood out over wide stiffened petticoats and was embroidered with precious stones. From the shoulders hung, in graceful folds, a

74

part of the dress which constituted the train. This also was emboridered as were the tiny satin shoes in which Doña Alcira encased her little feet.

Joanna piled her dark hair high on her head. It fell in soft curls on either side of her oval face and there were jewels to keep it in place. Great emeralds glistened on her ears and on her long fingers. A necklace of the same stones encircled the beautiful neck which Miajado had held tightly in his hands.

As she left the room, Doña Alcira thought of her lover. How angry he would be if he knew she was going out tonight! But he had no idea what hours were kept by the younger members of the Court. To him night was a time for sleeping, to them it was a time for feasting and merry-making.

Doña Alcira moved from her bedroom across the landing and on to the wide marble staircase which led down to the entrance hall. The whole house was magnificent with its embroidered hangings, its tapestry and pictures, its inlaid and carved furniture, its ivory, crystal and gold ornaments.

Doña Alcira had inherited it all from her father who had died two years previously. Her mother, the Duchess of Carcastillo, was still alive, but she was not strong and kept to her own rooms where few people saw her save her confessor and her most intimate friends.

'All mine!' Doña Alcira thought to herself, as she went slowly down the staircase, her hand on the ebony rail of the gold and crystal banister.

She looked at the pictures hanging on the wall. Each one was worth a fortune. Almost instinctively the fingers of one hand touched the emeralds round her neck. They were part of the family jewels, a collection which far exceeded in value those owned by the Queen.

At the foot of the staircase someone was waiting. At the sight of her he gave a funny little hop, skip and jump, and then with a childlike eagerness ran up the stairs to greet her.

'We are going to a party, Frivolo,' Doña Alcira said, laying her hand on the dwarf's thick head of hair.

He was a strange, grotesque and yet, at the same time, pathetic object, barely three feet tall; his head was larger than the head of a normal man; his body was smaller than that of a child. His legs and arms, foreshortened, fat and dumpy, were horrible in their appearance.

If anything was needed to accentuate and draw attention to Doña Alcira's beauty, it was Frivolo the dwarf whom she took everywhere with her. Dressed in vivid satins and velvets, he was the caricature of a human being; a terrible, almost bestial cartoon of what nature could produce.

Frivolo had been rescued from a circus where the Duke of Carcastillo had found him being cruelly and unmercifully treated by an acrobat who wanted him to walk a tight-rope. It was a physical impossibility for Frivolo with his ill-proportioned and malformed limbs to balance himself in any way. The acrobat had half killed him in an effort to teach him what he could never have learnt.

The Duke had bought the dwarf for a very small sum and brought him back to his home, not quite certain what he should do with his purchase, already feeling that he had been over-impulsive. He was, in fact, a kindly man who disliked brutality in any form, and it had seemed to him at the time that the only possible thing to do was to rescue the poor, badly treated creature.

But once he arrived home, the Duke found his new charge an embarrassment. The servants ran away shrieking at the sight of him, declaring he would bring the evil eye upon them. The Duchess begged him to keep the deformity out of sight.

'What can I do with the monstrosity?' the Duke had asked helplessly.

Doña Alcira supplied the answer. She had not been afraid, disgusted or repelled by Frivolo. He appealed to something twisted and malformed in her own mind. She saw all too clearly the sensation it would cause if Frivolo became her personal attendant and accompanied her wherever she went.

'The beauty and the beast!' She could hear her friends saying it. She could see with their eyes the contrast between her own exquisite and delicate beauty and Frivolo's outrageous, contorted ugliness.

The dwarf responded with a dog-like devotion which she accepted as she accepted the adulation of every man she knew.

Now, as he kissed her hand with his thick lips, his little pig-like eyes staring up at her from his moon-like face, she gave him a more kindly smile than those she usually accorded to her handsome and devoted admirers.

'A party? We go to a party?' Frivolo asked in his shrill, excited voice.

'Yes, a party,' Doña Alcira said. 'Don Carlos is giving it. You like Don Carlos, don't you, Frivolo?'

'No, no, Frivolo not like Don Carlos,' the dwarf said positively. 'Don Carlos slimy, greedy, wanting too much.'

Doña Alcira laughed. It was a good description of Don Carlos, and it never failed to amuse her that the dwarf was invariably right in his summing up of a person's character. He had a shrewdness which seemed to see past the usual superficialities of a person's make-up and strike on the truth which lay beneath the veneer of pleasantry and politness.

Don Carlos had, Doña Alcira knew, on more than one occasion made a fuss of the dwarf, giving him money and sweetmeats simply because he believed in that way he could curry favour with his mistress. But Frivolo was not deceived.

Don Carlos, Marqués de Estrada, lived in a comparatively small mansion not far from the Carcastillo Palace. It was rumoured that to keep himself in Madrid he extorted tremendous and quite illegal taxes from his estates in the south, but they were too far away for people to make inquiries or even to be sure of their facts. It was also said that Don Carlos could not have continued to keep up his mansion without the large sums of money he gained from gaming.

There were even those who whispered that the cards ran too often in Don Carlos's favour; that experienced gamesters, whose characters were beyond reproach, would not play with Don Carlos, and that he was forced to challenge young and inexperienced men to games of chance from which they invariably emerged the losers.

Such stories may perhaps have been lies or put about by those who feared Don Carlos's influence for quite different reasons.

As far as Doña Alcira was concerned, Don Carlos played only one role in her life. That was of a persistent and importunate lover. He had wanted to marry her ever since she was widowed, and not only, she told herself, because she was a great heiress. She had laughed at him, refused him, and told him he was wasting his time. Don Carlos continued his suit day in, day out, year after year.

The coach was waiting outside the front door to carry Doña Alcira and Frivolo to the party. It was drawn by four white horses. There was a coachman and a footman on the box and two powdered footmen standing up behind. Doña Alcira believed in travelling in state.

She settled herself comfortably on the cushioned seat, spreading out her wide skirts so that they should not be creased. Frivolo waited until she was settled, and then scrambled awkwardly up the steps into the coach. The footman was slow in helping him, and the dwarf, snarling like an animal, cursed him in the fluent, abusive argot of the streets.

He cast reflections on the legitimacy of the man's birth, on the virtue of his mother and the character of his father. When he had finished, Frivolo swaggered into the coach and clambered on to the seat opposite Doña Alcira, to sit there smirking, with his legs dangling.

Standing up behind the heavy coach as it drove off the footman who had been abused said to the other:

'The little swine! If I wasn't afraid he'd haunt me, I'd wring his neck.'

'You'd better be careful. She dotes on him,' the other footman replied.

'And that's not the only person on whom she dotes!' was the reply, with a wink.

The carriage went over a rut and the footmen hung on grimly. When they were on smooth ground again the second flunkey asked curiously:

'What d'you mean by that?'

His companion told him.

Doña Alcira and Frivolo entered Don Carlos's house slightly after one o'clock in the morning, but the party was only just beginning to warm up, and no one would have thought of leaving for another two hours.

As her arrival was announced in stentorian tones, Don Carlos sprang up from the table where he was playing cards and hurried across the room towards her.

He was a thin, unattractive-looking man with a long nose and eyes that were too close together. He was rude and autocratic to those he considered his inferiors, and over-gushing to those with whom he wished to ingratiate himself.

The hand which touched Doña Alcira's was, she noticed with faint distaste, hot and moist. He raised her fingers to his lips.

'Now the moon has come out and my heart is flooded with light,' he said.

'I am sorry to be late, my lord,' Doña Alcira replied formally. 'I had many matters to attend to.'

'You have come—that is all that matters,' Don Carlos began to say, but his voice was lost by the shrill remark from Frivolo:

'She was thinking of the Englishman,' he mocked. 'The Englishman who comes from across the sea to marry her!'

With a roar of laughter at this, the guests, who had all been watching with curiosity the meeting between their host and Doña Alcira, saw a dark angry flush suffuse Don Carlos's sallow skin.

'One can keep no secrets from Frivolo,' Doña Alcira said, as one might speak of a precocious but favoured child.

'When is this Englishman due?' someone asked.

'I had heard rumours of his arrival,' another replied, 'but until now I had not believed them.'

'I am not worried,' Don Carlos said in a low voice which only Doña Alcira could hear.

'You are not?' she questioned, a hint of surprise in the eyes she raised to his.

'No,' he answered, and there was an expression on his face which she did not understand.

'But why?' she inquired, puzzled and slightly intrigued despite herself.

'Because he will not come!' Don Carlos replied, and there was an expression of evil elation on his narrow face.

6

By the time Lord Lynke and Ventura arrived in Madrid they were tired of travelling, although the journey had been not too arduous. The inns at which they had stayed after that first disastrous night had been better appointed, and there had been no difficulty in obtaining a bedroom for Ventura.

At first, she found it hard to sleep, lying awake hour after hour imagining that each creak on the stairs was an assassin and each flickering shadow a murderer armed with a knife. But the days were long, the roads were rough, and soon she found that almost immediately after they had eaten their evening meal she was glad to fall into bed and sleep a dreamless, childlike sleep.

The weather had been fine and she saw little of Lord Lynke who preferred to ride his magnificent horses rather than be confined in the swaying coach. But they ate together, and it seemed to Ventura that, since she had saved his life, he treated her not only as an equal but as a companion. He spoke frankly and openly of the reason why he had been sent to Spain. He mimicked for her amusement the Duke of Newcastle's precise and pious voice, and even described Charlotte and spoke of his distress at having to leave her.

Ventura received these confidences with mixed feelings. She was neither innocent nor a fool. She was well aware that young men had clandestine love affairs and that married women sometimes betrayed their husbands. Nevertheless, what she had known vaguely in theory was very different from listening day after day to a man recounting his escapades and leaving her in no doubt that he hoped for further adventures of the same sort.

She wondered about the lovely, indiscreet Charlotte. Was she miserable and unhappy without her handsome, irresponsible lover? Lord Lynke had been gentleman enough not to mention her by name. But to explain why he had been banished from England it was necessary to tell Ventura that Charlotte was in waiting on the Queen. She was of noble birth Ventura thought to herself and wondered if it was fashionable in London for a noble lady to stoop to the folly of loving a man who was not her husband.

'When I marry,' Ventura told herself one night in the darkness, 'I shall want to love only the man to whom I belong.'

She felt herself shudder at the idea of intrigue and subterfuge, of stolen meetings, smuggled letters and guilty kisses. She thought of her father's and mother's happiness, of their delight in each other's company, of the expression of tenderness in their eyes when they looked at one another, and the way neither of them could bear to be parted even for a few hours.

'That is how my marriage will be,' Ventura vowed aloud.

Yet, shocked though she sometimes was by Lord Lynke's revelations of his wildness and dalliance, she was fascinated by all that he told her. She found herself encouraging him to reveal more and yet more of his past.

He told her how he had been thrashed at Eton because he had driven up to London to meet a lovely ballet dancer with whom he fancied himself in love. He related how he had been sent down from Oxford for bathing with a bevy of attractive young women in the College fountain after an uproarious party which had awakened half the town. He described to her visits to the stage door at Drury Lane and the night life in London, where a man could amuse himself in gaming dens and places which catered for every type of taste and interest.

Demned pretty love-birds at the White House,' he confided. 'Of course, one has to be up to snuff and well lined in the pockets or they soon give you the cold shoulder.'

As Ventura listened, wide-eyed, she realised that Lord Lynke was talking to her simply as an antidote to homesickness. He had forgotten who she was and never considered for a moment that, to a young boy, such knowledge was not particularly desirable. He was, in reality, talking to himself, living again in his thoughts the life which had amused him and held his interest, and for which he found the emptiness of the Spanish landscape a very poor substitute.

Only as they neared Madrid did Lord Lynke cease to live in the past and begin to anticipate the future.

'Are there any amusements in Madrid?' he asked a little petulantly their last night on the road.

'People who have been there say it is the gayest capital in Europe,' Ventura answered. 'The King and Queen live very quietly owing to His Majesty's ill health. But outside the Palace there is entertainment to tempt the most jaded tastes.'

There was a touch of sarcasm in her voice, and Lord Lynke said quickly with a twist of his lips:

'Are you really inferring that my tastes are jaded? It makes me sound cursed old.'

'Not jaded, but spoilt, m'lord,' Ventura answered.

Lord Lynke frowned for a moment, and then he laughed.

'You are certainly frank,' he said. 'If you were an English boy, I would box your ears for the impertinence; but because you say it, I have a feeling it might be the truth.'

81

'It is understandable—you have had so much,' Ventura murmured.

'Perhaps I have, Lord Lynke said slowly.

He got to his feet and walked across the floor of the inn to stand looking down at the flames of the log fire.

'I suppose, having always had money, I have never imagined what it would be like to be without it,' he said slowly. 'I was thinking last night how thin and emaciated you were when we first started this journey. You were just a mass of skin and bones, and now . . . have you looked at yourself in the mirror?'

'Yes,' Ventura answered.

'Then you see the difference,' Lord Lynke said. 'You are hardly recognisable as the same boy. That has been brought about entirely by the expenditure of a few *pesetas* a day on food. Food that I have always taken for granted, while you have been near to starvation!'

Ventura felt herself flush a little that he had noticed her. Day by day she had seen the difference in herself. The colour coming into her cheeks, the burnished sheen on her hair, the filling out of her face, the bones of her body ceasing to be prominent.

More than once she had looked anxiously at her figure lest it should betray her femininity, but she was still so slight, so slim, that it would have been hard for anyone seeing her in the disguising velvet suit and long brocade waistcoats, to suspect her of being anything but what she pretended.

'How little one knows of what goes on in the world,' Lord Lynke was saying. 'Am I more selfish or more self-centred than any other of my generation? I doubt it, and yet I suppose it seldom occurred to any of us to wonder what had happened to men who, like your father, were exiled in 1719.'

'Many are with Prince Charles Stuart,' Ventura murmured.

'But many have died,' Lord Lynke added, 'eating out their hearts with loneliness and poverty.'

Ventura said nothing, and after a moment Lord Lynke said:

'Won't you trust me, Venturo? Won't you tell me now, after we have been together all these weeks, who your father was?'

Ventura did not speak for a moment. It was as if she debated with herself whether she was right to break the

82

silence with which she had encompassed herself protectively ever since she had entered Lord Lynke's service.

Slowly she raised her eyes to his:

'It is not because I do not trust you,' she told him. 'It is because my father let no one know his real name. He was not only hiding from the English, it was something that he did not wish the Spaniards to know either. I do not know what it was. I only know that when he told me who he was, he made me promise to keep it a secret. "Later," he said, "I will tell you everything." He died without my learning any more.'

'So, you will not tell me,' Lord Lynke said.

He had an unaccountable curiosity to know the truth, but he told himself that in reality it was of little interest. The boy was a useful page and in Madrid might prove even more useful.

What did it matter if his real name was Cameron or McGregor? There had been enough Scotsmen fools enough to fight for the Old Pretender, and doubtless in time there would be many more foolish enough to fight and die for Charles Stuart. But because the boy was reluctant to trust him with his little secret, perversely, Lord Lynke was determined to learn it.

'We have been through quite a lot together, Venturo,' he said, with the charm which he could exert all too easily when it pleased him. 'You have saved my life, and I have a feeling that there are many other adventures, perhaps dangerous ones, ahead of us. I have told you a great deal, perhaps too much, about myself. I think it only fair that I should know a little about you.'

Still Ventura hesitated until, finally, Lord Lynke said with a note of irritation in his voice:

'Very well, if you prefer to keep your own counsel, I must accept it. I cannot force you to be friendly.'

'It is not that,' Ventura said in troubled tones. 'I was wondering what would be my father's wishes in the matter if he knew of the position in which I now find myself. But somehow I think that because you have done so much for me, because I am indeed so happy in your service, he would wish me to tell you the truth.'

She drew in a deep breath.

'My father was the Earl of Kinbrace.'

'Kinbrace! Euan Kinbrace!'

Lord Lynke repeated the name in amazement, and then he said:

'I remember him. He used to come and stay with my father when I was a child. He was a very distant connexion of my mother's. I remember hearing how he fought almost singlehanded against the King's men, then escaped with great brilliance and bravery. There was a price on his head; his lands in Scotland were forfeit. I remember now my father and mother talking about it, and my mother's distress at the thought that she would never see her kinsman again.'

'You knew him!' Ventura exclaimed softly.

'Yes, I must have been about eight or nine the last time I saw him,' Lord Lynke answered. 'He had red hair and astonishingly blue eyes. Now I know where yours come from!'

'My father always said that I had my mother's features, but his eyes,' Ventura smiled.

Lord Lynke sat down on the other side of the fire-place and stared at the boy opposite him. No wonder, he thought, he had said proudly that he was the son of a gentleman. There was no mistaking the breeding in that small aristocratic nose, clear-cut lines of forehead and chin, the proud carriage of the head and in the long, thin fingers and well-shaped legs. Kinbrace's son! He suddenly wished that his mother was alive so that he could tell her about it.

'But why should your father have been hiding from the Spaniards?' he asked. 'This country is very much in sympathy with the Old Pretender.'

'I wish I could answer that question,' Ventura answered. 'I only knew that my father must have had a good reason for remaining anonymous. We were very poor and he worked hard to get enough money to buy us the every-day things we needed. My mother worked, too. She embroidered and took in sewing from people in the town. She had learnt it from the nuns when she was a girl, and after my father was dead it was only this work of hers which kept us alive.'

Lord Lynke was attending with but part of his mind to what Ventura was saying. He was realising that the boy sitting opposite him was now the Earl of Kinbrace. An ancient title and one of which any boy might be proud, despite the fact that his father's ill-judged loyalty to the Stuart cause had resulted in his banishment from England.

'I suppose,' Lord Lynke said aloud, 'you would not like to enter Madrid under your own name? You are the Earl of Kinbrace, you know. It is revered in Scottish history. Would you not be wise to claim the title now before, perhaps, other people make pretensions to it?'

'No, no!' Ventura spoke quickly, with a note of agitation in her voice. 'I could not do that, I must not. I revealed my father's identity only to you. Please promise me, my lord, that you will not mention it to anyone.

There was no mistaking the pleading in the blue eyes looking up into his or the expression of strain on the little face, or in the feverishly twisting fingers.

Lord Lynke's lips tightened. There was something behind this, he thought, that had not been fully revealed. He had been told part of the secret but not all. What was the rest? He could not even hazard a guess.

'Very well,' he said brusquely, 'your secret is safe with me. You shall arrive in Madrid as we planned, calling yourself Euan Cameron, but I think you are mistaken.'

'I thank you, my lord,' Ventura said.

'I would rather you trusted than thanked me,' Lord Lynke said enigmatically. Then, without pursuing the subject further, he retired to his bedchamber.

Ventura tossed, wakeful and unhappy, in her own narrow bed. She wished she had not said so much, and then regretted that she could not have said more. She knew intuitively, without words, that Lord Lynke was disappointed in her, and she worried because she could not surrender her problems completely to his hands. He had been so kind, so generous, and yet she must fail him. With something like a sob she turned over and tried to sleep.

But in the morning Lord Lynke appeared to be in the best of humours. His journey's end was in sight, and Simon dressed him with particular care so that on arrival at the Palace he should create a good impression.

There was no doubt that the whole cavalcade was received with admiration as the heavy coach with its resplendent attendants and six magnificently paired horses swung through the gateway into the wide, open courtyard of the seventeenth-century Palace built in the centre of the beautiful park known as El Retiro. The grooms in attendance and even the soldiers on duty stared at it with undisguised admiration.

Flunkeys opened the door and let down the steps. And equerry covered in medals and with gold epaulettes came forward to bow and welcome Lord Lynke with a few well-chosen words.

The ancient Palace, which had been adapted, rebuilt and added to by the Kings of Spain since the eleventh century, had been burnt down three years earlier on Christmas night. Ventura was, however, tremendously impressed and almost overawed by the Palace which was to house the Court until Phillip V's building plans were put into execution.

They ascended a huge marble staircase beneath a ceiling of encrusted gold. There were attendants and Gentlemen at Arms posted all the way up the stairs and along the corridors.

Ventura, a few steps behind Lord Lynke, wanted to gape openmouthed at everything they passed, but Lord Lynke seemed completely indifferent to his surroundings. He was chatting jovially to the equerry about the journey, telling him of the roughness of the roads, the discomforts of the inns, and the almost record speed at which they had covered the distance between San Sebastian and Madrid.

Their guide ushered them into an ante-room embellished with colossal chandeliers and hung with rather unprepossessing portraits of previous Kings of Spain.

'If your lordship will graciously wait here, I will inform His Majesty of your arrival. He was asking the Queen only this morning when you might be expected.'

'I am most grateful for Their Majesties' consideration,' Lord Lynke said politely.

The equerry left them and Lord Lynke turned and winked at Ventura.

'Anxious to be polite, I see,' he said, in an amused voice. 'Well, it shows me that my uncle, the Duke of Newcastle, has kept his word. The least I can do in return is to get him what he wants.'

'What is that?' Ventura inquired.

Lord Lynke looked at her speculatively.

'I will tell you later,' he said. 'Don't let me forget.'

He walked round the room staring at the portraits. He stopped before one of a Spanish Queen and said:

'The Lord save us if all the *señoritas* are like this one!'

'I think, m'lord, you will find that Doña Alcira is very beautiful,' Ventura suggested.

She did not know why, but she could not help hoping that rumour had lied and that Doña Alcira would not be as gloriously beautiful as had been reported. It was not long before she was to see the truth herself.

The equerry returned and led them towards the Throne Room through ante-rooms crowded with courtiers. There was no mistaking the interest that Lord Lynke caused as he moved past wearing a resplendent coat of blue and silver brocade with a waistcoat embroidered in scarlet thread. There were diamonds twinkling in his lace cravat, a diamond ring on his finger; but, even so, compared with the Spaniards he was quite plainly dressed.

But he was by no means overshadowed. He had something, Ventura thought proudly, which made him quite independent of ornamentation. It was not only his good looks which commanded attention but his strong personality. No one could fail to notice him.

'The Englishman!' Ventura heard one or two people whisper as they passed; and then just as they entered the Throne Room she heard something else. She could not see the speaker. She was past him before she could look up at his face, and with tremendous effort restrained herself from looking back. What he said was quite clear: 'The Englishman! Don Carlos said he would not come!'

Don Carlos was going to get quite a surprise, Ventura thought. Then she could think of nothing except the fact that she was being presented to the King and Queen of Spain.

The Throne Room, with its red and gold walls, with its raised and canopy-covered throne, was too awe-inspiring to be taken in at first glance. But the man sitting on the throne and the woman by his side were merely surprising in that they appeared so homely.

Ventura had heard people talk so often about the Queen and her endless intrigues that she had expected someone quite different from the fat, rather tired-looking woman with swollen legs. Elizabeth Farnese had nearly lost all the beauty she had once possessed. Yet, the moment she began to speak it was obvious why she dominated her husband.

The King's weak, depressed voice quite clearly reflected not only his personality, but his wandering brain. The Queen, alert, voluble and charming, was all too obviously the real ruler of Spain. She was gracious to the point of being ingratiating to Lord Lynke.

'We are deeply honoured by your visit, my lord,' she said. 'His Grace of Newcastle has specially commended you to His Majesty's attention. You must dine with us this evening and tell us all the news of the English Court.'

'It is indeed gracious of Your Majesty,' Lord Lynke said.

'What's the shooting like in England these days?' the King asked in far-away tones.

'There is no shooting at the moment, Your Majesty,' Lord Lynke replied. 'But we had a good year with the partridges.'

The King said something to the Queen and she explained hastily:

'His Majesty is more interested in larger game—stags and wild boar; but you can talk about it later.'

She turned to the equerry.

'Take Lord Lynke to the Garden Salon. Doña Alcira is there and will, I know, be impatient to greet him.'

There was meaning in the Queen's glance as she looked at the Spaniard, and he led the way from the Throne Room after Lord Lynke and Ventura had bowed deeply to both Their Majesties.

The equerry led the way through several magnificent rooms. These were empty, but the room into which he led Lord Lynke and Ventura was filled with people. Here the Ladies of the Court were assembled and with them many of the officials and courtiers who were in waiting on Their Majesties after they had finished giving audience.

As Lord Lynke entered the long room which overlooked the gardens, several people round the door stopped talking and their silence affected those near to them, so that in a few seconds, it seemed to Ventura, the chatter had almost ceased.

Slowly the equerry paraded down the room until almost at the far end he paused in front of a group sitting by the window. There three ladies were gathered together, but one stood out among them so that there was no doubt who she was or to whom they were to be presented.

'May I present the Right Honourable Lord Lynke?' the equerry asked.

There was a pause before Doña Alcira rose to her feet and dropped a deep curtsy. From that position she looked up into Lord Lynke's eyes. She was lovely, Ventura thought suddenly—the loveliest woman she had ever seen!

'So you have arrived, my lord!' There was no hint of surprise in her voice, only a note of amusement.

Lord Lynke raised her fingers to his lips.

'I have arrived,' he repeated. 'But the journey has seemed a century long because of my impatience.'

'Your impatience for what?' Doña Alcira inquired.

Lord Lynke raised his eyebrows as if at the stupidity of her question.

'To meet you, of course, madame.'

She laughed at that, a provocative, enticing laugh, while her eyes flirted with him.

'You are a courtier,' she said, 'and I had always believed that Englishmen were inarticulate.' She glanced round the silent throng watching them. 'But you must meet my friends.' She murmured the names of the ladies who curtsied as Lord Lynke bowed, then she turned to the men.

'First, I must present someone who is most surprised at your safe arrival—Don Carlos, the Marqués de Estrada.'

Lord Lynke did not bow. Instead he looked straight into the sulky face and dark malevolent eyes of Don Carlos.

'The noble *Marqués* undoubtedly had good reason to suspect that I might fall by the wayside,' he said clearly.

Don Carlos did not answer. Ventura saw his fingers close convulsively over the hilt of his sword, then without a word he turned and walked away.

Doña Alcira threw back her head and laughed a little spitefully.

'He is jealous,' she said mockingly.

Lord Lynke raised her fingers once again to his lips.

'I am more than flattered,' he said softly. Then, as he straightened himself, he added: 'May I present my page? He comes from Scotland—Mr. Euan Cameron.'

Ventura made a Court bow which she had copied closely from the elegant performance of Lord Lynke. The ladies inclined their heads and made only the vaguest pretence at dropping a curtsy. Then, as she raised her head, she saw Doña Alcira's face. It was drained of all colour and there was a look of incredulous amazement in her eyes. But as she met Ventura's gaze, the expression on her face changed. The astonishment vanished, to be replaced with something else—something sinister, almost frightening.

'The name was Cameron, was it not?' she asked, and there was a note of insistency in her voice.

'Euan Cameron, at your service, my lady,' Ventura

replied, speaking as firmly and in the most masculine manner that she could manage.

Doña Alcira said nothing more. The colour was returning to her face; but the look she gave her made Ventura feel suddenly and inexplicably afraid.

7

'Not bad rooms,' Lord Lynke said approvingly. 'They obviously think I am of import!'

He walked round the large *salon*, inspecting the exquisite carved furniture, the bookcases filled with valuable volumes, and the pictures which graced the walls.

There was a big bedchamber, elegantly furnished, and beyond it, though not connected, was the room where Ventura was to sleep.

Her room was small, but even so, it was furnished with pictures painted by great Masters and hung with exquisite embroidered hangings which had been made for the Palace over a hundred years ago.

Lord Lynke stopped wandering, and taking off his sword, threw in on a chair, and then sat down on the sofa.

'Lord! How this kotowing tires a man!' he exclaimed.

It was not surprising that he was tired, Ventura thought. Since their audience with Their Majesties at noon, they had been calling on important personages, talking with statesmen, and making themselves pleasant to courtiers, without a stop.

Ventura had accompanied Lord Lynke everywhere except when he visited Sir Benjamin Keene, the British Minister.

'You may deceive the Spaniards with your English,' Lord Lynke said, 'but you won't get away with it if Sir Benjamin hears you. You stay outside in the coach and I will tell him you are indisposed.'

'I thought my English was so much better,' Ventura replied, piqued by Lord Lynke's words and not a little offended. She had tried so hard to imitate his manner of speaking, the intonations in his voice and the way in which he phrased a sentence.

'You're good!' he said approvingly. 'In fact, you are damned good, but I don't want Keene to go smelling a rat. Besides, if he did suspect that you were not Euan Cameron from north of the Tweed, he might talk about it. That is the one thing we want to avoid at all cost.'

They had had little time for conversation except in the coach driving through the crowded, picturesque streets to the British Ministry and back through El Retiro to the Palace.

Now Ventura told Lord Lynke what she had heard said as they passed through the antechamber.

Lord Lynke stroked his chin reflectively.

'It's obvious that fellow, Don Carlos, meant to prevent our arriving here,' he said.

'He may try again,' Ventura suggested anxiously.

'Somehow I doubt it,' Lord Lynke answered. 'If we had been murdered on the road, the news would have taken weeks in reaching Madrid, and by that time it would have been almost impossible to trace the assassin. But a murder here, under everyone's nose, would be a very different matter.'

'Yes, I can see that,' Ventura agreed, 'but at the same time I didn't like the look of Don Carlos. He ... he frightens me.'

'Chicken-hearted, eh?' Lord Lynke teased. 'Don't worry. I can deal with this fancy Spaniard now I know he is my enemy. I suppose he is an aspirant to the hand of the fair lady.'

'You think he wants to marry Doña Alcira?' Ventura questioned.

Lord Lynke nodded.

'I can see no other reason for his enmity. Oh, well! I don't blame him.'

'She is very beautiful,' Ventura said in a small voice.

'Very,' Lord Lynke said appreciatively.

He glanced at the clock over the mantelpiece.

'Five o'clock. I shall go and call on her. I hear they dine later in this country than in England. Five o'clock is an excellent hour for a *tête-à-tête*.'

He rose eagerly from the sofa, his tiredness forgotten. He went into his bedroom, pealed the bell violently for Simon, and demanded a change of clothes.

Ventura sat where he had left her. She was thinking of

Doña Alcira's face, wondering why she had changed colour, why there had been that strange look of astonishment in her eyes.

She could not have been mistaken. She had been watching the beautiful Spaniard all the time she was talking to Lord Lynke, noting the contours of that oval face with its magnolia skin; seeing, as only another woman could see, the tantalising enticement of those narrow eyes, and lips that seemed to have a faint mockery about their perfect fullness. Doña Alcira might flaunt her charms for all the world to see, but those charms were certainly worth flaunting.

'I am afraid of her,' Ventura told herself, and then knew that her feelings were deeper than that. Unreasonably and illogically, she hated Doña Alcira.

She looked towards the inner room where she could hear Lord Lynke talking to Simon. He is too good, she thought, for a woman like that; and yet, she asked herself, what had she against the King's ward? She was not sure, in fact it was nothing she could put into words; and yet she knew, with an intuition which came from some native, God-given wisdom, that Doña Alcira was bad.

'I hate her!' she whispered aloud, then shrank from the passion in her own words.

The door of the bedroom was opened and Lord Lynke came striding into the room. He had changed into a coat of cherry-red velvet trimmed with diamond buttons, which opened over a waistcoat embroidered with Tudor roses in pure silver thread. There were diamonds sparkling in his cravat, and diamond buckles on his shining black shoes.

'I shall come straight from Doña Alcira to dinner,' he said. 'You must meet me in the ante-room. Anyone will tell you the way, and don't forget, you stand behind my chair during the meal. Do you recall your duties?'

'I hope so,' Ventura answered, and then added with a little smile: 'I am afraid, m'lord, of letting you down and making you ashamed of me.'

Lord Lynke put a comforting hand on her shoulder.

'Don't worry,' he said. 'Any mistakes you make will be attributed to your barbaric upbringing. Sir Benjamin tells me that the Spaniards think of us in England as a most uncultured people.'

He walked towards the door, and then turned back.

'You have done unconscionably well, so far,' he said, with a smile which made Ventura's heart turn over in her breast. 'I was proud of you at the Audience today. Don't forget the blood that runs in your veins is as fine as that of most of the people who treat you as if you were nobody—if not finer.'

'Thank you.' Ventura could hardly say the words before he was gone.

She stood looking at the door through which he had passed, feeling a little glow of pleasure because he had commended her. It was so like him, she thought to say something like that in case she was smarting from an insult she had received just as they were leaving the Garden Salon.

Ventura had been following closely behind Lord Lynke. A rather important-looking lady had attempted to walk between them. Frightened of being left behind, Ventura had pressed forward, only to receive a flick of the lady's fan straight in her face.

'Impertinent boys should not be allowed in here,' she had said in an audible voice to her companion: 'In the old days this room was kept for gentlemen.'

On Ventura's lips had hovered for a moment a rude retort. Lord Lynke had glanced over his shoulder in a warning manner, and she had followed him without a word.

Now she knew he had tried to salve her pride, and he had succeeded. He was proud of her. She felt like dancing at the thought, but then she remembered where he had gone, and her spirits fell again. Quite suddenly she wanted to cry. Slowly she went out into the passage which led to her own room.

Lord Lynke was humming a tune beneath his breath as he walked down the wide staircase to the front door. Simon had already ordered the coach and it was waiting for him. The horses were being fulsomely admired by the flunkeys.

When Lord Lynke directed the coachman to Doña Alcira's house, he saw a knowing look on the faces of those in attendance, and realised with a sudden sense of irritability that there was likely to be nothing private about his love-making where everyone at the Spanish Court was concerned.

'Dammit! 'Tis like being at a playhouse,' he swore to himself as the coach started off.

He had a sudden impulse to change his mind, then

realised it would cause even more comment if he did so. It would be expected that he should call at the earliest opportunity on the lady he had travelled many thousands of miles to see. In fact, it might seem rude if he waited until the morrow.

The coach travelled swiftly through the beautiful park, past stone fountains, Grecian temples and elaborate grottoes; but Lord Lynke was deep in his own thoughts, forgetting, for the moment, even Doña Alcira, but thinking instead of his interview with Sir Benjamin Keene.

'Your uncle, His Grace of Newcastle, has told me, by code of course, thay you are prepared, if it is possible, to help me discover what is the Queen's motive behind her new and quite unexpected pleasantries towards our country,' Sir Benjamin said.

'You think there is a reason other than peace?' Lord Lynke asked.

'If peace was what Spain really required, why did Patino, Chief Minister to Their Majesties, build up the most powerful fleet in the whole world? He died last year, but Don Sebastian de La Quadra is carrying on his plans and his ideas, and I tell you, m'lord, I do not like what I see and hear.'

'You think it might mean a fresh bid for Gibraltar?' Lord Lynke inquired.

Sir Benjamin made a gesture of helplessness.

'I do not know. If I did, it would be better. All I am completely and absolutely convinced of is that there is something afoot.'

Lord Lynke had felt both his interest and his curiosity were aroused. It would be amusing, he thought, if he could find out what Sir Benjamin had failed to discover. But how he was to do this he had not the slightest idea.

The coach drew up at the enormous entrance to Doña Alcira's palace. Flunkeys in magnificent uniforms of purple and green came hurrying to open the door of the coach and help Lord Lynke to alight. He was escorted up wide marble steps and in through an archway, which reminded him of entering a cathedral.

Lord Lynke was shown into an enormous, rather ornate *salon* and told that Doña Alcira would be informed of his arrival.

Alone, Lord Lynke stared about him. The room was magnificent, and yet he had a sudden longing for his own rooms at Hatharton Castle. The *salon* that his mother had redecorated would seem very plain compared with this baroque magnificence, but he knew that he preferred it, just as his own favourite room—a book-filled library—was more to his taste than all the glories and luxury of the Courts he had visited either in England or abroad.

He thought of his dogs lying in front of the fire and wished with all his heart that he was home. In Hatharton there would be no intrigue, no fears of assassination, and no dark-eyed woman to be placated. He had a yearning that was almost a physical pain for the Norman castle where he had been born. Then the door opened and he forgot everything but the present as he followed a resplendent major-domo up the marble stairs to the first floor.

He guessed that Doña Alcira would see him in her own rooms. It was not the first time by any means that he had visited an attractive woman at this particular hour and found her resting, yet not too fatigued to see him. He expected to be admitted and there was a cynical little smile on his lips as the major-domo opened the door and announced him.

He walked in and saw Doña Alcira lying—as he had expected—on a couch drawn up in front of the fire. She was wearing a négligé of fine, almost transparent material which fell around her in soft folds, yet did little to conceal the exquisite curves of her slim figure.

The couch on which she reclined was different from any Lord Lynke had seen before. Low, almost as if it were of Eastern origin, it was little more than a mattress raised a few inches from the floor and piled with cushions embroidered in silk and covered with priceless antique lace over rose-pink satin.

The room, too, echoed the seductive intimacy of the couch. The walls as well as the windows were draped with soft satins and gossamer fine material. Incense was burning somewhere and its faint, exotic fragrance seemed to permeate everything so that Lord Lynke felt his senses swim a little as he came forward and bent down to kiss Doña Alcira's hand.

She drew back her head to look up at him, and he realised that her hair was unbound and fell over her shoulders to make a background for the whiteness of her skin. It was very long and very fine—a silken sheaf in which a man might bury his face and forget everything but his own desire.

'I did not expect you so soon.' Her voice was very low

and yet, at the same time, there seemed to be another meaning in the words—an enticement, an invitation.

'Did you really believe I could stay away?'

She smiled at this and her eyelids dropped, her long dark lashes sweeping her cheeks as though she was shy, and yet Lord Lynke had the impression that it was not shyness but triumph that she concealed.

She moved her feet a little to one side and he understood that she was inviting him to sit down on the edge of the couch. As she moved, he could see that her feet were bare, the soles of them soft pink, the high arches of her insteps proclaiming her aristocratic lineage as they were crossed, one over the other.

'Tell me about yourself!' It was the voice of a siren, of a woman who knows that no man can resist that irresistible subject—the story of his own life.

'What do you want to know?'

Lord Lynke was not thinking of what he was saying. He felt that he was being swept into a whirlpool of passion and seduction so that he had no time to think, no time to consider anything but his own emotions.

He had never for one moment dreamt that he would be received in such a manner on the first occasion of his visit. He had been told by several people that the ladies of Spain were strait-laced and that they were chaperoned always by their *duennas*. Also that a man had to be very careful what he said or he would find himself facing the unsheathed swords of brothers and fathers.

He told himself that Doña Alcira was a widow and therefore not subject to the same conventions as a virgin, but, even so, the scene was a surprising one.

'I would rather talk about you,' Lord Lynke parried.

'You are interested?'

It was a question that he could answer, easily.

'Very interested. You are very beautiful.'

'I am glad you think so. I was afraid that you would only love English women—pink and white, with blue eyes and fair hair. Pah! They are insipid, and yet, no doubt Englishmen love them and ask for nothing more.'

Lord Lynke had a sudden memory of Charlotte—pink and white, with blue eyes—and yet no one would have called her insipid. Then, quite unexpectedly, he found himself remembering two blue eyes he had just left. Blue eyes, shining and happy because he had paid the owner a compliment, and then, as quickly, becoming perplexed and anxious as he left the room. Impatiently he put such thoughts from him.

'You are very different from what I expected,' he said honestly.

'And what did you expect?' Doña Alcira asked.

It seemed to Lord Lynke as if his senses had cleared a little. The incense was not so oppressive. The whirlpool into which he was falling had suddenly receded a little. He was on the brink of it and yet he could still think fairly clearly.

'You know why I have been sent here?' he asked.

'The Queen wishes us to marry,' Doña Alcira said pleasantly. 'Do you think you would like that?'

'It is for you to answer that question,' Lord Lynke said.

Doña Alcira looked at him from under her eyelashes.

'How can I know?' she asked. 'I do not know you—we must get to know each other. I want to learn of what you are thinking, what you are feeling, and if I am someone you could perhaps . . . love a little.' Her voice was soft and warm.

Lord Lynke bent forward and took her hand in his.

'You are a very unexpected person,' he said.

'Am I?' She drew him a little towards her. 'I am not a fool. I know that you have come here to marry the estates and the fortunes of the Dukes of Carcastillo. I am to marry the peace and goodwill of England. But why should we not enjoy what we have to do? Why should we not amuse ourselves as well as please the governments of our countries?'

Lord Lynke bent his head to kiss her hand. He was astounded by her frankness and yet, at the same time, he could not help seeing the logic of it. It was then that he realised suddenly that somehow, almost imperceptibly, she had changed her position. His lips were on her hand but her mouth was not very far away. She was looking up at him, her white shoulders so close that he could almost feel the rise and fall of her breasts. He lips were parted and her breath was coming quickly.

As he bent forward to find her mouth, something caught his eye. Something in the corner of the room, standing out despite the soft lights and the faint haze from the incense . . . then the whirlpool closed over his head.

He found himself sinking deeply into it, conscious only of the soft arms entwining his neck, of a soft body pressed closely to his, lips that gave him kiss for kiss, of long dark silken hair falling like a screen around them both. . . .

It was an hour later that Lord Lynke came hurrying into the ante-room where the Court was assembled for dinner. He was only in time by a split second for, even as he took his place in the line of those awaiting the arrival of Their Majesties, the door at the far end of the room opened and the Lord in Waiting appeared, walking backwards before the entrance of the King and Queen.

Ventura heaved a sigh of relief as Lord Lynke appeared. Her eyes went to his face, but his expression told her nothing. She wondered what reception he had received from Doña Alcira and again felt that stab of fear, or was it, she asked herself, jealousy? She almost laughed at the idea, and realised that this was the longest time, except when they had been asleep at night, that Lord Lynke had been out of her sight.

During the journey she had not been able to talk much to him, but at least she had been able to see him riding beside the coach, sometimes going a little ahead, but always coming back. He had been there—that was what had mattered. Now, she was to be left behind.

It was ridiculous to mind, and yet it seemed to her that the hours he had been away with Doña Alcira had been the longest she had ever experienced.

'It is because I have grown used, these past weeks, to knowing he was there!' she told herself. 'He has taken away my loneliness. He has become the one person in my life on whom I can rely.'

As they moved into dinner, Ventura saw the ladies of the Court casting shy glances and smiling at Lord Lynke. It was obvious that they wished to make his acquaintance. And when he was seated at table, he had an extremely pretty Princess on one side and a young, vivacious Duchess on the other.

Standing behind his chair, Ventura could hear the conversation very clearly and realised that both the women were doing their best to flirt with the handsome Englishman.

Their method of approach was so obvious, so blatant, that she wondered if any man could be so stupid as not to realise that they were over-flattering him and making fools of themselves. Yet, she thought scornfully, Lord Lynke seemed to enjoy it. More than once his laugh rang out so that the Queen looked down the table a little wistfully as if she was remembering her youth and wanted to know what the joke was about.

Dinner was a long, elaborate meal. Course followed course—all of them served on gold plate. The wine flowed freely and as soon as a guest had taken a sip from a glass it was replenished.

Ventura found herself growing very tired. She began to be afraid that she would fall asleep where she stood, or perhaps faint from exhaustion. That, she knew, would be disastrous. The thought of such a thing happening made her straighten herself.

When at last dinner was over, the company moved into the King and Queen's private sitting-room, and the equerries and pages were told to remain in the ante-room.

'They usually talk for about an hour until Their Majesties retire,' an equerry told Ventura.

She sat down in a high-backed chair which was hard and uncomfortable, and hoped that it would help her to keep awake. She hadn't been there more than a moment when she heard one of the men say something very rude about 'a little beast'. It was said in a low voice as if the speaker did not want to be overheard, but, turning her head, Ventura realised of whom he was speaking.

Coming wandering into the room was the most grotesque dwarf she had ever seen. He took no notice of the rest of the company who spoke to him as he passed, but came towards Ventura, his big hands swinging by his sides, his big head seeming too large and too heavy for his puny body.

He came up to Ventura's chair and put his big, clumsy hand on her arm. She wanted to shake it off but she felt it would be insulting. At the same time she realised to her surprise that the hand was strong and heavy and by no means as weak as it looked.

'Come with me. You are wanted,' tht dwarf said in Spanish.

Ventura shook her head.

'*No comprendo*,' she said slowly and hesitatingly as if it were the one sentence in Spanish that she knew.

'He wants you to go with him,' the equerry who spoke English told her.

'Where to?' Ventura asked.

'He is Frivolo, Doña Alcira's page. I expect his mistress wishes to see you.'

'I must wait for my master,' Ventura answered firmly.

'You must go with him,' the equerry insisted. 'Doña Alcira always gets what she wants. A summons from her is the same as a Royal command.'

Reluctantly Ventura rose to her feet, and the dwarf, gesticulating and beckoning, led her from the room. As she went, Ventura heard the sneering and laughing whispers which followed them.

'Don't tell me that Doña Alcira has started cradle-snatching?' someone asked. There was some spiteful laughter before another voice said: 'They will all be competing in the bullring before they have finished!' There was a roar at this and Ventura wondered what it meant.

The dwarf led her along the passages and through ante-rooms until they came to another part of the Palace. Here, there were smaller and more intimate rooms which Ventura guessed were used by the Queen's Ladies-in-Waiting. They passed through several until they came to one a little bigger and more ornate than the others. The room was empty save for Doña Alcira sitting in a high-backed chair in front of a writing-table.

Ventura stood just inside the room; the dwarf shut the door behind her.

'Come here, to the writing-table near me!' Doña Alcira said in Spanish.

She was wearing an elaborate satin gown and resplendent jewellery, and the sharpness of her voice was out of keeping with her appearance.

Ventura was just about to obey when she remembered who she was supposed to be, and remained where she was.

'*No comprendo, Madame,*' she said politely.

Doña Alcira turned her head.

'Come here,' she said in English.

Ventura obeyed her, coming up to the table and standing there attentively.

'Who are you?'

Ventura bowed.

'Euan Cameron, *Madame.*'

'Where do you come from? Who are your parents?'

'I come from Scotland. My parents live near Perth.'

'What is your father like?'

Ventura thought quickly. She did not know why but it was obviously unsafe to tell the truth.

100

'He is six feet tall, dark, with a black moustache which is now going a little grey,' she improvised.

Doña Alcira said nothing. She was watching Ventura in a strange, searching manner. Quite suddenly, she spoke in Spanish:

'There's a snake behind you! Jump or it will strike!'

Ventura did not move.

'*No comprendo,*' she said stupidly.

Doña Alcira rapped with her fingers on the table.

'How long has your father lived in Scotland?'

'All his life,' Ventura replied, 'as did his father before him.'

Doña Alcira made a gesture of impatience.

'You can go,' she said. 'I only hope you have been telling the truth.'

'Why should I tell you anything else, *Madame*?' Ventura asked.

'Go!' Doña Alcira commanded, and Ventura bowed and obeyed.

Outside the room she realised that she was trembling and her forehead was wet. She put up her finger to touch her face and then saw that the dwarf was watching her. He was lurking in a corner of the passage where she had not noticed him. He looked evil and frightening, she thought.

Quite suddenly, she knew she could stand no more. She started to run, not looking back to see if anyone was following her. Just running wildly, carelessly, using only her instinct for direction, and wanting, more than anything else, to get away both from the dwarf and his mistress. She was breathless as she reached a landing that she recognised. A moment later she found the door to the ante-room.

The equerries and pages were sitting where she had left them. At her entrance they looked up full of curiosity. Then, as Ventura stood there, her breath coming quickly, she saw to her utter relief that the doors at the far end of the room were opening.

Their Majesties were retiring to bed; but beyond them, like a harbour in a rough sea, a light shining in the darkness, Ventura saw Lord Lynke approaching.

He was looking for her, and her heart gave a sudden leap of gladness because, once again, she felt safe.

8

Ventura was tired. The Court Ball seemed to have been going on for a very long time. At first, she had been entranced by the magnificent dresses, the glittering jewels and the elaborate formality of the scene. The great gold and white ballroom, its glittering chandeliers lit with a thousand tapers, was a perfect setting for the beauty of the women and the gallantry of the courtiers.

Sitting in an obscure alcove where the pages were allowed to watch their masters, Ventura thought at first that this was a fairy-tale come true; then, as if the scales dropped from her eyes, she was forced almost against her will to see the truth. Beneath the glitter, the pomp and the spendour of the party there was unhappiness, malice and evil.

She saw the Queen scheming even while she was at play, consulting with the Ministers and, quite obviously, giving commands and instructions that the King was too weak to refute.

Ventura had heard that the King was interested now only in Farinelli, an opera singer who for the sum of fifteen hundred guineas was employed to sing to him every night. No one else was permitted to hear him any longer, and to please an audience of one he must sing the same songs over and over again.

Among the throng of dancers Ventura caught sight of Don Carlos. He was scowling darkly and she saw that his gaze was resting on Lord Lynke who was partnering Doña Alcira.

Lord Lynke stood out, Ventura thought proudly. It was not only his broad shoulders, his height and his handsome face which distinguished him, but something more intangible, more difficult to put into words.

There was something clean-cut, something intrinsically decent and trustworthy about him which made Ventura feel that he was like a breath of fresh air in an over-scented, over-heated atmosphere. All around her there were passions smouldering beneath the surface. Greed and avarice were but thinly disguised by paint and powder.

Perhaps, she told herself, it was Doña Alcira who made her feel that way. There was no doubt that the King's ward was looking her best tonight. She wore a dress of gold lamé lined with orange velvet. Her bodice was cut very low to show the valley between her breasts. She wore a necklace of pearls and diamonds and a great wealth of the same stones was entwined in her dark hair. She was radiant, she was beautiful; and yet, Ventura thought, there was something evil about her beauty. What it was she did not know. She only knew she mistrusted and, if she was truthful, hated Doña Alcira.

She saw Lord Lynke's face as he looked down at the Spanish beauty. 'He is infatuated with her,' Ventura thought and felt suddenly as if someone had thrust a dagger into her heart. She told herself that, logically, she should be pleased that Lord Lynke was to marry someone he loved, and yet every instinct in her body told her that she should warn him. About what?

She remembered the hardness in Doña Alcira's voice when she had questioned her. She remembered the expression on her face. Here was no soft, tender woman who would respond to love. Passion was a different thing, but how could she explain that to Lord Lynke?

She overheard going on around her the conversation of the other pages. One said to the other:

'The Englishman is enjoying his visit here.'

The other laughed.

'He is apparently prepared to share his favours!'

'I don't suppose he knows he is doing so,' the other retorted.

The first page sniggered.

'Miajado knows. I hear he was so distrait at the fight yesterday that the bull's horns tore the back of his coat; but the crowd roared, thinking he had done it on purpose. My friend who was there said he was like a sleep-walker.'

'Be careful what you are saying!' the page whispered, with a glance towards Ventura.

'The Englishman's page does not understand Spanish,' his friend retorted.

Ventura did understand, and with her brows knit she was thinking furiously. The pages had spoken of Miajado. She was well aware who he was. There was no one who lived in Spain who had not heard of his artistry, his

103

brilliance, which made every other matador seem clumsy. Miajado was a hero. He was also extremely handsome.

Bit by bit, like the pieces of a jigsaw, the things Ventura had heard fell into their places. The remark of the courtiers as Lord Lynke walked through the ante-room to be presented to Their Majesties; the giggles and the sniggers of the pages on various occasions; the cynical smiles of those watching Doña Alcira and Lord Lynke together.

Did Doña Alcira know that she was talked about? Ventura wondered. Perhaps, like other women all through the ages, she imagined that she kept her love affairs secret; but nothing was secret in palaces, and nothing was secret where a hero of the people was concerned.

A look, a glance, a word spoken by mistake was enough to set the gossips talking. And then, how easy for someone to see Miajado slipping like a shadow in through the doorway of Doña Alcira's palace! Yes, everyone would be talking and the only people who did not know what was being said would be Doña Alcira, Miajado and, of course, Lord Lynke.

'What can I do? How can I tell him? How can I warn him?' Ventura asked herself; and the problem kept her thoughts busy until at last, when she was almost dropping with fatigue, the King and Queen retired and the ball came to an end.

Even though Their Majesties had withdrawn from the glittering throng, the younger members of the Court still kept on talking and chattering, while some made their way towards the supper-room and the card-tables.

'I must go home,' Doña Alcira said to Lord Lynke.

'So early?' he asked.

'It is nearly two o'clock,' she replied.

'I have lost track of time while I have been talking to you,' he said.

She smiled up at him, her eyes under her long lashes mysterious and inviting.

'May I escort you home?' he inquired.

'And set all the gossips talking?' she questioned.

'What do they matter?' Lord Lynke asked, his voice deep with a sudden passion.

There was something about this woman that fired his desires. There was something exciting about her that seemed to challenge him and to which he could not help but respond.

'You are too impetuous!' Doña Alcira protested.

'Let me come with you tonight!' Lord Lynke begged insistently.

She shook her head.

'No, I am fatigued. Come to me tomorrow at four o'clock and we will talk about ourselves.'

'Why not now?' Lord Lynke pleaded.

As they spoke, they had reached the doorway and Ventura, seeing that Lord Lynke was leaving the room, had come from the alcove and was standing quietly behind him. Doña Alcira turned her head and looked directly into Ventura's eyes. It was a glance of hatred and of something else which made Ventura stand suddenly still as though she had been struck in the face by a cruel blow.

'Go to bed ... and take your page with you!' Doña Alcira said.

Her voice was sharp and peremptory; then, without another word, she swept away down another corridor, her wide skirt and long train rustling behind her like a snake. Lord Lynke watched her with a puzzled expression on his face, and then he turned to Ventura.

'That appears to be a command!' he said, 'so we had best obey it.'

He detached himself from the crowd and with Ventura at his heels, walked down the wide corridor which led from the ballroom to the less formal side of the Palace. At length they found their own staircase and began to climb it.

'Are you tired?' Lord Lynke asked.

'A little,' Ventura answered.

'Did you hear anything of interest?' It was a question Lord Lynke invariably asked.

For a moment Ventura hesitated. Should she tell him of the pages' conversation? she wondered, and then decided against it. It was too embarrassing, too intimate a matter for her to reveal; but before she could lie and say nothing, Lord Lynke noticed her hesitation.

'There was something!' he said quickly. 'What was it?'

'Something of little import,' Ventura parried.

'Everything is of importance if it concerns me or my country,' Lord Lynke answered. 'What did you hear?'

Still Ventura hesitated. But this time they had reached the landing outside their room. Lord Lynke thrust open the door of the sitting-room.

'Come in!' he commanded.

Ventura obeyed him, wishing she had been quicker with her replies, wishing, most of all, she had nothing to tell.

The fire was still burning in the grate and Lord Lynke gave the log a kick with his foot so that it burst into flames. There were only two tapers still alight in the sconces on either side of the chimney-piece, but they were enough for Lord Lynke to see Ventura's face clearly.

It was a sensitive face, he thought. The expressions chased themselves across it very clearly, and he knew now that she was striving to conceal something from him. He leant one arm against the mantelpiece and looked down at her.

'Well!' he said, 'I am waiting!'

'It was . . . only a few words,' Ventura faltered.

'About whom?'

Ventura looked away into the fire.

'About . . . Doña Alcira,' she answered in a very small voice.

'What about her?' Lord Lynke inquired.

'They said . . .' Ventura began, then broke off to stammer: 'It was . . . nonsense . . . quite untrue, I am sure . . . and . . . really not worth repeating.'

'What was it?'

'They . . . connected Doña Alcira's name with that of . . . Miajado.'

Ventura dare not look up into Lord Lynke's face as she almost whispered the words. She felt she could not bear to see either his anger at the gossip or his disgust at her for having repeated it.

'Miajado?'

It was a question.

'Yes, that was the name.'

'Who is he? Have I met him?'

'No, no, m'lord! He is a bull-fighter.'

'A bull-fighter!' Lord Lynke put back his head and laughed. 'No wonder you thought the story ridiculous. A bull-fighter indeed, to look at Doña Alcira, or any lady of the Court for that matter!'

Then suddenly he was silent. He was remembering something, remembering what he had seen that first evening in Doña Alcira's room, remembering what lay in the chair beside the door, as though someone had left the room hastily and forgotten to take it with him. A small object, nothing distinguishable or unusual about it save that it was there in Doña Alcira's room—a matador's hat!

Abruptly Lord Lynke straightened himself and walked across the room to pour himself a drink from a side table.

'Undoubtedly a nonsensical tale,' he drawled. 'You can go, Venturo! Good night.'

Ventura stood looking at him miserably. He was angry with her. It was what she might have expected.

Lord Lynke put the stopper back in the decanter.

'I said that you could go!' His voice was like the lash of a whip.

Ventura turned and went blindly towards the door. She reached the handle, pulled the door open and slipped through it. Outside in the passage she paused. She could not bear to go to bed like this, knowing that he was cross with her, perhaps hating her for what she had told him.

She had an impulse to go in again and beg his forgiveness, to tell him that she did not believe the story, to tell him—if it would make him happy—that the story had no foundation in fact. Then, as she stood there palpitating, undecided as to whether she dare brave him again, she heard Lord Lynke walk across the room and into his bedchamber, slamming the door behind him. There was nothing for Ventura to do but go to bed.

Miserably she went into her small room and began to take off her clothes. The room was in darkness save for the light of one small candle. In the shadows she felt she could see Doña Alcira all too clearly, watching her with hate in her eyes, her lips tightened into a cruel line.

What had she done, she asked herself, to incur such enmity? For a woman whose position and beauty gave her everything in the world, did she really suspect that Ventura had been told to spy on her? Why else had she tried to trap her into speaking Spanish? Why else that questioning as to whether she was, in fact, what she pretended to be?

Ventura was shivering, not so much with cold but from some unnamed fear, as, finally, she slipped her long white nightgown over her head and then knelt on a *prie-dieu* to say her prayers.

Always in the past her prayers had brought her comfort and peace. She was always certain that when she prayed she drew nearer to her mother. Her comforting protection and love which was with her always was even closer when her heart was raised to God.

But tonight that sense of peace and understanding did not come to Ventura. Instead, she felt merely apprehen-

107

sive. Of what and why she did not know. She only knew it was there. A fear she could neither name nor understand. A fear that was heavily overshadowed by her unhappiness because Lord Lynke was annoyed with her.

She prayed for a long time. The taper flickered and went out, but the room was not in darkness because the moon, which had been behind the clouds all the evening, had now come out in all its silvery majesty. It shone over the gardens which lay beneath the windows, on the lake turning it to molten silver, and then crept in through the open window to make an arrow of silver across Ventura's dark carpet.

'Why am I afraid?' Ventura was whispering. 'What is there to frighten me? Help me, Mother, help me, wherever you are! Let me feel that you are near me. Oh, please, please, don't go away from me!'

It was a cry from the very bottom of her heart. Even as she said it, she heard a sound outside the door. For a moment she thought she must have been mistaken; then she knew with some sixth sense, which did not require hearing or seeing, that someone was outside. Someone was waiting there, listening.

She felt her heart give a sudden, frightened thump. There was something horrible in the very silence, and in knowing that whoever it was outside did not wish the fact to be revealed, but must stand there listening and waiting.

Ventura felt herself begin to tremble, and with a sudden shock she remembered that she had not bolted the door. She had come into the room, oblivious of everything but the fact that Lord Lynke was angry with her.

Usually, she locked or bolted her door for fear someone should come in and discover that she was not the boy she was thought to be. She had always been afraid that Lord Lynke, impatient for what he wanted, would come into her room to fetch her rather than send Simon, who would always knock politely before he presumed to enter. But tonight she had forgotten.

There was no movement from outside and Ventura, despite her quickly beating heart, began to think that she had been mistaken. There could be no one there—she must have been imagining it.

Then a board creaked, just a faint, almost inaudible creak, and yet she knew that someone had shifted the weight from one foot to the other.

Quite suddenly, with a courage she was far from possessing, Ventura crept towards her bed. It was only a few steps from where she had been praying. It was a narrow bed set against the wall, but it was canopied and curtained, and it was impossible to see even in the moonlight whether anyone lay in it or not.

Swiftly, almost in one movement, she thrust her pillow down beneath the sheets, and then moving with her bare feet absolutely silently across the carpet, she slipped out of the room on to the balcony and hid behind the shutter. She pushed it until it was open a little, leaving her space to stand just behind it, and yet through the crack to see quite clearly into the room she had left.

It was cold on the balcony. Ventura did not feel it. She was conscious only of the dryness of her mouth and the feeling of constriction in her throat, the pounding of her heart.

Then, through the crack in the shutter she saw, though very faintly, the door at the far end of the room begin to open. It moved so slowly and so silently that at first she thought she must be dreaming. The aperture grew wider—wider, wider, until the door was open enough to admit the body of a person. As she watched, Ventura felt that she must scream from sheer terror. Although the door opened, no one apparently came into the room.

Everything she had ever heard or read about ghosts came creeping to her mind. She felt that her hair was standing on end and that she would faint from sheer terror. Then round the foot of the bed, which had hidden the bottom of the door from her sight, she saw something moving.

For the moment she could hardly believe her eyes, though, as she stared, it drew farther into the room and she saw it for what it was. It was the dwarf—Doña Alcira's dwarf Frivolo. Moving almost unbelievable quietly despite his short legs and heavy, ungainly figure, he drew nearer to the head of the bed.

Ventura put her hand to her throat and stifled a scream. A long, thin knife was held in his mis-shapen hand. A knife that glittered in the light from the moon, which showed her, too, the expression on his horrible, grotesque face—an expression of lust, evil and—murder!

She knew then that he would not be deceived by the pillow. She knew then that he would search for her and find her, and the knife would be plunged deep into her

109

breast and his horrible face would be near to hers in triumph.

Wildly—like a trapped animal—she looked for a way of escape. The balcony was small—a tiny square piece of stonework jutting out only a few feet from the window. There was a row of balconies all along this side of the Palace. Every window on the first floor possessed one, but they were not joined one with the other. There was a gap of over three feet between each one, and below, a direct fall on to the flag-stones of the terrace.

It was a jump which Ventura would never have considered for one moment under normal conditions. She was afraid of heights, afraid even of looking down from the tower of a church or the roof of a high building; but now terror of the dwarf drove every other thought from her mind save that of finding Lord Lynke and invoking his protection.

She would be safe with him, she knew that—knew it with every fibre of her body. She could think of nothing else save to get to him, to find sanctuary with him from the death which stalked her room.

Without even considering the consequences should she fall, she scrambled on to the stone balustrade of her balcony, swayed for a moment in the night breeze, and jumped.

She thought there was a guttural cry behind her. She thought she heard the clatter of the dwarf pushing against the shutter, but she did not look around. She caught hold of the balcony of Lord Lynke's bedchamber, and holding on to it with bleeding fingers, she somehow scrambled to safety.

She heard her nightgown tear, she felt the sharp stone cut her knees—she did not care. Somewhere through the window was Lord Lynke and he would save her.

She burst through the curtains and looked wildly towards the bed, but it was unslept in; and then she saw Lord Lynke spring to the writing-desk, his hand going out towards his sword, which he had thrown with his coat negligently across a chair.

'Save me! Oh, save me!'

Ventura could not hear the anguish in her voice as she sped across the room, a pathetic figure in her torn night-gown, her unbound hair tumbling about her face. She flung herself into his arms, clinging to him, trying to tell him what had happened, making only unintelligible sounds in her terror and panic.

He stood immobile for a moment, his arms around her and then he bent down and picked her up in his arms. Just for a moment he hesitated as though in utter astonishment; then he carried her to the sofa and set her down gently, and would have released her had she not held on to him.

'Don't go, don't go! He is there, with a knife! He is trying to kill me—the dwarf! The dwarf!' The words were a moan.

Very gently Lord Lynke disengaged her fingers.

'He won't come here,' he said quietly. 'I am going to get you a drink.'

He poured her out a glass of wine, and when she would have pushed it away, said firmly: 'Drink it! You have had a shock.'

Custom made her obey him and as she felt the wine course down her throat and still the trembling of her body, her panic subsided. It was only as she handed the glass back to him and saw his eyes on her that she realised what she had done.

'Oh!' Instinctively her hands crossed themselves over her breasts, and her blue eyes beneath the tumbled hair were wide as she looked up at him.

Lord Lynke set down the glass.

'How could I have been so blind?' he asked.

Ventura looked round her.

'I . . . must have . . . something . . . to wear,' she stammered.

In answer, Lord Lynke picked up a beautifully embroidered shawl which lay over the back of a sofa. Carefully, he put it round her shoulders, and Ventura pulled it round herself with a little feminine gesture that women have made since the beginning of time.

The shawl covered her torn nightgown and scarred knees. She was so undeniably feminine, so obviously a woman with her little pointed face and dark fringed lashes that Lord Lynke rubbed his fingers across his eyes and wondered if he was seeing things now or whether he had been demented in the past to have ever believed that she was a boy.

'I am sorry,' Ventura said, breaking the silence. 'The dwarf frightened me so much that I forgot everything else

111

except that I must escape from him. Why should he want to kill me?'

Lord Lynke shook his head.

'I have not the slightest idea,' he replied. 'But I daresay we can find out. Perhaps Miajado sent him!'

He gave her a little smile as he spoke the Matador's name, and Ventura knew that, without words, he apologised to her for his anger earlier in the evening.

'Frivolo would not take orders except from his mistress,' she said.

'Then Doña Alcira must have sent him,' Lord Lynke answered.

There was a pause before he added:

'But still, that does not make sense. If Doña Alcira does not want to marry me, she has only got to say so; and, in any event, she would not be allowed to marry a bullfighter.'

'She hates me!' Ventura cried. 'You remember that I told you how she tried to trick me into admitting I understood Spanish? I thought I had convinced her, but tonight, when she looked at me, I saw hatred in her eyes! Why? Why?'

'She said: "Go to bed, and take your page with you",' Lord Lynke said almost below his breath. His lips tightened and he rose to his feet and walked across the room to get himself a drink.

'It is a mystery which time will doubtless unravel for us,' he said, then, with the glass in his hand, he walked back to the sofa to stand looking down at Ventura.

'What am I to do about you?' he asked.

'About me?' Ventura looked up at him quickly. 'You mean I must go away, that you won't keep me any more?'

Even as she said the words, she realised what it would mean for her to part from him.

'You can't imagine that I could really have a girl as a page do you?' Lord Lynke said, with a faint twist to his lips, and added: 'But, my God, the trouble if it is discovered! Can you imagine what they will say at Court if it gets known that I have brought a girl here disguised as my page—a girl whom I have never met until a few weeks ago when I arrived in Spain?'

He put his hand to his forehead as if to wipe away his troubles.

'I've been in some devilish bad scrapes before, but this undoubtedly beats the lot!'

'But if you send me away, won't they think it very strange?' Ventura asked timidly.

'That's just it,' Lord Lynke replied. 'If I send you away, I've got to explain what has happened to you. If I keep you, I am deliberately putting my head into a noose as far as my life is concerned in any Court—Spanish or British.'

'I'm sorry,' Ventura murmured meekly.

'Sorry!' Lord Lynke shouted. 'And so I should think! I've done a lot of dam-fool things in my life, but even I couldn't think up anything as stupid as this one. A girl smuggled into the most respectable Court in Europe!'

He threw back his head and laughed.

'It's no use, I can't help seeing the funny side of it!'

'I never thought of it getting you into trouble,' Ventura said.

'What did you think then?' Lord Lynke inquired.

'I wanted to go to Madrid,' she answered. 'As she was dying, my mother told me to go there—she died before she could tell me why. I determined, if the opportunity arose, to do as she wished. Besides, I wanted food to eat and clothes to wear, and I also wanted to be with you.'

Lord Lynke sat down in the chair and looked at her.

'Why didn't I guess? Seeing you now, I think I must have been blind—or drunk, not to have realised that you were a girl.'

'People see what they expect to see,' Ventura told him philosophically. 'Besides, I was so thin—just skin and bone—Señor Padilla thought of dressing me as a boy; he said that, as men like curves, no one would think for one moment that I was a woman.'

'You're certainly less angular than when we first met,' Lord Lynke said with a smile.

'Perhaps if I didn't eat anything, it would be safer,' Ventura suggested.

'There is nothing safe about it,' Lord Lynke replied. I think the best thing would be to say that we have had word that your parents are ill and that you have to return to Scotland immediately. I will then send you back in the coach to San Sebastian.'

Ventura gave a little gulp, and then she was on her knees beside him looking up to him with her eyes full of tears.

'Don't send me away. Please, please, don't send me away,' she pleaded. 'I'll be careful. I'll do anything you want, but please let me stay with you.'

Her tears overflowed and ran down her cheeks.

'Please let me stay,' she repeated, her voice breaking on the words.

Almost without thinking, Lord Lynke's arm went round her.

'Now listen, Venturo,' he began. 'And that isn't your name, I suppose? Don't cry, dammit? I never could abide a woman in tears.'

'Then say that I may stay,' Ventura sulked.

'All right, then, you can stay—anything you like—only stop weeping and making a mess of my shirt!'

Ventura looked up at him, her smile like April sunshine coming through a storm.

'Do you mean that?' she whispered.

'I suppose so. I have grown used to you and I would miss you if you were gone. At the same time, if anyone gets to hear of this, I'm finished! Do you understand? Finished! I shall have to spend the rest of my life in the West Indies or some such outlandish place!'

'But if I explain to everyone that I had deceived you, that you thought that I was a boy . . .'

'Do you suppose anyone would believe that?' Lord Lynke inquired. 'And, what's more, a fine fool I should look if they did! A man of my years and experience ought to be able to recognise a female when he sees one!'

'I'll be very, very careful,' Ventura promised.

'You'd better!' he cautioned. 'And by, the way, what is your real name?'

'Ventura,' she answered. 'It means "luck". My father and mother believed, when I was born, that I should bring them luck.'

'It is something you won't bring me if anyone finds out about you,' Lord Lynke answered.

'Why should they make so much fuss about it?' Ventura wondered. 'I know it's wrong for a man to have a girl as a page, but you've come here to marry Doña Alcira. They couldn't imagine that . . .' She hesitated for loss of words.

Lord Lynke put his fingers under her chin and turned her face up to his.

'You are very innocent, my dear, of most people's imaginations,' he said drily, 'if you think that under the circumstances they would not credit you with being my mistress.'

Ventura moved away from him sharply and her face went crimson.

He looked at her ruefully.

'I suppose I oughtn't to have said that,' he remarked. 'But, dammit, I've got in the way of speaking openly to you, saying what I think. It's going to be devilish difficult to choose my words now!'

'I don't want you to,' Ventura cried. 'Please be just as you have always been. Forget that I am a girl!'

She got to her feet, holding the shawl tightly round her.

'I will go back to my room,' she said, 'if you will, please, look to see if he has gone.'

'It will give me great satisfaction to find him there!' Lord Lynke remarked. 'But I feel that is too much to hope.'

He picked up his sword and, drawing it from its scabbard, walked across the room, the firelight shining on the uncovered blade. It made Ventura remember the knife in the dwarf's hand. She felt herself shiver. She waited for Lord Lynke's return. He was back in a matter of seconds.

'There is no one there,' he said.

'Thank you for looking.'

She stared up at him and thought how strong and tall he seemed. Why was she afraid, when he was there to protect her?

'Go back to your room, now,' Lord Lynke said quietly. 'Bolt the door and I will sleep with mine ajar. If anyone comes along the passage, I shall hear.'

'There is no need for that,' Ventura said. 'He will not come again tonight. He knows that I went to you for protection.'

'And for God's sake, don't attempt to jump like that again!' Lord Lynke said. 'If you had fallen, you would have broken your neck!'

'I would rather have done that than be killed by the dwarf,' Ventura said.

'I'll settle up with him one day!' Lord Lynke promised.

Ventura turned the handle of the door.

'Good night, and thank you.'

'Good night,' Lord Lynke replied, looking at her. 'I still can't believe that you ever deceived me, but perhaps in the morning you will seem like a boy again.'

'Everyone else will think so,' Ventura promised.

She slipped from the room, but he came to the door and watched her go into her own bedchamber.

Ventura rammed home the bolt and, for added protection, set the back of a chair under the handle of the door, then she lit a candle and, carrying it across the room to the mirror, stared at her own reflection.

Since she had been in the service of Lord Lynke, her hair had grown considerably and was curling on to her shoulders now. Because she was better in health, it was soft and wavy around the temples; there were more glints in the darkness of it added to what there were before.

Her face had filled out, the bones were no longer sharp and ugly. But she still had a kind of spiritual look, a kind of transparency which came not only from lack of food, but from an inner spirituality which had guided her all her life.

Then she stared into her own eyes. They were vividly blue in contrast to the dark lashes surrounding them, and in them Ventura saw what lay hidden deep and secret in her heart.

'I love him!' she whispered. 'I love him! I didn't know it until now.'

9

Ventura entered the sitting-room a little shyly. She had lain awake all night wondering what she should say and do when she faced Lord Lynke again.

Looking back on the panic and terror which had driven her to make the dangerous leap from balcony to balcony and to fling herself unthinkingly into his arms, she wondered how she could have been so foolish.

Her fears now seemed out of all proportion to what she had risked in letting Lord Lynke guess that she was not the boy she pretended. Yet the alternative would have been to face the dwarf with his deadly dagger. That, she knew, would have been impossible for her. She had neither the courage nor the stamina that a real boy might have had.

She tried to think what else she could have done. Had she screamed from the balcony, would Lord Lynke have come to her rescue in time? It was all problematical, and what really mattered was not only the fact that Lord

116

Lynke now knew her for what she was, but also that she had discovered her own love for him.

'I love him, and he must never guess it,' she told herself as she dressed.

'I love him, but I must hide it,' she whispered as she walked down the passage to the sitting-room.

Only when her hand was on the handle of the door did she realise how great an effort it was to enter the room, to know that his eyes would look at her, perhaps in anger, or at least in irritation, because she had forced him into a false and uncomfortable position. With a composure she was far from feeling and carried forward by a defiant desperation, she walked in.

Lord Lynke looked up from the breakfast table. He was consuming a plate of well-done lamb chops. There was a roast chicken in front of him and a collation of cold dishes on the adjacent sideboard. Two footmen, resplendent in their royal uniform, were waiting upon him, and Simon stood hovering in the background in case his services should be required.

'Good morning, m'lord.'

Ventura's voice was hardly above a whisper and she felt her heart sink as she saw the expression on Lord Lynke's face.

'Good morning!'

The inclination of his head was brief and his voice was curt.

Ventura slipped into her seat at the table. A footman proffered a silver dish which contained sweetbreads tastefully cooked with mushrooms. She waved it away. Other dishes were brought for her inspection, both Spanish and English, but in the end she had only a little fruit and a slice of freshly baked bread and wild honey.

The meal continued in silence. Finally, Lord Lynke rose and walked towards the fire-place, dismissing the footman with a flick of his fingers. Simon went into the bedchamber and closed the door behind him. Ventura was alone with her master.

'I have been thinking,' Lord Lynke said, breaking the silence, 'of what action I should take with regard to last night.'

'Action, m'lord?'

'Yes, action,' Lord Lynke repeated. 'It is impossible for me to do nothing, to allow anyone in my employment to be subjected to a murderous attack while ... er ... he is

117

under my protection. The fact that you were not hurt and that no damage was done has nothing to do with the matter. The dwarf came to your room, and that is enough.'

'I beg of you, m'lord, to make little of it,' Ventura pleaded. 'Only I saw the dwarf. If it is denied that he was there, it will simply be my word against his.'

Lord Lynke appeared not to have heard her.

'I shall speak to Doña Alcira and ask her for some explanation of why one of her servants should show you such enmity.'

'She will laugh at you!' Ventura said firmly.

Lord Lynke turned to look at her, it seemed to her, for the first time that morning.

'Laugh?' he queried. 'Why should Doña Alcira laugh?'

'Because she is a woman, and because she will be clever in concealing her feelings!' Ventura answered quickly. 'If she has reasons for getting rid of me, she will certainly not admit it, especially as the attempt was a failure.'

'Why should she wish to get rid of you?' Lord Lynke inquired. 'Why should she even notice you?'

'I have no idea,' Ventura replied. 'And yet, there is some reason, I am sure of it. I have known it from that first moment when we met her in the Garden Room. She stared at me then and her face was drained of colour.'

'Nonsense!' Lord Lynke ejaculated. 'Now I know you are imagining things; but I cannot credit that it was merely imagination which drove you to leap across the balcony between your room and mine. I measured the distance this morning. It is over a yard? How could you have been so foolhardy?'

'As you accuse me of being imaginative, there is no point in answering that question, m'lord,' Ventura answered bitterly. 'And why should you believe me? It is obviously far easier for you to take the word of Doña Alcira!'

She rose as she spoke and, leaving the table, crossed the room to stand looking out over the garden. She was suddenly very near to tears. It was bad enough to be tired and dispirited after a sleepless night, to feel shy and embarrassed because Lord Lynke knew that she was a girl and not a boy; but to have him questioning her veracity and practically accusing her of lying—that was too much.

Lord Lynke watched her for a moment, then a faint smile twisted his lips.

'You sound annoyed with me.'

Ventura did not answer, and after a moment he added:
'I apologise. Does that satisfy you?'

With an effort Ventura checked the tears rising in her eyes and the sob in her throat.

'Yes . . . yes . . . thank you, m'lord.'

'Very well then, get your hat! We go to visit Doña Alcira.'

Ventura turned at that in surprise.

'So early?'

'The Spaniards start their day earlier than we do,' Lord Lynke replied; 'then they make up for it by their siesta. Doña Alcira will undoubtedly be awake, and I have a feeling this matter is urgent.'

'Why?' Ventura asked.

'Because, having failed once, the dwarf, or whoever is instructing him, may try again.'

'You cannot imagine for one moment that Doña Alcira will tell your lordship anything or admit to being in any way implicated!' Ventura remarked a little scornfully.

'I am not so stupid as you appear to imagine,' Lord Lynke retorted. 'I do not always gain information from what someone says, but from how they look. There is an old adage which says: "Watch their eyes".'

'I have done that,' Ventura said, 'and that is why I know that Doña Alcira hates me!'

'Yet, why should she?' Lord Lynke asked. 'What can you matter in her life?'

'Do .. you think ... do ... you imagine,' Ventura stammered, 'that . . . she . . . guessed about me?'

'It is impossible!' Lord Lynke said. 'Quite impossible! Yet even if she has guessed the truth—it is not a matter for murder!'

There seemed nothing for Ventura to say, so she stood silent, her blue eyes, circled with dark shadows, fixed on Lord Lynke's face. Her face was very pale and she had been at pains this morning to drag her hair severely back from her forehead and tie it tightly in the black bow that she wore at the nape of her neck.

There was nothing, she had thought, feminine about her appearance; and she would have been surprised if she had known what Lord Lynke's thoughts were at the moment. It was those which, perhaps, made his voice unusually sharp as he said:

'Get your hat ... and be quick about it! This damned chatter is getting us nowhere!'

Obediently Ventura hurried from the room, and as she did so, she heard him shout for Simon to bring his coat and sword.

A few minutes later they were driving through the budding greenery of El Retiro towards the town.

Something had put Lord Lynke into a disagreeable mood. In the coach he put up his feet on the opposite seat and sat scowling, his eyes inscrutable, his mouth a tight line.

'He loves her!' Ventura told herself, 'and that is why he is angry at having to talk with her on such a disagreeable subject.'

She felt as if something was weeping inside her at the thought, not of Lord Lynke's anger, but of his love for Doña Alcira. She was sure, quite sure, that the Spaniard was bad, through and through. She had nothing to substantiate such an idea. It was only a feminine instinct which enabled her to sum up another woman and know, without any need of proof or even hearsay, that she was evil.

She thought of that lovely, oval face with its dark eyes and full, greedy mouth; and she longed with a longing which was actually selfless to save Lord Lynke. And yet, what could she do? What could anyone do, if a man was caught in the toils of a woman who was far more subtle and clever in the art of seduction than ever he was likely to be?

Impulsively, forgetting everything but her love for him, Ventura put out her hand and laid it on his arm.

'Please be careful.'

Lord Lynke turned his head in surprise.

'What do you mean by that?' he asked.

His words threw Ventura into a confusion.

'I do not know exactly,' she answered. 'It is only that I am . . . afraid for you.'

'For me?' Lord Lynke queried, and then he laughed. It was gentle, kindly laughter, and the expression on his face had changed as he said:

'Since we first met you have twice acted as my rescuer. First from being robbed, then from being killed. Is this the third time?'

Ventura blushed.

'I do not know,' she said. 'I only have a feeling that you should be careful of what you do, both now and in the future, where . . .'

Ventura hesitated and could not bring herself to finish the sentence.

'Where Doña Alcira is concerned,' Lord Lynke finished for her.

Ventura dropped her eyes.

'Yes,' she said. 'Yes, that's what I feel.'

'Oh, to hell with all women!' Lord Lynke exclaimed.

It was an expression that seemed to burst from his lips, and then he added:

'Look at this nonsensical tangle I am in at the moment, and why? All because of women! Charlotte, Doña Alcira and you! I wish you were all at the bottom of the sea!'

He spoke with a sincerity which could not possibly be denied; and then, before Ventura could reply, the coach drew up outside Doña Alcira's palace.

Flunkeys opened the door, and Lord Lynke stalked up the steps with Ventura following behind him.

A magnificently attired major-domo informed them respectfully that Doña Alcira would be advised immediately of Lord Lynke's arrival, but her Excellency was at the moment engaged.

'Tell her it is of the utmost import,' Lord Lynke said.

The major-domo bowed, and they were shown into a large, ornate salon on the ground floor. The walls were lined with books; but everything about it proclaimed luxury and wealth so that even the smallest ornaments were of rare and fabulous craftsmanship or of gold and silver set with precious jewels.

Lord Lynke did not sit down as he had been invited to do but roamed restlessly about the room looking at the books and ornaments.

'I have not the slightest idea for what I am searching,' he said, 'but at the back of my mind I feel there is something I should discover.'

'The major-domo came back and bowed.

'Doña Alcira will see m'lord,' he said.

Lord Lynke turned to Ventura.

'Wait here!' he ordered her, and followed the major-domo from the room.

Alone, Ventura did what Lord Lynke had done. She walked round the room searching for something although she did not know what it was. Vaguely, at the back of her mind, she remembered her father talking of how he had once been in a room lined with books, in which a secret doorway operated amongst the shelves. It was a story he had told her when she was a child, ornamenting the adventure stories that she loved with real reminiscences of where he had been and what he had done.

'There was a little spray of roses carved along the ledge of the bookshelf,' he said. 'One pressed the centre of the third rose from the left, pressed it hard, and the door would open. It was covered with books like the rest of the room, and when it was in place it was impossible for anyone to guess there was a door there ... a perfect hidey hole!'

Looking at the shelves, Ventura realised with a little shock that on one side of the room there were small trailers of flowers carved on them. She looked again. Yes, there were roses amongst them!

She felt a sudden surging excitement. Could the memory of her father's story have come to her at this moment as an indication of what she would find? She pressed her fingers on the rose nearest to her, and then realised that the flower was not a rose but a marguerite.

She moved slowly down the room. Marguerites and all sorts of other flowers were quite discernible, but nothing which looked like a rose. She moved on, searching carefully; and then, as she got almost to the centre of he room, she saw that the pattern of the flowers had altered. Now there were roses amongst the carving!

With her heart beating quickly she counted three roses from where the pattern altered and pressed her finger hard into the centre of it.

Ventura had been somehow so certain by now of what she would find, it was hardly a shock when there was a click, and part of the bookcase swung open. The door was there, just as her father had described it!

She stepped forward. Nothing in the world would have prevented her at that moment from passing through the secret doorway in search of what lay behind.

She had expected steps or a passage but, instead, she found herself in a small room. It was a disappointment to find that it led no further. Just a small room, stacked with odd pieces of furniture, a broken chair, a file of papers.

Ventura stood looking around her, and as she did so, she saw the door close quietly behind her. It made a sound almost like a sigh. She turned round apprehensively, but she saw at once that the door would open quite easily from this side. She pushed it and felt it give under her hand. The mechanism of the secret catch, she decided, was so delicately and beautifully made that the door remained open only long enough for someone to pass through.

She glanced at the papers on the chair. They looked old and rather musty manuscripts, but she wondered if there was anything amongst them that she should read for either Lord Lynke's sake or her own. She hesitated, and then she heard a voice say:

'If Your Excellencies will wait here, I will inform Doña Alcira of your arrival.'

The words were so clear that Ventura could hardly believe that she had heard them through the thickness of the secret door. Someone, she knew, had come into the outer room. She wondered whether it would be best to reveal herself or remain hidden.

It would look strange, she thought, for the English page of Lord Lynke to be poking and prying about in the secret chamber of Doña Alcira's house. But until the people next door moved, she was trapped. Should she confront them boldly, pretending she had found the door open and had just wandered casually through it?

While she was wondering what to do, a man's voice said in Spanish:

'I think, Don Carlos, your estates are going to be very useful to us.'

'They are entirely at your Grace's disposal.'

Ventura started. So Don Carlos was there in the outer room. It was then that she saw a light coming through the wall beside the door, and understood how she could hear the voices so clearly.

The small room itself was lit by a skylight of opaque glass let into the ceiling, but this light was different. It hinted of the sunshine which had been flooding the outer room when she and Lord Lynke entered it. She went nearer, and understood. A piece of the wall had been cut away, leaving exposed half a dozen books which backed into the library. They were set a fraction of an inch apart so that it was possible to see past them into the room beyond.

Ventura understood all too clearly why this smaller room had been built. It was typical, she thought, of the Spanish mind, which loved intrigue and suspected the integrity of everyone, even the closest friends. A man could listen to what was being said and never be discov-

123

ered. A man could trap both his friends and his enemies by such methods.

Peeping now, between the volumes, Ventura saw that there were three men in the outer room. One was Don Carlos, splendidly dressed, his too-close-together eyes turning fitfully from one man to the other. The man he had addressed as 'your Grace' Ventura recognised immediately as the Duc de Montemar, the fire-eating Minister of War. The other she was doubtful about, although she was certain she had seen him at Court.

'How many troops do you think you will need to accommodate on Don Carlos's estates?' he asked now.

He spoke with a rather affected voice and Ventura suddenly remembered who he was. The Count of Montijo, who had been pointed out to her as the ambitious, continually intriguing President of the Council of the Indies.

'Five to six thousand should be enough,' the *Duc* replied.

'The garrison at Gibraltar is not large, and of course you will have the support of the fleet,' Don Carlos remarked.

'You think the English have no idea of our plans?' the Count of Montijo asked.

The *Duc* pulled his beard.

'None at all,' he replied.

'The difficulty is the fleet,' the Count went on. 'If we sail twenty or thirty ships of the line into the Mediterranean, the English are bound to suspect that something is afoot. That is why I suggest we must have time. Let our ships come out of harbour one by one and move round into the Mediterranean casually, keeping to the African side until they have received your signal.'

'I think, personally, I can manage the attack alone,' the *Duc* said rather pompously.

'It must be a combined attack, my dear *Duc*!' the Count of Montijo said firmly; 'and above all, nothing must be done hastily or prematurely if we are to be successful.'

'How long do you think it will take to get the fleet to the Mediterranean?' Don Carlos inquired.

'The way I visualise it—two or three months,' the Count replied. 'That is, of course, after we get the Queen's consent.'

'Do you really think it is wise,' the *Duc* asked, 'to trust Doña Alcira?'

The Count flung out his hands.

'Whom else?' he inquired. 'I dare not ask the King in the Queen's presence. He is, as you know, bitterly opposed to war in any form. And I never see the Queen alone.'

'Could you not request an audience with Her Majesty?' the *Duc* inquired.

'And have the whole Court speculating as to what I was asking of her?' the Count of Montijo inquired. 'I dare not do anything unconventional without causing talk which might defeat our plan from the very onset.'

'Do you think that Doña Alcira will succeed in this project?' Don Carlos inquired.

'The Queen is fond of her,' the Count replied, 'and she has the opportunity of being alone with Her Majesty in her bedchamber or wherever women talk. It is our only way, I assure you.'

'You are right!' the *Duc* said. 'There must be no talk, whatever happens. Remember, Torre Nueva is convinced that our finances can stand no conflict of any sort. Only last night he said to me: 'I am shutting down on your budget, my dear *Duc,* for there will be no more war!'

'The *Marqués is a fanatic on the subject*!' the Count growled.

The door opened and the major-domo stood there.

'Doña Alcira will be with Your Excellencies in a few moments. In the meantime, she begs you to honour this house by partaking of some refreshments in the dining hall.'

'An excellent idea!' the Count said.

They all three followed the major-domo from the room.

This, Ventura knew, was her opportunity to get back into the outer room unobserved. She moved away from the wall, cast a look at the papers on the chair, and decided it was too dangerous to linger longer even though they might be of interest.

At that moment her eye was caught by a picture hanging on the farther wall—a picture which made her stare at it incredulously. For a moment she could not believe her eyes, for it was unmistakably a picture of herself!

She drew nearer to it, everything forgotten except that she felt that she was moving in some strange dream. It was only the head and shoulders of a girl, and yet she might have been staring into the mirror at herself.

There was the same pointed face, the same tiny straight, aristocratic nose. The same square forehead. The same full, red mouth. Then she realised that the eyes were different. Her eyes were blue, unmistakably blue but the eyes in the picture were dark.

She glanced at the plaque set into the carved gilt frame and read: *Doña Anna Louisa*—1718. It was then she realised who it was! Her mother! A portrait of her mother, painted when she must have been the same age as she herself was now. No wonder that for a moment she had mistaken it for a portrait of herself!

'You have your mother's face and my eyes.' She could almost hear her father's voice saying it to her, but she had not entirely believed him. Her mother had been so ill, the lines of suffering and unhappiness spoiling her beauty after she had been bereaved. Now Ventura could see her as she had been in the full bloom of her beauty.

Her mother! Ventura stood staring at the picture, oblivious of everything else. It was almost as if her mother stood there, that she could put her arms around her and hold her close. It was as if she had come back to life and the security and protection which had gone when she died was once again restored.

Ventura put out her hand and touched the painted cheek.

'Mamma!' she whispered 'Mamma!'

Only as her fingers touched the cold canvas did she awake to reality.

Hot and fast the questions threw themselves at her brain. What was the portrait of her mother doing here? Why should Doña Alcira possess it? And how had her father known of the secret door unless he, too, had been in this house?

They were questions which left Ventura bewildered. She could not even begin to formulate an answer to them. She could only feel as if her brain was reeling. As if the only sane and sure thing was the picture of her mother on the wall.

She looked at it as if for strength; and then, because it could not help her, she turned and hurried from the secret room out into the empty ante-room.

The door closed behind her softly, and almost silently. She turned back to look at it. It was completely indiscernible. Was it really there, she wondered—or had she dreamt it?

She knew suddenly that she must find the answer to her questions; that someone must explain to her what it was

126

all about. She could not wait! She must find Lord Lynke. She must tell him what had happened and show him the picture.

Without thinking and without considering anything but the urgency of her own problem, Ventura ran across the room and pulled open the door. The great hall was empty.

Ventura, on her other visits, had learned that Doña Alcira's rooms were upstairs. She would have asked imperiously any servant who had appeared to lead her to them. But the major-domo and his flunkeys must have all been in attendance on the Ministers and Don Carlos, for there was no one about.

Ventura hurried up the wide ebony and crystal staircase to the first floor. There, the landing divided and she could go right or left along corridors decorated in silk brocade and gold, with innumerable doors and passages opening out of them. Right or left? Ventura did not give herself time to think which would be the best way to take.

Driven by an urgency that she could not control, she ran left, down a corridor where, at the far end, were huge double doors covered with coloured carving and surmounted with an elaborate coat-of-arms. This, Ventura decided, must be Doña Alcira's room.

She knocked sharply on the door. As she had expected, a woman's voice bade her enter. She opened the door and stood for a moment, a little dazzled by the sunshine that was pouring in through several big unshuttered windows.

Then, as her vision cleared, she saw that the room, a symphony in soft pastel shades, was occupied by only one person—an old lady with white hair, sitting in an armchair by one of the windows. There were flowers all round her and at her feet were several pet dogs, on her lap a puppy. She glanced towards Ventura standing in the doorway, and said in a soft, gentle voice:

'Come in, young man. What can I do for you?'

'A thousand apologies, *Madame*,' Ventura answered, 'but I have come to the wrong room. I was looking for Lord Lynke, who is visiting Doña Alcira.'

'And who is Lord Lynke?' the elderly lady asked in a voice that seemed to have a hint of amusement in it. 'No, no!' she added as Ventura would have turned towards the door. 'Come and tell me who he is. I am interested.'

'He is my master, *Madame*,' Ventura answered, coming a little farther into the room as she was commanded, but wondering impatiently how she could get away. She wanted Lord Lynke. She must see him. She must tell him about the picture.

'That is no answer!' the elderly lady insisted. 'Now ... let me think ... Lynke. It sounds English to me!'

'It is English, *Madame*,' Ventura replied, and realised, even as she spoke, that she had been speaking in Spanish.

For the first time since she had come to Madrid she had forgotten the part she had to play. For the first time—when someone had spoken to her—she had answered unthinkingly, replying in the language in which she had been addressed.

'I am ... sorry, *Madame*, I ... must go,' she stammered, thinking only to escape, to get away quickly before she committed herself further. Already she was beginning to realise what she had done, and the consequences if Doña Alcira learnt that, after all, she could speak and understand Spanish.

'I ... must go!' Ventura repeated.

The old lady looked up at her as she stood now not far from her chair; and suddenly her face changed. She stared at Ventura blindly, her eyes searching her face. Then impulsively her hands came out to her.

'Anna!' she cried in a voice that was both broken and happy. 'Anna Louisa! You've come back! Oh, my baby, you have come back to me!'

10

Doña Alcira looked up impatiently when there came a knock on her door. She was tired, for Miajado had visited her the night before and had only crept out of the house as dawn was breaking.

Since her father's death Doña Alcira had administered the Carcastillo fortunes and she had found that her work connected with the estates increased day by day. She could, of course, have turned everything over to the attorneys as other women would have done in her place, or she could have appointed one of her many cousins to be in charge of her affairs, but Doña Alcira trusted nobody.

She had long suspected that her father, being too easy

going had been cheated by those he most trusted; and one of the first things she did when she took over was to dismiss old employees and servants who had been in positions of trust for over a quarter of a century. It was not surprising therefore that Doña Alcira was not loved by those whose wages she paid.

She was well aware that the morning was to be a heavy one. The overseer of the vineyards was to be told what improvements he must make on his returns of last year. The stables were costing too much, and Doña Alcira was determined to check and re-check the food that was being bought for her horses and also the heavy bills for coach repairs, which seemed to her out of all proportion.

She was aware, as well, that the Duc de Montemar and Count of Montijo would not have asked her to see them if it were not a matter of great importance. She was not quite sure what they required of her, but she had a faint idea that it was somehow connected with their avowed hatred of the English. The *Duc* had shown, quite clearly, that he was against the idea of her marriage with an Englishman unless he were of Royal descent and could bring with him as a marriage portion the fortress of Gibraltar.

This brought Lord Lynke to Doña Alcira's thoughts, and for the first time since she had awoken that morning her face seemed to soften and the look of hard suspicion vanished, which was habitually in her eyes when she was dealing with her personal affairs.

She had not expected this Englishman to be so attractive. She had been prepared to despise him; to find him oafish and a bore. Instead, she found Lord Lynke had a polish and a sophistication which made even Don Carlos seem gauche and uncultured. He had, too, a physical attraction that it was impossible to deny.

Doña Alcira thought of his kisses, and her dark eyes narrowed sensuously and her lips parted while her breath came a little quicker. She wanted him! She was even prepared to believe that she loved him. At any rate, because of him, she had finished with Miajado.

She had intended to tell the matador so last night; but when he had come to her, smart and glittering in a new suit trimmed with silver threads and sequins, she had found her senses captured once again by his primitive beauty. There was, she thought, something irresistible in those broad shoulders and narrow hips, in the feline grace

129

of a body which could sway by only a hair's breadth and yet escape the points of a bull's horns.

She had meant to dismiss Miajado; yet, when he was there, the words died on her lips and she thought only of his kisses. It seemed to her last night that their passion flared so brightly that it consumed itself and then, as far as she was concerned, died away to leave nothing but ashes.

"What is it?' she asked impatiently as a servant stood at the open door.

'His Excellency Lord Lynke craves an interview with you, m'lady.'

Doña Alcira hesitated. The table before her was piled with papers, accounts, bankers' statements, letters which required an answer and many other matters, all craving her attention. Then she caught a glimpse of herself in a long silver-framed mirror which was set between the windows.

She saw that her face was almost breath-takingly beautiful; there was a faint touch of colour on her cheeks to throw into contrast the magnolia texture of her skin, while her eyes were dark and mysterious beneath eyebrows like a raven's wings.

There was the flash of diamonds in her ears. Her wrists seemed weighted down with the same stones, and her dress rustled soft and silken as she moved across the room towards another mirror before which lay a dozen creams and lotions with which she accentuated the beauty that nature had already given her.

'I will see Lord Lynke in my boudoir,' she said. 'Pull down the sun-blinds and light the incense bowl before you admit him.'

'It shall be done, m'lady.'

The servant bowed and closed the door behind him.

Doña Alcira stood for a moment, a faint smile on her face. It was a smile of joy anticipated, and also one of triumph! Yes, Doña Alcira told herself, she had no further use for Miajado. He was finished, as many better bred men before him had been finished, because, over-night as it were, she no longer had need of them.

She thought of Lord Lynke and knew that he could give her so much more than Miajado had been able to do. It was not only a satisfaction of the senses that she required, but something else as well. Something which would engage

130

her busy, active brain, her interest and perhaps, even, her ambition.

She wondered what Miajado would do. Would he cry and plead with her, as many of his predecessors had done? Would he threaten vague, ugly threats which had no possible chance of fulfilment? She somehow expected the latter course. Miajado was not a weakling either to humble himself or to take his life as one of her lovers had done; and yet she was well aware that she was about to deal him a body blow. He loved her. He had never known a woman quite like her before. What would be his reaction?

Callously, with a little shrug of her shoulders, Doña Alcira dismissed Miajado from her thoughts. He was no longer of the least importance to her. It was Lord Lynke who mattered. Lord Lynke, who was so impatient to see her that he could not wait until the hour prescribed, but had come here hot-foot.

She touched her face with powder, put a further hint of salve upon her red lips, and then moved slowly and confidently towards the door which led into her boudoir.

The sunlight had been excluded, but the room was banked with flowers, and mingled with their fragrance was the faint, sweet insidious perfume of incense.

Lord Lynke was standing by the mantelshelf and Doña Alcira watched him for a moment before he realised that she was there. He was in profile to her, and she liked the sharpness of his chin, the firmness of his mouth. He had none of the grace of Miajado, but his looks appealed to her more. There was something so brutally masculine about him that she felt herself thrill because, beside him, she was weak, soft and feminine.

'This is an early visit, m'lord!'

She contrived to make her voice sound surprised.

Lord Lynke turned abruptly.

'Your servant, *Madame*,' he said formally. 'I was compelled to speak to you. My apologies if my call is inconvenient.'

'I am busy, very busy,' Doña Alcira replied, 'but never too busy . . . for you.'

Her voice was soft and yet caressing, eager; and, as he kissed her hand perfunctorily, she wished that he would kiss her lips.

'What I have to say,' Lord Lynke said, 'is unpleasant, but, unfortunately, must be said!'

'Unpleasant?'

Doña Alcira's eyes were wide, and then suddenly she knew why Lord Lynke had come! She had not seen Frivolo this morning. The dwarf was a nuisance when she was busy, and she had given her maids instructions that he was not to come to her room until she sent for him.

She wished now that she had seen him before she had granted an interview to Lord Lynke. She had spoken to Frivolo yesterday, explained what she wanted done, told him to take his opportunity when the occasion arose. She had not expected him to act so swiftly; but now she realised that he must have gone to Lord Lynke's rooms last night!

Well, what did it matter? The sooner, the better as far as she was concerned. It was only that she would have liked to be more prepared, to have known exactly how the deed was done.

'What has happened?' she asked soothingly. 'You look worried. I want everything in Spain to enchant you. Your cares and troubles should have been left behind you with the fog and cold of England.'

Lord Lynke's expression did not alter, and she saw that her words had not swept the frown from between his eyes.

'I came to speak to you about your dwarf,' he said.

'Frivolo?' Doña Alcira questioned with just the right amount of surprise in her voice.

'Yes—if that is what you call him!'

'What can he have done to offend you?' Doña Alcira asked. 'Oh, I know he is tiresome at times and often his humour is ill-placed and irritating, but he makes me laugh and that is why I keep him. I have not always got a great deal to laugh about.'

Her tone was wistful, her expression that of a woman who is often hardly used and in need of someone to protect her.

'Last night your dwarf made an attack on my page!'

'Not little Euan Cameron,' Doña Alcira cried. 'Oh, but I cannot believe it! What can have happened? What can the boy have done to annoy poor Frivolo?'

'I thought perhaps you could enlighten me on that matter,' Lord Lynke said.

'I? But how should I know?' Doña Alcira questioned. 'I am appalled if what you tell me is the truth. Frivolo sometimes takes these wild, unreasonable dislikes to people. Usually, it is because he is jealous. I know that once he threatened Don Carlos, but he was a man. Euan Cameron is different. Poor little boy! How could he defend himself?'

'How, indeed?' Lord Lynke said grimly.

Doña Alcira put up her hands to her face.

'It is too terrible to contemplate?' she cried. 'I am ashamed and very angry. Frivolo shall be sent away at once! He must be banished to my estates in the south.'

She gave a very realistic little sob, and then put out her hands towards Lord Lynke.

'You must forgive me for not realising before that the dwarf was dangerous, she said. 'I will find you another page; and as for poor little Euan, we will give him a magnificent funeral.!'

'A funeral?' Lord Lynke questioned.

'Yes, we must be careful not to let anyone know what really happened to him. Perhaps you could say he had an accident or suffered from a weak heart. We would not wish, of course, to cause a scandal which would perturb and upset Their Majesties. No, no, it could all be arranged quite simply. A weak heart, is, I think, the best story.'

'You've got it all thought out, haven't you?' Lord Lynke said slowly.

"We must act swiftly!' Doña Alcira insisted. 'How wise you were to come here to me before you did anything else! The boy is dead, therefore there is no point in making a fuss about it—in letting too many people know what has occurred. I will send my own servants to lay out the body.'

'That will be quite unnecessary!' Lord Lynke replied.

'But of course you must let me do everything,' Doña Alcira said quickly. 'I feel as if it was my fault the poor child has died. If Frivolo hadn't belonged to me, then he might have been alive at this moment. It is a terrible thought, isn't it? But what has happened cannot be undone. We must only be careful to see that it does not in any way cause difficulties or arouse hard feelings between your country and mine.'

'You need not concern yourself about that,' Lord Lynke replied. 'You see . . . Euan Cameron is not dead!'

There was a little pause.

'Not dead?' Doña Alcira's voice was sharp.

'No, he is alive.'

Doña Alcira's face had gone very white. Lord Lynke

thought for a moment that she would faint; then with what was an obvious effort she said:

'Whom have you sent for? What doctor have you called to him? Tell me quickly! It is of the utmost import!'

'There was no need for a doctor,' Lord Lynke said slowly and suavely. His eyes were watching her. 'Euan, I am thankful to say, is unscathed. He escaped from your dwarf by the hazardous method of jumping from the balcony of his bedchamber on to the balcony of mine.'

'But it is impossible! No one would dare to attempt such a feat!'

'Nevertheless, Euan attempted it and succeeded; and so, for the moment, there is no need to bury him!'

'I cannot credit such a story!' Doña Alcira said.

'And I cannot credit why your dwarf ... your personal attendant ... should attack my page without a very good reason! What was that reason?'

Doña Alcira spread wide her hands.

'How should I know?'

'Well, suppose we have the dwarf here and ask him?' Lord Lynke suggested.

'No! No! We cannot do that!' Doña Alcira exclaimed. 'Frivolo is not normal. He is, in some ways, a simpleton. In other ways, as crafty as an animal. It would not be wise to question him and, anyway, we are unlikely to find the truth.'

'I should like to try!' Lord Lynke said.

'No!' Doña Alcira almost spat the word at him.

'Why not?'

'Because I say so!'

'That, I may say, is a very feminine answer!' Lord Lynke commented. 'Shall I tell you what I think?'

'If you desire to do so!' Doña Alcira replied.

'Then, I think,' Lord Lynke said slowly, 'that you knew that your dwarf was likely to make this attack on Euan Cameron!'

'I knew?' Doña Alcira repeated, her voice rising angrily.

'Yes. You knew!' Lord Lynke repeated. 'What is more, I have a suspicion that you commanded him to do it!'

'You must be crazed!' Doña Alcira said scornfully. 'Why should I be interested in your page? Why should it matter to me whether he lives or dies?'

'Unfortunately, I do not know the answer to that,' Lord

Lynke said. 'But I can assure you that I intend to find out!'

Doña Alcira suddenly lost control of herself.

'Get out of my house!' she screamed. 'Go away from here! Leave me! How dare you insult me by your insinuations, your vile accusations of which you have no proof! The King shall hear of this!'

Lord Lynke bowed.

'Most assuredly!' he said. 'For I intend to tell His Majesty myself.'

He bowed again and walked towards the door. It was only as he reached it that Doña Alcira put out her hand as if to stop him.

'W ... wait!' she said in a faltering voice. 'W ... wait! Can we really be saying these cruel things to one another over a page—an unimportant boy who cannot matter greatly to either of us?'

'His safety matters to me!' Lord Lynke said frigidly.

'But ... but not to the extent that you must quarrel with me,' Doña Alcira replied. 'Surely I matter to you more than this mere boy?'

There was a distinct pause before Lord Lynke replied. Then, in a voice which held a hint of genuine surprise, he answered:

'I am not at all sure of that!'

Before Doña Alcira could speak again he had left the room, closing the door behind him.

For a moment she stared blindly at the spot where he had stood, her fingers clenching and unclenching themselves. Then she flew into a wild, hysterical rage which those who attended on her knew only too well.

Choking with tears, her lips muttering foul and filthy oaths, she ran around the room snatching up valuable ornaments from the tables and smashing them against the walls so that the broken pieces fell in all directions. Then she beat on the furniture with her clenched fists until they were bruised—till finally, panting with exhaustion, she fell to the ground to lie there screaming and sobbing until her attendants came to minister to her.

Lord Lynke walked slowly down the staircase, his mouth set in a grim line, his eyes hard as steel. He glanced around him, hoping he would catch sight of the dwarf, determined that if he did so, he would shake the truth from him even though he killed him in the effort. But

135

there was no sign of Frivolo. In fact, there was no one about.

He opened the door of the room where he had left Ventura and saw that it was empty. For a moment he thought he must be mistaken. He looked behind the chairs and in the deep window-seat as though she might have concealed herself; then, with a sudden shock which was almost a physical blow, he realised there was no sign of her.

What had happened? he wondered. Had he been unwise to leave her here? He could not credit that the dwarf or anyone else would commit a murder in broad daylight. Yet, the fact remained, Ventura was gone!

Lord Lynke's hand went instinctively towards his sword; then some hard core of common sense told him he had got to be more subtle. Using violence, making a scene, demanding the return of his page at the point of the sword might be an ill-judged action which could have disastrous consequences. He had to pretend, at any rate until he knew more, that his feelings were those of any ordinary man whose page was not waiting for him as he had been commanded to do.

Lord Lynke crossed the room and tugged hard on the bell-pull. It was several minutes before it was anwered— minutes which seemed to Lord Lynke to tick by like centuries. Then a flunkey appeared.

'Inform my page, Mr. Cameron, that I am ready to depart,' Lord Lynke said.

The footman who had been the one on duty in the hall when Lord Lynke arrived, looked round the room as if he expected to see Ventura lurking in one of the corners. Then he bowed and disappeared.

It was several more minutes before the major-domo came to the door, but which time Lord Lynke was tapping impatiently with his foot on the floor.

'Your page cannot be found, Your Excellency.'

'But he must be found!' Lord Lynke replied. 'What can have happened to him?'

'I have no idea, Excellency. He was here in this room when I last saw him.'

'Then he must be somewhere in the house,' Lord Lynke said. 'Set a search for him. If he is not at my side within five minutes, I will search the house myself!'

The major-domo looked horrified as well as astonished at Lord Lynke's threat.

'I cannot understand, Your Excellency . . .' he began.

Lord Lynke dismissed him with a sharp 'Find him!'

The major-domo disappeared, but Lord Lynke felt that it was impossible for him to wait where he was. He walked into the hall. Should he go up to Doña Alcira's room again? he wondered. Should he force her to give orders for Ventura to be returned to him? He would do that if it was necessary.

He glanced at the clock, an ornate piece of French workmanship standing at the foot of the stairs. One minute had passed. What could have happened to Ventura? Could the dwarf have carried her off? Could he have come upon her unawares and stabbed her before she could call out for help?

Lord Lynke remembered that the hall was empty when he came downstairs. Ventura might have screamed and no one would have heard her. Perhaps, even at this moment, her body was lying concealed under one of the sofas. It required all Lord Lynke's will to prevent himself from rushing round the house, bursting open doors.

Three minutes had gone. There was no sign of the major-domo.

'Dammit!' Lord Lynke said aloud. 'I have got to do something! I cannot just stand here while she is murdered!'

His hand went once again to his sword and at that moment he saw Ventura at the top of the stairs.

He had never believed it was possible for him to be so glad to see anyone. He felt as if a sudden ton-weight of anxiety had been lifted from his shoulders. And then because he was so glad to see her, because the relief was so great, he felt irritated because she had caused him so much anxiety.

'Where the hell have you been?' he asked angrily as she reached his side.

He had forgotten she was a woman. He had forgotten everything save that this small, white-faced 'boy' had caused him the greatest anguish he had ever experienced.

'I was looking for you,' Ventura said simply.

'Come on, let us be quit of this place,' Lord Lynke replied roughly.

He strode across the hall at such a rate that Ventura had to run to keep up with him. He pulled open the door and the flunkeys in attendance in the outer hall hurried forward with their hats.

The coach was outside, the horses prancing and fidgeting at having been kept waiting. Lord Lynke got in and sank back against the cushioned seat. Ventura sat opposite him. The horses started off in the direction of the Palace.

'Now, doubtless, you can excuse your actions,' Lord Lynke said acidly.

He could not explain to himself why, but it would have given him great pleasure to beat Ventura for the anxiety she had caused him. He was too angry to notice how pale she was or that there was an almost dazed expression in her eyes.

'I'm sorry if you are incensed with me, m'lord,' Ventura said humbly; 'but I went to look for you because I had news of such import that I felt it could not wait!'

'And what was this stupendous news?' Lord Lynke asked, a sarcastic note in his voice as if he would be surprised that it could be anything but trivial.

Ventura took a deep breath, and then glossing over how she had found the secret chamber, she told him that she had stepped inside it and that the door had closed behind her. She went on to describe how the men had come into the room that she had just left, and how she had been able to see them from behind the books and listen to their conversation.

Ventura had a good memory. When they had been too poor to afford teachers for her, her father and mother had taught her by simple methods. One of them had read aloud a chapter from the Bible or a book that was well written and made her repeat what she had heard. In this way she acquired an acute and retentive memory, and she was able to repeat to Lord Lynke almost word for word the conversation she had overheard between the three men.

Lord Lynke sat in silence until she had finished speaking. Then he brought his hand down on his knee with a hard slap.

'Ye Gods!' he exclaimed. 'This is what Sir Benjamin has suspected all along, and he is not mistaken! He must send a messenger post haste to London. What will Walpole say to this I wonder? And even my revered uncle will be astonished! The question is, shall we be in time?'

'Don't forget,' Ventura answered, 'that Doña Alcira has to obtain the permission of the Queen.'

'That gives us a short respite, at any rate,' Lord Lynke

138

agreed. 'But once she has obtained it, the ships will start slipping out one by one.'

He bent forward across the carriage and took Ventura's hand in his.

'Thank you, Ventura,' he said. 'You have done something which may not only save Gibraltar for England, but also save the rest of the world from Spain.'

He threw himself back with a gesture of satisfaction then said hastily:

'They could not have guessed in any way that they were overheard?'

Ventura shook her head.

'I see no reason why they should suspect there was a secret chamber in the room, or if there were that there should be anyone in it.'

'It was clever of you to discover it,' Lord Lynke said. 'What made you suspect it was there?'

'I think I was just lucky, m'lord,' Ventura answered evasively.

She did not want at the moment to discuss with Lord Lynke how the story her father had told her had led her not only to the catch which opened the secret chamber, but also to the picture of her mother.

She thrust aside the questions which concerned herself, but she knew that sooner or later she would have to face her own position.

For the moment, at least, Lord Lynke was happy. She had gained for him the information he had most wanted. She had paid back the debt that she owed him for his kindness in bringing her to Madrid. She had even, in some way, made reparation for having deceived him and pretended to be what she was not.

As the coach rumbled on through the park and back to the Palace, Ventura sat in a golden daze of happiness because she knew who she was. She had learned that the old lady in the sun-filled room was her grandmother! That her mother had been the elder daughter of the Duke and Duchess of Carcastillo, and that she had run away because she had been forbidden to marry an impoverished, exiled Scot who had taken refuge in Spain after he had fought for James Stuart.

But it was all very well to know these things. It was, Ventura thought, far more difficult to prove them. It was true that the old Duchess had recognised her and thought that she was her mother come back again.

But Ventura had realised as she talked with the old lady that in many ways her senses and her memory were fading. She could remember the past very clearly. It seemed to her only yesterday that her daughter had run away with the red-haired Earl of Kinbrace. She could recall how distressed the Marqués de Torre Nueva had been, to whom Anna Louisa had been officially engaged. She could remember her husband's anger which had gradually abated and become anxiety and distress when all efforts at finding their eldest child had failed.

All these things were very clear to the Duchess, but when she came to speak of present-day things it was very different. She could not remember the names of the King and Queen. More than once she spoke of Doña Alcira as if she were a little girl in the schoolroom. She did not know the Royal Palace had been burned down, and at first it had been difficult for Ventura to convince the Duchess that she was her grand-daughter and not her daughter.

Ventura knew now why Doña Alcira had wanted to kill her. She gave a little start as she realised the carriage had drawn up at the Palace door. Lord Lynke, who had been silent for some time, said:

'I had best go to Sir Benjamin right away! I shall leave you here because I think it unwise for him to see you. I shall tell him your story and persuade him that it is unnecessary for you to repeat it to him in person. It is not going to be easy, but we don't want explanations as to why Sir Roderick Lane, for whom my uncle wrote letters of introduction, has become Euan Cameron. We don't want him to think it strange that Mr. Cameron seems more Spanish than English; and above all, we don't want him to be suspicious that the aforesaid Mr. Cameron is rather effeminate-looking.'

'No, no, of course not!' Ventura said quickly.

Lord Lynke smiled at her.

'Don't think I am not grateful or that I am in any way belittling what you have done. But I do think it best for you to keep out of Sir Benjamin's sight.'

'I never imagined doing anything else,' Ventura announced.

'Then go upstairs to our rooms and don't for Heaven's sake get into trouble until I return! If you are afraid, lock the door or tell Simon to keep you company.'

'I shall be all right,' Ventura said.

She got out of the carriage and smiled at Lord Lynke, then slipped through the huge door. Lord Lynke gave the order to drive to the British Embassy, and the coach went back the way it had come.

Upstairs in her own bedroom Ventura stared across the sunlit gardens without seeing them. It seemed to her as if she were looking back into the past, understanding so many things which had been inexplicable before. Of one thing she was quite certain. Her mother had never regretted that she had run away.

Ventura remembered the poor little house in which they had lived.

The way they had to consider every peseta. The times when they had been hungry and their clothes had been mended until nothing more could be done to them. And yet she knew, looking back, that her mother would not have changed any of it for the luxury and magnificence of the home she had left. She had loved the man with whom she had eloped, and he had loved her with such devotion and selflessness that every sacrifice became a joy because it was shared.

Now Ventura knew what her mother had meant when she said with her dying breath: 'Go to Madrid!' She had wanted her child to do what she had never been able to do in her lifetime—to make reparation for the sorrow and unhappiness she had caused her parents.

Her mother had meant to go back herself. But she had spoken of letters. Now Ventura guessed what those letters contained. Yet she had searched and searched and never found a trace of them. There was nowhere where they could have been hidden. She wondered whether her mother had been mistaken. Perhaps she had meant to write a letter to her parents, and as she was dying had imagined she had done so.

Ventura walked across the room and picked up the jewel-case which had been the only thing she had refused to part with. She looked at the initials on it and understood them for the first time. 'A.L.C.' And the crest above it belonged to the Duke of Carcastillo. Would this be considered sufficient proof of her identity? She doubted it. Anyone could buy or steal a case of this description.

She thought of Doña Alcira's hard face, of her questions, of the legal representatives she could pay to denounce as an impostor an impudent gutter-snipe who

141

had first pretended to be a boy and was now pretending to the estates of Carcastillo.

No! If she was to come forward and say who she was, she would want something better than a likeness to her mother and a jewel case which was empty except for a wooden crucifix.

Ventura opened the box and took out the crucifix. Gently she ran her fingers over it, remembering how often her mother had prayed before it.

'Help me, God, to prove who I am,' she prayed. 'It is what Mamma would have wanted for me—to be at home with my own people. I think she would also have wanted me to be a girl again. Please, God! Hear my prayer!'

The words were simple enough, but the intensity came from the very depths of her heart. She felt the tears flood her eyes as she laid her face against the jewel case.

'If only you could speak!' she whispered.

Then she turned from the window to carry it back to the chest-of-drawers where it habitually stood. The sunshine, glittering on her tears, made the world appear suddenly patterned with rainbows. The polished floor was slippery and she was tired from the long, sleepless night. She slipped. She struggled to keep her balance, but the box fell out of her hand. It seemed to shoot high in the air, and then crash downwards on to the parquet.

Ventura gave a gasp of dismay. The delicate inlay would be damaged, and the box was the only link left with her mother. Then with a little cry she stood staring at the box. The fall had dislodged a narrow drawer which had been concealed in its base. It had opened to disclose on its velvet surface, two letters.

11

Ventura stared at the letters for a long time.

'How could I have been so foolish as not to find them?' she asked herself.

But she saw now that the secret drawer was well hidden and the tears came into her eyes as she stared at her mother's writing in beautifully formed, clear letters. One letter was addressed to the Marqués de Torre Nueva, and above his name was written: *In case my father is dead or will not receive Ventura.*

'She thought of everything,' Ventura told herself with a little sob. Then, gathering the letters in her hand, she stood in the sunshine holding them close against her breast.

Quite suddenly she saw how imperative it was for her to act cleverly. The one thing she must not do was to embarrass Lord Lynke or place him in the false position of having to explain her presence. Whatever else happened, she must not harm him by scandal or gossip.

Ventura felt as if her new-found love for him was something which made her ready to make any sacrifice if it were to his advantage. She would tear up the letters and destroy them. She would remain as she was—a foundling of the gutters of San Sebastian to whom he had given his protection. And yet, she asked herself, would that really be to his advantage?

She thought of Doña Alcira's face, her eyes, cold, hard and venomous. She thought of her tight lips, and knew that she must save Lord Lynke from her if from nothing else.

She felt a sudden thrill of triumph. She could challenge Doña Alcira and take from her the power and the wealth which she obviously loved so well. At the same time, Ventura knew she must be careful. Doña Alcira had already made one attempt upon her life. It was unlikely that she would fail the second time.

Ventura shivered a little at the thought of her terror last night when she had watched the dwarf come creeping into her room. She wondered what Lord Lynke had said to Doña Alcira this morning, and thought how strange it was that they had forgotten to speak of it in the excitement of other things.

'He will tell me later,' Ventura thought, and decided in that instant what she must do. There was no time to be lost. Doña Alcira knew her for what she was. She was bound to make another attempt to dispose of her. If then it was discovered that Lord Lynke's page was a woman disguised as a boy, it would discredit him at Court. It would make him an outcast as far as the King and Queen were concerned and all the members of their entourage. He might even be exiled from England.

It would perhaps suit Doña Alcira to reveal her knowledge and dispose of both of them in that manner; and once she had done so who would listen to Lord Lynke's explanations? And who would believe that the girl in boy's clothing was Doña Anna Louisa's daughter? No one would credit such a story for an instant, and Doña Alcira, the favoured ward of Philip V, would remain supreme and unchallenged as the owner of the Carcastillo fortunes.

'I must go to the *Marqués*!' Ventura said aloud, looking down at his name written on the envelope. She wished she could remember what he looked like. She must more than once have been in the same room with him, and yet his features escaped her.

She could hear the Duchess saying in her soft, rather vague manner:

'Your mother was betrothed to the Marqués de Torre Nueva. She was content to marry him until she met your father, and then she declared that if she could not wed this penniless Scot she would enter a nunnery.'

How fascinating the story sounded, Ventura thought. She wanted to hear more and yet more, but she had not dared to linger too long with the Duchess. She could only beg her to keep silent—to speak of her visit to no one. If she did so, Ventura thought suddenly, even she herself might be in danger from the greed and enmity of her own daughter.

Speed, speed, speed! That was above all what was necessary. Ventura put her hands to her head. She had so much to do. She had to cease to be Euan Cameron. She had to become Ventura Stuart, daughter of the Earl of Kinbrace. She had to find the *Marqués*, convince him of her identity and persuade him to fight her battle for her against Doña Alcira.

That was what she must do for herself. On the other hand, as far as Lord Lynke was concerned, she must dispose of Euan Cameron so that not for one moment would anyone connect his disappearance from Madrid with the arrival of Lady Ventura Stuart.

Ventura took a deep breath, then she went to her writing-table and scribbled a note. It did not take her long. Her face was white as she wrote. Her eyes were dark with pain. She realised that with every word she penned she was raising a barrier between herself and the man she loved.

She had one last desperate temptation to do nothing, to let events take their course, to stay with Lord Lynke. She might be of little consequence in his life, but it was something to be near him, to see his face, to hear his voice, to feel the touch of his hand upon her shoulder.

'I love him ... how much I love him!' she whispered aloud. And then, because she was driven by the passing of time, she sprang up from the chair and ran to the door. First, she must have woman's clothes.

A little way down the corridor, in a suite of rooms somewhat similar to their own, was housed the Countess de Fernando. She was young and pretty and had only recently been appointed a lady-in-waiting to the Queen. Ventura had often seen her coming up the stairway or passing along the corridor to her rooms, and she had thought how elegant and well dressed the Countess was, and then learnt that she was French.

'Her gowns are made in Paris,' another lady-in-waiting had said enviously. 'How can we expect to compete!'

Ventura had noticed that the Countess was very small and slight, and had decided, almost unconsciously, that they were about the same size and height.

The Countess's wardrobe was so extensive that it was said that, although she had been at Court for over three months, she had not yet worn the same gown twice. In which case, Ventura told herself she was not likely to miss one.

She stood listening. This part of the Palace was very quiet. It was time for the midday meal and all the maids and valets would have gone downstairs for it. Very quietly Ventura crept along until she came to the door which led into the Countess's suite. She knocked softly. There was no answer.

Had there been one, she decided to say she had come with a message from her master. But her knocking provoked no response, and after a second she turned the handle of the door. It was unlocked and Ventura found herself in the sitting-room, which was almost identical in shape to the one occupied by Lord Lynke.

She wasted no time looking round, but fled across the room into the bedchamber. This, too, was empty, and it took her but a moment to open one of the long wardrobes which flanked an entire wall of the room. As she pulled open the door, the Countess's gowns fluttered with the rush of air as though they were flowers bowing before the wind. Red, pink, green, orange, purple, blue. There was every colour imaginable—all fashioned by the skill and artistry known only to the French designers.

Ventura wasted no time in looking at the more colourful gowns. She picked the plainest she could see, which was of deep blue satin, embroidered with tiny flowers. There was lace fringing the square *décolletage* and dropping gracefully below the short sleeves, but, even so, it was a simple dress compared with the majority of the others.

Ventura threw it over her arm. She opened another wardrobe and found a dark cloak such as the ladies of the Court wore on informal occasions when they visited the theatre or pretended to be disguised from the curious eyes of the crowd. Shoes, stockings, petticoats! Almost instinctively, Ventura seemed to know where she would find what she wanted; and then, as unobtrusively as she had come, she slipped away, having closed the doors of the wardrobe behind her.

It was not stealing, she told herself as she returned to her bedroom. It was merely borrowing something in an emergency. She would return the things to the Countess later or, if she ever had the chance, make it up to her by some other means. She did not think that the pretty little French woman, if she knew the whole story, would grudge her one gown.

Quickly Ventura made the things up into a bundle. Then she slipped the letters she had obtained from the secret drawer into the wide pocket of her page's coat and went from her own room into Lord Lynke's.

She stood for a moment looking round her. It was severe in its masculinity, and yet she felt that because he had occupied it he had left an indelible impression there. A pair of his gloves was lying on the dressing-table. Ventura picked them up and held them for a moment against her cheek. Then she kissed them—soft, yet passionate kisses of farewell.

Almost guiltily she glanced at the clock over the mantelpiece. Time was passing. She must be ready to go. She went into the sitting-room and pealed the bell. She waited a few seconds and pealed it again impetuously. A minute later she heard Simon coming, running up the stairs. He was breathless as he hurried into the room.

'You rang, sir?' he asked; but there was surprise in his voice because it was obvious that he expected such an impetuous summons to have come from his master, not from a mere page.

'Yes, Simon, I rang,' Ventura said. 'I am sorry if I have interrupted you in the middle of your meal, but it is of import. I have had a message to say that my uncle is desperately ill. I have to leave immediately for San Sebastian.'

'I am sorry to hear that, sir,' Simon said gravely.

'I have been informed that there is a coach leaving Madrid in twenty minutes' time,' Ventura said. 'I shall be able to obtain a seat. Will you tell his lordship, when he returns, what has occurred? I have left him a note, but I had not time to write much.'

'I understand, sir, and I'll tell his lordship,' Simon said.

'I am only taking a few things that I can carry with me,' Ventura went on. 'Would you be kind enough to pack my clothes in my trunk so that they can be ready for me on my return or could be sent to me by carrier to San Sebastian.'

'I will see to that, sir,' Simon replied.

'Thank you.'

Ventura held out her hand.

'Good-bye, Simon. Thank you for all you have done for me. I am exceedingly grateful.'

'That's all right, sir. Glad to have been of service,' Simon answered, shaking her hand with a grip which hurt. 'And I'm sorry about your uncle and hope that you will get there in time.'

'I hope so too,' Ventura said gravely.

'Shall I see you to the door, sir?' Simon asked.

Ventura had anticipated this question.

'No, thank you,' she said. 'I have made my arrangements; and his lordship asked me to tell you to lay out his blue velvet coat and silver vest. He will be back to change in a few moments.'

'Very good, sir.'

Ventura escaped from the room. Putting out Lord Lynke's things, she knew, would keep Simon engaged while she got downstairs. She put the bundle which contained the Countess's clothes under her arm and went down the broad staircase; but on reaching the ground floor instead of proceeding to the front door she hurried down a long corridor which had a number of small waiting-rooms opening out of it.

Here were places for the attendants who came with

147

ambassadors or envoys from other countries when they sought audience with the King. Sometimes they were forced to wait for hours on end. Sometimes they would come back, day after day, until their master's presence could be brought to His Majesty's attention. As it was below the dignity of the secretaries, chaplains, aides-de-camp and other personnel to sit with the servants, and their betters would not accept them, these small waiting-rooms were provided for them.

Ventura glanced into one and found a stout monk reading a breviary. She closed the door and opened another. Two women sat there chattering vivaciously. A third room was empty. She went into it and shut and locked the door behind her.

It took her but a few minutes to divest herself of the velvet suit which the tailor in San Sebastian had made for her. She slipped it off, throwing it nonchalantly on the floor, and then, with a shiver of pleasure, began to dress herself as a woman again.

It was not easy for her to fasten the dress which did up at the back, but somehow she managed it. There was a mirror over the mantelshelf, and standing in front of it Ventura arranged her hair. It had grown very much longer since she had been in Lord Lynke's service. Her fingers were skilful enough to twist the sides into the fashionable curls, to pile the rest high upon her head in the very latest mode amongst the Court ladies.

Then she drew the dark cloak over her shoulders, pulling up the hood so that it framed her face becomingly, and effectively disguised anything inadequate about her finished toilet.

It took her only a moment, once she was ready, to bundle the page's clothing into a cupboard which opened out of the panelled walls of the room. The Countess's shoes were a fraction too big, but they did not prevent Ventura from walking very elegantly and with a grace that was entirely feminine, down the passage and through the wider corridors which led to the front door.

The flunkeys looked up at her approach, expecting her to give her name so that they could call a coach. Ventura shook her head.

'I am leaving much earlier than I expected,' she said to the major-domo. 'My carriage will not yet have returned for me. Can you suggest any possible way that I can get into the town?'

The servant was only too ready to be of assistance.

'There are coaches that have been waiting here for several hours, *señorita*,' he said. 'The exercise will do the horses good.'

Ventura smiled at him. He hurried away and procured a coach that she recognised as belonging to the Italian Ambassador. She thanked the man who had brought it and asked him to tell the coachman to drive to the house of the Marqués de Torre Nueva.

As they drove through the park, Ventura found that her heart was beating quickly while at the same time her mind felt surprisingly cool and unagitated. Everything, so far, had gone exactly as she had planned. She only had to force her thoughts away from Lord Lynke and what he would say when he read her note.

She wondered if he would miss her, even a little. He had been glad enough to talk to her on the journey to Madrid; but now that he had found his feet in Spain, now that there were all too many people ready to fête and befriend him, perhaps he would scarcely notice her going.

She felt a little sob rise in her throat at the thought. It was hard to love someone so much and know how little one mattered in his life. Perhaps he would even be glad that she had gone, so that he need no longer be anxious lest someone should discover that she was not a boy. Perhaps he would say 'Good riddance!' or, worse still, say as so often before: 'To hell with all women!'

Should she stay with him after all? Fiercely, Ventura wiped the tears from her eys, bit her lip and told herself to stop being a fool. This was no time for sentiment. No time for weakening because her heart was given to a man who was betrothed to her own aunt.

The carriage was driving into a huge courtyard. Ventura could see a magnificent mansion and felt her fingers grow cold at the thought of what lay before her; but it was with admirable self-possession that she managed to step from the carriage and say to the major-domo who bowed to her:

'I have unfortunately forgotten my purse. Kindly reimburse the coachman for bringing me from the Palace. I will arrange matters with the *Marqués*.'

Her orders and her grand manner impressed the majordomo so that he said to the coachman, 'Wait!' and led Ventura into the house.

'You have an appointment, *señorita*?' he asked.

'No, but the *Marqués* will see me,' Ventura said confidently. 'Inform him that the daughter of Doña Anna Louisa desires an audience with him.'

The major-domo repeated the description in a mystified manner then he left Ventura alone in a magnificent *salon* decorated with rose brocade and hung with pictures which seemed to Ventura even more magnificent than those in the King's Palace.

She could not help thinking that these were the surroundings that her mother could have had if she had been prepared to take as her husband the man who owned them. Then the door was opened and a tall, middle-aged man with iron-grey hair and tired lined face came into the room.

Ventura swept him a curtsy. As she rose, he put out his hands and drew her close to him so that he could look down into her face.

'So it is true!' he said. 'You are Anna Louisa's daughter! I should have known you anywhere.'

'Do I look like her?' Ventura asked with a smile.

'Exactly as she was the last time I saw her,' the *Marqués* answered, 'except for your eyes.'

He gave a little sigh and then drew Ventura to a sofa.

'Come and sit down,' he said. 'I can hardly believe that you are not your mother; and yet you know the questions I want to ask. How is she? Why has she not come herself?'

'Because she is dead,' Ventura answered, and saw the pain in his eyes. 'But she meant me to come to you,' she added more softly and held out the letter to him.

Only a few streets away from the Marqués de Torre Nueva's house Lord Lynke was in consultation with Sir Benjamin Keene. At first the English Minister found it hard to believe the story which Lord Lynke related to him.

'It is impossible!' he said. 'I cannot believe that the Duc de Montemar would lend himself to a plot that is not only unethical but foolhardy in the extreme. He cannot imagine that the British fleet would allow any extensive movement of ships without being aware of it, and he must know that at Gibraltar our look-outs are continually on the alert.'

'That is as it may be,' Lord Lynke said a little testily, 'but this is what they said in the hearing of my page, and from what I hear of the Count de Montijo he is continually hoping for war.'

'Yes, I have thought that for some time,' Sir Benjamin said. 'And, frankly, I have never trusted the *Duc*. When Patino was alive, he kept him in order. His death was a tragedy for Spain, although I am not certain that we British should not be grateful that his finest ambition did not materialise.'

'And what was that?' Lord Lynke asked.

Sir Benjamin's eyes twinkled. 'The acquisition of Gibraltar!' he said.

'Then surely the *Duc* is carrying on Patino's schemes?' Lord Lynke suggested.

'I imagine so,' Sir Benjamin said; 'but even then I can hardly credit that he would sink to associate with Don Carlos.'

'Necessity can make for strange bedfellows,' Lord Lynke quoted, 'although I must say Don Carlos would not be my choice however pressed I might be!'

'Nor mine!' Sir Benjamin said. 'But what you have told me necessitates immediate action. I must send a courier hot-foot to the coast.'

'We have a little time in hand,' Lord Lynke warned him. 'First, Doña Alcira has to get permission from the Queen. Secondly, the ships are to slide out one by one so as to deceive our naval commanders.'

'I suppose you are absolutely certain that this boy could not have imagined all this?' Sir Benjamin asked. 'I don't want to seem incredulous, but the whole thing seems to be rather peculiar. Why should your page, who is English and never been to Spain before, manage to find his way into the secret chamber which you tell me is hidden behind the Duke of Carcastillo's library? I am not suggesting for one moment this chamber is not there. They exist in most Spanish houses and palace, but what I want to know is, how did the boy find it?"

'It does seem odd,' Lord Lynke replied slowly. 'But I am prepared to believe Euan Cameron.'

'I think that before I send my courier I'd best see this page of yours,' Sir Benjamin said. 'You tell me that you mentioned to him that you were anxious to discover any secrets that concerned Great Britain. Well, the boy may have wished to curry favour with you. He may have wanted to produce a sensational story. We must eliminate such possibilities before we rush into actions which may have very big consequences.'

'Yes, I see your point,' Lord Lynke answered. 'At the same time, I am prepared to stake my honour that the boy is entirely reliable.'

'Well, I'd like to have a word with him,' Sir Benjamin said.

'I'm afraid that is not so easy,' Lord Lynke replied.

'Why?' Sir Benjamin inquired.

Lord Lynke walked restlessly across the room.

'The boy is shy. He trusts me; but he has never met you and would not, I feel, be particularly happy to confide in a complete stranger. I am afraid, Sir Benjamin, that you must take the story from me.'

'But ... I cannot understand your objections, m'lord!' Sir Benjamin expostulated. 'I am not going to cross-examine the boy or make him uncomfortable in any way. I just want to talk to him in a friendly manner, to hear the story from his own lips, and to form my own judgement.'

'Well I am afraid it is impossible!' Lord Lynke said.

'Impossible!' Sir Benjamin was obviously astounded. 'But what can be your objection?'

'I have given you my reason,' Lord Lynke answered. 'When I came here, my uncle asked me to find out what I could and to report to you any matters which seemed to me of significance. Here is something which I consider very significant—news which should be carried to my uncle with all possible speed. How I obtained that information is, I consider, quite irrelevant.'

'Upon my word! Your lordship is making things very difficult for me,' Sir Benjamin said. 'You come to me with a story which, to put it mildly, is sensational. It is something which strikes at the very root of the peace which we have recently negotiated between Great Britain and Spain. It is a story which discredits the War Minister and throws suspicion on Her Majesty herself. You cannot expect me to swallow it without question ... without making inquiries ... without being absolutely convinced in my heart that it is not a fabrication of lies!'

Lord Lynke yawned ostentatiously.

'I am not concerned, Sir Benjamin, with what you believe or do not believe,' he said. 'This story as it stands should be carried to my uncle post-haste! If you do not do so, then I must disclaim all responsibility for any consequences which may come from your omission.'

As Sir Benjamin did not speak, Lord Lynke bowed.

'I bid you good-day, sir,' he said; and before the Minister could answer, he stalked from the room.

Only the fire in his eyes revealed the anger that was seething within him as he descended the steps of the Embassy and walked towards his coach which was waiting outside. He was just about to step into it when he heard his name called by Don Francisco de Varis, the Minister of the Marines and Indies whom Lord Lynke had met several times at Court.

'Where are you going?' he inquired jovially.

'I was thinking of going back to the Palace,' Lord Lynke replied.

'You are not going to the bull-fight?'

'I hadn't thought of it.'

'Then come with me,' Don Francisco invited. 'I am to watch it from the Royal balcony and I am told that Miajado is facing a bull which is twice the size of any animal we have seen for years.'

'I shall be glad to come with you,' Lord Lynke smiled.

He had no particular desire to see a bull-fight, but he did wish to see Miajado. He was curious about the fellow.

The Plaza Mayer, a rectangle where the bull-fighting took place in Madrid, was crowded with people, as were the balconies of all the houses. The Royal box was empty save for Don Francisco and Lord Lynke; and as the sun slanted down on the spectacle before him, Lord Lynke could not help but find it surprisingly beautiful.

The flowers and shawls of the ladies, the colourful dress of the men, the procession of bandoliros, picadors and matadors in their gold embroidered jackets, knee breeches and magenta cloaks, made it look like a scene in the ballet.

For the moment Lord Lynke forgot his anger with Sir Benjamin, his disgust with Doña Alcira, his worry over Ventura. He found himself warming towards the Spaniards as they cheered and clapped beneath him, waving their handkerchiefs and laughing with the happy abandonment of children; and then the bull-fight began.

It was obviously a very successful one from the point of view of the crowd. Bull after bull was despatched with ease. The matadors were skilful and graceful, and Miajado himself, when he appeared to a roar of applause which seemed to shake the very roofs of the houses, was as brilliant and as daring as his reputation.

But offset against this was the slaughter and damage to the horses. Three horses, one after the other, were disembowelled, and Lord Lynke began to feel sick.

He loved his horses more than anything else he possessed. To him, horseflesh was something noble, something to be cherished, something to be respected. The poor broken old crocks in the bullring could hardly be compared with his own magnificent animals; and yet they, also, were the friends of man, and he felt a sudden fury for the manner in which they were being treated.

He could control himself enough to feel that it would be useless to protest and still more useless, and merely humiliating, to make a scene. There was nothing he could do but watch the slaughter and hate the men who were responsible for it.

He appreciated Miajado's skill, but the horses which died in agony or were taken away to be patched up and appear again counted immeasurably more than the bulls the Matador sacrificed so brilliantly.

With relief, Lord Lynke saw that the death of the sixth bull meant the end of the performance. He listened impassively as the crowd went wild over Miajado. He watched the bull-fighter parading the arena with his cap and sword in hand, being showered with flowers and jewels, scarves and mantillas, gloves and cravats. The spectators seemed to be speaking with one voice, and the noise seemed to go on and on interminably.

Lord Lynke turned from the balcony.

'Thank you for your hospitality, Don Francisco,' he said formally.

'You have never seen a bull-fight before?' his host inquired.

'No. This is my first,' Lord Lynke replied.

Inwardly, he vowed it would be his last. The sight of those horses would haunt him all his life. He refused the wine Don Francisco's servants were offering him. He hurried down the stairs of the house, which was called *Panaderia* and belonged to the Guild of Bakers.

It took his coach a long time to get through the crowds surging into the streets away from the arena, laughing and talking and all in high spirits because of the spectacle that Miajado had afforded them.

Lord Lynke had a sudden nostalgia for England, for the

race-course at Newmarket, the horses streaking past, their coats shining like satin, their grooms waiting to rub, brush and look after them as though they were children. He felt he had nothing in common with people who, beneath their gaiety, could be so cruel and so utterly brutal to an animal as noble as a horse.

Altogether, the day had been extremely unsatisfactory, Lord Lynke thought. He felt irritation again at the thought of Sir Benjamin's attitude, although he could not help knowing that the Minister was not really unreasonable in his demands. He thought of Doña Alcira, and almost instantly the image of Miajado came to his mind. They were two of a kind, he thought savagely, and, as far as he was concerned, they were welcome to each other!

The coach drew up outside the Palace. Lord Lynke got out with a scowling face and ascended the stairs without speaking to anyone. He was suddenly impatient to see Ventura, to tell her what had occurred, to hear her exclamations of dismay at Sir Benjamin's behaviour. Perhaps she would think of a solution for that problem, at any rate.

He flung open the door of the sitting-room; but there was no one there, and almost immediately Simon appeared in the door of the bedroom to take his hat and sword.

'Send Mr. Cameron to me!' Lord Lynke commanded.

'Mr. Cameron has gone, m'lord. I thought you knew, m'lord, about his uncle.'

'What uncle? What are you talking about? For God's sake explain yourself, man!'

Simon looked flustered, as he always did when Lord Lynke shouted at him.

'Mr. Cameron said his uncle was desperately ill, m'lord, and that he had to leave for San Sebastian at once! I thought he had told your Lordship, as he said you required me to lay out your blue and silver.'

'My blue and silver!' Lord Lynke ejaculated.

'Yes, m'lord, and he left you a note.'

'Why didn't you say so at once! Give it me! Where is it?'

'It is here, m'lord.'

Simon almost ran across the room with the note on a salver. Lord Lynke took it from him as if it was something distasteful; then as Simon waited, he snapped:

'You can go! And see that I am not disturbed.'

'Very good, m'lord.'

Simon withdrew and shut the door quietly behind him.

Slowly, almost heavily, as if he had suddenly grown older, Lord Lynke sat down on the chair. Then, with fingers that seemed curiously stiff, he opened the note and read what Ventura had written to him.

12

Doña Alcira closed the door very quietly behind her, then stood in the centre of her bedchamber breathing as if she were on the very edge of exhaustion. She had exerted her will to control her feelings to such an extent that now when at last she was alone, every nerve in her body was still tense.

Dragging one foot behind another as an old woman might have done, she walked across the room to stand staring into the mirror as though she looked at a stranger.

She still could not believe it was true; still could not credit that her whole world had crashed about her ears. And all because the knife that should have been planted firmly in the breast of the usurper of her powers had failed to find its mark.

Why had she not struck that first evening when, in the Garden Room at the Palace, she had seen Anna Louisa's face swim before her startled eyes and thought that she saw a ghost? She had imagined then that she must be dreaming. Afterwards she had thought that it could not really be Anna Louisa's child, but perhaps some by-blow of her father's or of one of his relations which had the family features.

She had always been utterly convinced in her own mind that Anna Louisa was dead. When the search for her and the penniless Scot failed and the *Duc's* servants reported that there was no sign of them in the whole length and breadth of Spain, Doña Alcira had been quite certain that Anna Louisa was dead. How else could she have lived, with no money, with a husband who dare not reveal his identity, with no prospects ahead of them save of penury and obscurity?

Doña Alcira could never have faced either of those things; and the fact that Anna Louisa's disappearance left the Carcastillo estates in her hands filled her with such delight and joy that she hardly spared one thought of regret for her lost sister.

Even during her father's life-time she had intrigued and schemed to get more power into her own hands. She loved to know that she was in command, that those who served her were afraid of her, that those who offended her must pay the utmost penalty that it was in her power to impose.

She was a hard, almost tyrannical mistress. She was often cruel and frequently unjust. The tenants on the great Carcastillo estates, who not only served her father but loved him, murmured amongst themselves that it was a bad day when the old *Duc* died and Doña Alcira took his place.

But they would not have dared to express those sentiments openly; and as Doña Alcira drove them harder and harder, extracting higher taxes and more work from them, they could only suffer miserably in silence and wonder how long they could endure under the strain.

Doña Alcira dismissed many of her father's overseers and replaced them with younger, hard-faced types who knew little about the countryside and less about the families they commanded. The only person who dared to remonstrate with Doña Alcira about what she was doing was the Marqués de Torre Nueva.

Towards the end of his life the *Duc* had sought not only friendship but advice from the man to whom his elder daughter had been betrothed and from whom she had run away to marry another. The two men grew very close to each other, and the *Marqués* became more and more concerned with the finances and interests of the Carcastillo estates.

Doña Alcira ended this the day after her father died.

'I will manage my own affairs personally,' she told the *Marqués* proudly.

He knew too much about Doña Alcira not to know she was speaking the truth. He bowed to her and left the Palace without a word; but his heart was sore for all those who had trusted his friend, and *Duc*, and who he knew would now suffer.

It would have been hard for any man, let alone one who loved and understood the country folk of Spain, to

157

watch in silence Doña Alcira's methods, but the *Marqués* forced himself not to interfere. He knew better than most people what Doña Alcira was really like at heart. He had not gone to the Carcastillo Palace day after day without seeing that the sweet and gentle exterior she kept for the court and for the guests whom her father entertained hid a very different character.

Doña Alcira was too clever ever to become the subject of public gossip. The King, the Queen and even the more spiteful members of the Court found little to relate about her. It was known, of course, that she had suitors, but only the servants and the *Marqués* knew of her many lovers. Only they were aware of her fits of temper, of her cruelty to those who offended her, of her ruthlessness if anyone crossed her.

But there was nothing the *Marqués* could do about it until Ventura came to his house carrying a letter from the woman he still loved after eighteen years' separation.

When Doña Alcira had been told that the Marqués de Torre Nueva wished to see her, she was surprised. The *Marqués* still visited her mother because the Duchess clung to him and, despite anything her daughter could say, preferred to take his advice on anything that concerned herself.

Never since her father's death had the *Marqués* deliberately sought out Doña Alcira. She met him sometimes by chance going upstairs to her mother's suite. They would come face to face in the Royal Palace or, most uncomfortably, would find themselves seated next each other at a dinner party. On these occasions the *Marqués* was always polite; but Doña Alcira knew that he despised her, and she hated him with a violence which made her sometimes plan to herself some diabolical revenge in which he would plead for her mercy.

'You are sure you are not mistaken?' she asked her maid when she received his message. 'It is the Marqués de Torre Nueva who wishes to see me?'

'*Si, si*, the *Marqués*, m'lady.'

'I wonder what he wants,' Doña Alcira muttered to herself.

She would never have admitted it even in her frankest moments of self-examination, but she was afraid of the *Marqués*. He was the one man who could look at her coldly and dispassionately and on whom her beauty apparently had no effect. Nevertheless, because she could never believe that her feminine wiles could evoke no response from a member of the opposite sex, Doña Alcira glanced at herself in the mirror before she went downstairs.

What she saw was peculiarly satisfying. Her dress of heavy brocade was embroidered with seed pearls and trimmed with bunches of velvet ribbon specially procured from France. Its colour of deep emerald green set off her white skin and her dark hair, and to enhance her beauty still further, she was wearing the jewellery she had recently ordered from the finest goldsmith in Madrid.

A necklace of black pearls and diamonds was matched by bracelets, ear-rings and a huge corsage. The jewels had cost a fortune, and the peasants on the Carcastillo estates would have to sweat to pay for them.

Doña Alcira smiled in the mirror. What did it matter what the *Marqués* would say when she still had the assets of youth and beauty and her great wealth as a background for them? She swept down the stairs and into the great *salon* on the ground-floor with her head held high, ready for a fight, ready to deny the *Marqués* whatever he should ask of her.

But as she entered the room her heart turned to stone. She had only to take a quick look at the girl standing by the *Marqués's* side to realise what had happened. She had only to see that sweet face that was so exactly like her sister's to know that she must have been demented not to have struck sooner.

The *Marqués's* voice was quiet but Doña Alcira felt herself writhe because she guessed that, though he did not in any way show it, he must be glad that she was to be deposed.

'Lady Ventura Stuart, your niece and the daughter of your sister, Doña Anna Louisa, has brought me letters which reveal, without any question, her identity,' the *Marqués* said.

If she had not seen Ventura before, if she had not already known who she was, Doña Alcira might have betrayed her feelings. But although she felt the blood drain away from her face and lips, she was able to give an exhibition of play-acting which would have done credit to any professional. She even kissed Ventura and, taking out her handkerchief, wiped her eyes when she learned how Anna Louisa had died.

'I have already sent for the attorneys,' the *Marqués* went on. 'You will recall that your father—my most beloved friend—left me sole executor of his estates and fortune. I shall require, of course, an accounting for all that has been spent during your administration.'

'Of course,' Doña Alcira said with a smile that seemed to hurt her like a knife-thrust.

'Tonight Lady Ventura will stay at the Chancellery as my guest. Tomorrow we will make arrangements for her to move here to her rightful home. I am now going to take her up to see your mother.'

'Then it would be best for me not to come with you,' Doña Alcira murmured. 'It is not wise for poor Mamma to have too many visitors at the same time.'

She turned to Ventura with what was quite a creditable effort of pleasantness.

'Good-bye, dear niece,' she said. 'We shall have many things to talk about tomorrow.'

Ventura dropped a curtsy shyly. She was not deceived by Doña Alcira's manner and she saw the hatred in her eyes even though it was carefully veiled from the *Marqués*. She was wondering desperately how she could stave off the moment when she must come to live in the Palace.

She was well aware that to sleep under the same roof with Doña Alcira was to put herself completely in her aunt's power. Doña Alcira would not make the same mistake that she had made before. The next time there was an attempt on her life, it would not be a failure.

Whatever else happened, Ventura thought a little hopefully, Doña Alcira would not dare to murder her in cold blood. That would be too difficult to explain. But there were other ways of disposing of a person besides sticking a knife into them.

As Ventura went up the stairs towards the Duchess's suite she felt herself shiver apprehensively. Today the *Marqués* might be a good bodyguard, but what, she wondered, would happen tomorrow? She had a sudden longing for Lord Lynke. For a moment she could almost feel his arms around her. How closely he had held her that night when she had fled to him in terror from the dwarf, forgetting what she had to hide, oblivious of the fact that she was lightly clothed, galvanised only by her terror.

She had wanted him at that moment with a longing which had never left her since. The mere thought of him now started her heart beating. It was with an effort that she forced herself to listen to what the *Marqués* was

160

saying as they walked down the corridor which led to the Duchess's rooms.

As they opened the door, there was the sound of birds twittering, and they found the Duchess sitting—as Ventura had found her before—in the sunshine, but her hands were clasped over a painted miniature of Anna Louisa.

For a long time it seemed to Doña Alcira that she could think of nothing and see nothing but Ventura's pointed face. She knew now that she had always hated Anna Louisa even when they were children together.

It was Anna Louisa who was good and Alcira who was naughty. It was Anna Louisa who was loved by their nurses and governesses and servants. It was Anna Louisa to whom their mother held out her arms so eagerly and who brought a smile to her father's eyes.

From the very moment of her birth, it seemed to Doña Alcira, the things she most wanted to possess were denied to her because of Anna Louisa. She had always been greedy, always possessive. She wanted everything. She didn't want to share her toys or her friends or her affections. She wanted them to belong to her and to her alone.

Alcira was several years younger than her sister. Between them there had been two sons, but they had not lived. Nor had the two boys whom the Duchess had borne before Anna Louisa. The Duchess was delicate and it had seemed to her a miracle when Anna Louisa lived, the first of her children who had done so. Then Alcira was born and although the Duchess wanted to love her second daughter just as much as her first, the child had never seemed to evoke the same tenderness and the same overwhelming love which Anna Louisa seemed to command so effortlessly from everyone she knew.

When Anna Louisa ran away. Doña Alcira was just beginning to be conscious of her own beauty and, because of it, she had been glad that her sister had gone. And her gladness had increased when she realised what a difference Anna Louisa's disappearance was to make to her status in life.

With all four sons lying buried in the family vault, the two daughters were left to inherit one of the greatest estates and finest fortunes in Spain. When Anna Louisa was finally presumed to be dead, Doña Alcira had told herself that now at last she reigned supreme in the family. Now at last she had everything. And yet she had been mistaken! Out of the past, almost out of the grave as it were, this child of Anna Louisa's had come back to frighten and oppose her.

'She shall not do it. She shall not!' The numb feeling which seemed to have sapped all vitality from Doña Alcira was passing. Now she felt as if life was creeping back into her face. Now she felt her spirit returning. She knew then that she was not going to take this lying down. She would fight back and she would win. Somehow, by some method, she would rid herself of this tiresome girl.

She sprang up from the chair into which she had sunk. How absurd it was to feel frightened or downcast! Her niece would not last long; and until the brat died, she must be clever enough to make the world believe that she welcomed this upstart's arrival.

She crossed the room, took a gold key from a hidden place and opened an iron box that she kept hidden behind a sliding panel. It was filled with money and jewels, but there was something else there, too. Something packed away in a velvet case—a collection of little bottles and powders.

There was a glint in Doña Alcira's eyes as she looked at them. An Italian lover had given them to her. He had come to the Court at the Queen's invitation. A man of great power and importance, but also a man of learning. He had told Doña Alcira how he had studied the methods of the Borgias.

'There are unfortunately but a few records of the poisons they used.'

'But there are some?' Doña Alcira questioned.

He nodded.

'Only a very few, and even historians are not certain that our descriptions are correct.'

'Surely the question is, do the poisons work?'

'There is no doubt about that,' he said with a glint in his eyes.

She had known then that she must obtain the information from him. He had been reluctant to tell her more, but she had coaxed it from him, learning of his perusal of old manuscripts, of the experiments of trained and trusted alchemists in his private laboratory, of the resulting poisons which they had tested and proved by the only really successful method—on human beings. Finally, of course, he had given her a sample of each of the different poisons

162

with instructions never to let anyone know that she had them in her possession.

With her long, sensitive fingers, Doña Alcira picked up the phials one by one. She could hear her lover's voice describe them as he had done when he had given them to her.

'This one is creeping death. It defies analysis in the dead body, but the victim gets weaker every day until he just fades away.'

Doña Alcira fingered the phial and then put it back in the case.

'This poison is instant,' she heard him say as she picked up another. 'One or two drops in food or in drink, and a few seconds after it is taken it is all over. A little choke perhaps, a sudden gasp as if for breath, then—death!'

There was a third phial and Doña Alcira caressed it softly.

'This one is the safest of all,' the Italian had told her. 'taken in the food, the victim runs a high fever. There is nothing extraordinary in that. The doctors prescribe their medicines, which will have not the slightest effect. On the third day the heart stops beating.'

Doña Alcira smiled and, putting the phial down on the table, she locked the other poisons away in her iron box and replaced the key.

The only difficulty she could see in this scheme was that someone who could be absolutely trusted must place the poision in the food that Ventura was to eat. It would not be safe, she knew, to confide in the maids. Many of them in the house would have been here when Anna Louisa was a girl. They would be full of sentiment and excitement because her daughter had returned to the Palace, and the younger servants were untrustworthy.

There were too many new ideas in Spain nowadays. Young people talked in almost a revolutionary manner; and, although no one was foolhardy enough to do so in Doña Alcira's hearing, she was somehow subtly aware of this new trend of thought which seemed to her to strike at the very root of the feudal system.

'No, it would have to be someone absolutely trust-worthy; yet who was there who would do her bidding without question, without repeating to anyone else what they had been told to do? She knew then that it would have to be Frivolo. He had failed her once, but there was no reason why he should do so again. She had told Lord

163

Lynke that she would send him away, but, of course, she had no intention of doing so.

The thought of Lord Lynke brought an expression to Doña Alcira's face which would have frightened those who knew her well. Lord Lynke was at the bottom of this, she thought. She had forgotten that for the moment. It was he who had brought Ventura to Madrid disguised as a boy and then had sent her to the *Marqués* decked up in woman's clothes and calling herself by her proper name.

With a cruel smile on her lips, Doña Alcira knew suddenly how she could expose and humiliate Lord Lynke. She had not forgotten his treatment of her. He should be made to suffer for that, and so should Ventura.

She sat down for a moment to plan what she could do. Her fingers tapped restlessly on the polished top of the table beside her. Her eyes were suddenly alight with evil and her depression had vanished.

It would not be becoming, she thought, for her to go to the Palace and tell the Queen openly that Lord Lynke had passed off a girl as his page. To denounce them would make her appear spiteful. She must be careful for fear people treated her with less respect because she was no longer as wealthy and as important as she had been.

'I will be subtle,' Doña Alcira told herself. She would ask for a special audience with the Queen alone, and then, because of their long affection for each other, because of her position as the King's ward, she would beg the Queen's help.

'There is no one to whom I can mention this except yourself, Ma'am,' she would say in a soft, worried voice. 'But you are so understanding that I feel as if I could speak to you as to my own mother. It is the danger to which my poor niece has been exposed that perturbs me. Supposing she is with child, what then must I do about it?'

If she put it to the Queen in that manner, Her Majesty would quite certainly realise what an insult had been perpetrated on the Court. She would feel that Lord Lynke had abused Royal hospitality and insulted the Court of Spain.

Doña Alcira smiled to herself. That would even up her score with him, at any rate; and after that she could deal with Ventura.

She picked up the phial, then put it down again. It was going to be hard to wait even a day or so before she used it. Then she reached out her hand and rang the little gold bell which summoned her maid. The door opened almost immediately. Joanna must have been waiting, wondering why she had not been sent for before.

'I want Frivolo here, at once!' Doña Alcira said sharply.

Joanna obviously wished to speak of something else, but when she saw her mistress's face she went out without speaking and shut the door behind her.

Doña Alcira moved across the room, and from a drawer in a table by the window she drew out a thin leather riding-whip. It was Frivolo's fault that she was suffering as she was, she thought. He must be punished for his stupidity. He must be made to realise, too, that when she gave an order, she meant it! He had been told to kill, and the girl had eluded him. Now she had got to organise all over again the job that he had been told to do.

Ventura would not smile for long. Lord Lynke should never have her! He had been sent out from England to marry the owner of the Carcastillo estates. Perhaps he was chuckling, to himself, thinking how easy it would be now that Ventura owned them. He was going to be disappointed!

Doña Alcira swished the riding-whip and heard it cut through the air with a sharp whistling sound which somehow gave her evil satisfaction. She would like to whip and torture Ventura before she killed her. It was a pity that that was impossible. Perhaps her death would hurt and distress Lord Lynke. That, at least, was some consolation.

She thought of his face, aloof and disdainful, and felt herself shaken with sudden rage. He too had eluded her. He too had turned away from her.

'Why, why is this happening to me?' Doña Alcira asked the empty room, and heard her voice echo back at her.

She looked round at the treasures with which she had surrounded herself. The gold ornaments, exquisite pictures. The china, the silver, the ivory, the crystal. She looked at the silken rugs upon the floor, the inlaid furniture, the crystal and gold sconces.

Her eyes rested on her jewel-case standing on the dressing-table. She thought of the rubies, the emeralds, the sapphires and the diamonds lying there in their beds of velvet, many of them heirlooms—all of them bought with Carcastillo money.

She would not give them up, she would not part with

165

them. They were hers! Hers! And she would keep them if to do so she had to kill and destroy every one of her enemies.

All this because of one man and one girl! She felt her rage rising up in her, bubbling and fermenting in her mind until it seemed to possess her.

At that moment the door opened and Frivolo came in. He was frightened. Doña Alcira saw that at once and it gave her a curious pleasure to see him sidling towards her, his mouth hanging open, his eyes darting nervously from side to side.

'Frivolo's come. Lady wants Frivolo?' His voice, sometimes deep, sometimes high, was quavering. He had seen the whip in her hand and his fat fingers closed and unclosed.

'Come here!' Doña Alcira commanded.

He came a little nearer to her, eyeing her as an animal eyes its master when it knows it is to be punished and yet must obey his command.

'Why did you not kill when I told you to kill?' Doña Alcira asked.

'Frivolo go,' the dwarf answered. 'Page not in bed. Frivolo stab, but no one there!'

'You let him escape, you silly fool!' Doña Alcira said.

She reached out as she spoke and slashed the dwarf across the face with her whip. He gave a little shriek of pain and put up his hands to his face.

'When I tell you to do a thing, you should do it!' Doña Alcira said. 'If the page was not in bed, why did you not find him?'

'He on the balcony. He jump before I reach him.'

Doña Alcira's eyes narrowed.

'So! It was true!' she said. 'She jumped from balcony to balcony. She was clever! Cleverer than I thought. I must be careful.'

She was talking to herself and then she saw Frivolo peeping at her as if he thought she might be forgetting him. She slashed at him once again.

'You disobeyed my orders,' she said, 'and because of it, I am going to give you a beating you won't forget in a hurry.'

She raised her whip as she spoke and hit him again and again. He began to cry and, falling down, whimpered at her feet; but still she went on, the wiry whip whistling through the air, the blows falling on his contorted, grotesque body, and leaving huge weals across his pale round face.

'Stop, lady! Stop!' he begged piteously, but Doña Alcira hardly seemed to hear him. She was crazed with her own anger, with her own hatred for everything and everybody that stood between her and what she wanted. She was fighting invisible forces which seemed prepared to destroy her. She was fighting Anna Louisa, the *Marqués* and Lord Lynke as well as Ventura. She had to hurt someone for what they had done to her, and Frivolo must suffer.

After a while his cries got less and he seemed almost unconscious when finally she flung her whip away and left him bruised and bleeding on the floor. The whip had caught the corner of his eye and the blood was pouring from it. His lips were beginning to swell and the lobe of one ear was torn.

Doña Alcira flung herself down on the couch. The energy she had put into whipping the helpless dwarf had exhausted her; but, even so, her punishment of him was not at an end. She turned her back to him so that she could not see him and after a while she heard him begin to stir, to move his tortured body, and she decided to hurt him still further.

'You are no longer any use to me,' she said in her hard voice. 'Tomorrow, or perhaps the next day, I shall send you back to the circus.'

She heard him give a little gasp of fear.

'No, lady, no! Frivolo do what you say. Frivolo kill anyone—everyone, but not go back circus.'

'But you are no good. You can't kill! You fail to kill when I tell you. The page got away.'

'Frivolo kill him now, now, now!' Frivolo cried.

'He is no longer there,' Doña Alcira replied. 'He has gone.'

'Frivolo find him!' the dwarf whispered.

'No, no, it is too late,' Doña Alcira replied. 'You can go back to the circus. Perhaps your old master will find a use for you.'

'No! Circus kill Frivolo! They very cruel. Frivolo die!'

Doña Alcira shrugged her shoulders.

'What does it matter to me! You are too stupid to do what I want, to carry out my orders.'

'No, no! Frivolo good. Frivolo do what you say. Frivolo kill quickly, no mistake.'

She could hear the dwarf shuffling along the floor to get

167

nearer to her. He was sobbing in a heart-broken manner. It was salve to her own hurt feelings that she could manage to inflict so much pain on another.

For some time nothing was said and then at last Frivolo pleaded again:

'Please. Frivolo stay ... Frivolo good now. Not go circus.'

'No! You go back to the circus!' Doña Alcira said. 'You are no use to me!'

Again there was silence, and then in a tone which would have been heroic if he had been anything but a grotesque absurdity, Frivolo said:

'Frivolo rather die!'

'What does it matter if you can't kill?' Doña Alcira answered.

'Frivolo can kill!'

'I doubt it!' Doña Alcira said.

She could hear the dwarf breathing heavily as if in agony. She heard him shuffle awkwardly to his feet.

'Frivolo kill!' he said. 'Frivolo not go circus!'

It must have been intuition which made her turn round sharply. He must have been just about to strike, for the dagger was held high above his head. She gave a scream, but even as it left her lips she knew it was too late. He had been in the very act of bringing down the long, pointed knife into her back. Now, instead, it entered her breast.

She felt the sudden pain shoot through her. She felt a sudden surprise that this should be happening. She saw the dwarf's wild, tortured eyes and knew in that split second that she had driven him too far; he was mad—completely and utterly mad—and there was nothing she could do about it.

Slowly, mercifully, the darkness of death and oblivion closed over her tortured thoughts.

13

Lord Lynke spent a wakeful night. As the hours passed, he grew more and more restless until finally he arose from his bed and walked backwards and forwards across the room.

For the first time in his life he was frustrated to a point that was long past anger and irritation, and instead made him merely desperate.

How could he find Ventura? In his mind he went over every possibility—going in search of her; appealing to the King; even returning to San Sebastian.

At times he cursed her because her note had not been more explicit.

I must go away because it is expedient for your sake as well as my own, she had written.

He had never seen her writing before and somehow the delicate, pointed letters made him think of her little pointed face and big blue eyes. How often had he seen those eyes cloud and become misty when he had been unduly harsh with her? How often had he surprised a look of devotion which had fed his vanity until he began to take it for granted? Fool that he had been, idiot and imbecile to take anything on its face value!

He went over and over the times they had met, the talks they had had together, the adventures they had experienced; and he began to see how utterly he had relied on Ventura's companionship, on the way she listend to him, on the manner in which she managed always to be there when he wanted her yet was so self-effacing when he did not.

She was so small, so helpless! And then he thought of the dwarf and swore aloud that he would kill anyone who harmed her.

Up and down the room he paced until the pale glimmer of light between the curtains told him the dawn was breaking. He flung wide the windows and asked the sleeping world where she was. Was she in danger? Had she perhaps become involved in yet another dangerous adventure from which this time she might not emerge victorious?

'Let me find her! Let me find her!' he said aloud to the heavens, and it was the nearest to a prayer that he had come for a very long time.

The difficult thing was that he had not the slightest idea where to look. If Ventura had told Simon she was returning to San Sebastian, it was quite evident, Lord Lynke thought, that that was the last place to which she was likely to go.

Then where else? Was she afraid of Doña Alcira? He thought she must be, and felt suddenly so murderous that his hands clenched and unclenched themselves as if they squeezed a warm, rounded neck and throttled the life from it.

'If she harms Ventura, I will kill her,' Lord Lynke vowed.

Simon brought him his breakfast; but he could not eat, thrusting the rich dishes aside and taking only a glass of light wine to quench his thirst. Simon looked at him anxiously, but forbore to comment. He knew only too well what that dark scowl on his master's forehead foreboded; he knew the signs of anger about the tightness of his lips; and he wisely kept silent.

Lord Lynke was just rising from the breakfast table when there came a knock on the door. Simon went to open it. A flunkey in resplendent uniform handed him a note. Simon carried it across to his master.

Lord Lynke opened it indifferently. He had the idea it was one of the usual Palace invitations to dinner or to view the private theatricals with which the King and Queen were very occupied at the moment.

Then as he glanced at it he became more interested. The letter was signed 'Torre Nueva'. He read the brief lines through more carefully; then turning to the waiting flunkey, he said in Spanish:

'Tell your master I will be pleased to wait upon him in one hour.'

The man bowed and Simon closed the door.

'My clothes immediately!' Lord Lynke commanded.

He walked into the bedchamber and dressed quickly, so preoccupied with his thoughts that he hardly noticed what Simon had put out for him.

What did the Marqués want with him? he wondered. It was obviously a matter of urgency or he would not have written as he did. Could it be something connected with Ventura? Lord Lynke dismissed the thought. No, it was far more likely to be some national matter.

His thoughts turned to Sir Benjamin Keene and he cursed softly. In his anxiety over Ventura he had forgotten the Minister's refusal to accept her story, to believe that the Duc de Montemar and the Count de Montijo were plotting against Gibraltar. It was typical of British obtuseness, Lord Lynke thought, that after having asked for information, they should refuse to believe it when it was given to them.

He glanced in the mirror as he tied his cravat. There were dark lines of sleeplessness under his eyes and his expression was unusually grim.

'I am ready,' he said briefly to Simon. 'Have you ordered the coach?'

'It will be at the door, m'lord.'

Lord Lynke buckled on his sword and picked up his hat.

'I do not know what time I shall be back,' he said. 'and if anyone inquires, I can make no engagements for this evening or tonight.'

'Very good, m'lord.'

Vaguely at the back of Lord Lynke's mind was the idea that when he had seen the *Marqués,* he might go in search of Ventura. Where or how he had no idea; he only knew that somehow, by supernatural means if necessary, he must find her.

The carriage carried him through the park until they reached the narrow streets of Madrid. The *Marqués* was living in the Chancellery, an imposing building outside which were sentries in their brilliant red and blue uniforms.

Lord Lynke was evidently expected, because he was bowed to the doorway and taken down the corridors away from the official audience chambers to the *Marqués's* own private apartments.

Lord Lynke found his host in a small but charming room overlooking the garden. The French windows were open and through them there was a vista of spring flowers and orange blossom. As Lord Lynke was announced, the *Marqués* rose from his desk where he had been writing.

'It was good of you to come so quickly, my lord,' he said in excellent English.

'I gathered from Your Excellency's note that the matter was urgent,' Lord Lynke replied.

'It is,' the *Marqués* said. 'I have, unfortunately, bad news. It is my painful duty to inform you that Doña Alcira is dead.'

'Dead!' Lord Lynke ejaculated. 'I had expected many things but not that!'

'Yes, dead!' the *Marqués* repeated. 'She was murdered last night by her dwarf. The servants did not find her until early this morning. When they did so, they communicated with me immediately.'

'It seems incredible,' Lord Lynke said. 'Is there any reason why the dwarf should have committed such a crime?'

'That we shall never know,' the *Marqués* replied. 'The poor little beast—one can hardly think of him in any other terms—threw himself off the roof of the house. Those who saw him do it said that he was quite mad. The crime must have turned his brain.'

'I must thank Your Excellency for telling me this,' Lord Lynke said.

'I was executor to Doña Alcira's father,' the *Marqués* explained. 'That is why I am so intimately involved with what has happened. And now there is something else I must relate to you.'

Lord Lynke raised his eyebrows.

'Not another crime I hope,' he murmured.

He was finding it hard to credit that Doña Alcira was really dead. At the same time he could not help feeling slightly relieved. This would solve his own difficulties, his own conviction that under no circumstances, however advantageous either to England or himself, would he consent to be her husband.

'No, not another crime,' the *Marqués* said. 'Won't you sit down?'

He indicated a chair and seated himself on the high-backed sofa which faced it.

Lord Lynke settled himself comfortably. He supposed that he should show some expression of his distress, but it went against the grain for him to act anything he did not feel. And so he said nothing, merely waiting attentively for what the *Marqués* should choose to tell him. The Spaniard seemed to choose his words with difficulty.

'You came here, my lord,' he said at length, 'to win Doña Alcira because it was the wish of our Queen and your Government for closer association between our countries. Doña Alcira was chosen by Her Majesty because she was one of the richest women in Spain, having inherited, as you know, the vast estates and great wealth of her father, the Duc of Carcastillo.'

'Yes, of course,' Lord Lynke said a little abruptly. He felt all this was slightly embarrassing.

'The truth was,' the *Marqués* went on, 'that before Doña Alcira died she had learned that she was not, in fact, the heiress that we all believed.'

Lord Lynke raised his eyebrows.

'The estates are bankrupt?' he questioned.

'No, no! Nothing of the sort,' the *Marqués* replied. 'The estates are intact and so is the great bulk of the Carcastillo fortune. But Doña Alcira should not have inherited them, for the simple reason that the child of her elder sister, Doña Anna Louisa, is alive.'

'This must have been a shock to Doña Alcira,' Lord Lynke said.

'A very considerable shock,' the *Marqués* agreed. 'The point I am trying to make, my lord, is that although Doña Alcira is dead there is not need for the Queen's plans to go awry. The heir to the Carcastillo fortune is of marriageable age. She is, too, a very charming and a very beautiful young woman. What I am suggesting to you is that you merely transfer your affections.'

Lord Lynke rose to his feet and walked across to the window. For a moment he stood with his back to the *Marqués*, looking out on the sunlit garden, and then he said abruptly:

'No! I am sorry, it cannot be done.'

It was the *Marqués* turn to look surprised.

'You mean that because your affections were engaged by Doña Alcira . . . he began.

'My affections are engaged, but not by Doña Alcira,' Lord Lynke replied. But that is of no interest to you, Your Excellency. My answer to the proposition is, no. I was sent out to achieve a certain object. It is not my fault that Doña Alcira is no longer with us so that I can press my suit. To be honest, I had no desire to do so; and had she continued to be alive I doubt if I could have gone through with the marriage. As it is, I now consider myself free—free to love and marry where I wish.'

'I respect your feelings, my lord,' the *Marqués* said.

It was obvious that the interview was at an end. Lord

Lynke bowed. But even as he did so there came an interruption. The door opened and a light voice asked:

'Is Your Excellency alone? Because I would speak with you.'

Lord Lynke turned abruptly and then stood very still. A girl was standing in the doorway. She was wearing a dress of cream satin caught with tiny velvet bows of strawberry pink. There was one string of perfect pearls around her neck. Otherwise she was without jewellery.

But there was no need for ornamentation. Her beauty was arresting. Her hair, swept up in the latest fashion on top of her tiny head, fell in ringlets on either side of her face. It was a tiny, pointed face and her eyes were very big and very blue.

She had seen Lord Lynke and the sight of him seemed to have turned her to stone. She was standing still, hardly breathing; and then, when it seemed that the silence between them was endless, the *Marqués* broke it.

'I am not alone, Ventura,' he said. 'But that is no reason why you should not come in. I want you to meet Lord Lynke, who is from England. May I present Lord Lynke—Doña Ventura, granddaughter of my dear friend the Duc de Carcastillo.'

As if he were pulled by strings, Lord Lynke managed to bow, and then Ventura sank in a deep curtsy to the floor.

'Lord Lynke was just about to leave us,' the *Marqués* went on. 'But perhaps you can persuade him to stay a little longer and partake of some wine and refreshments.' He glanced from one to the other and added with a little twist of his lips: 'Or perhaps a walk in the garden would be more to his lordship's taste.'

'Yes, the garden,' Ventura said in a strangled voice. 'Would you not honour it with a visit, my lord?'

'Yes, yes, of course! I shall be charmed,' Lord Lynke said.

Ventura walked through the french window, and, stiffly, Lord Lynke followed her. The *Marqués* watched them go; and then, smiling a little to himself, he went back to his desk.

Ventura and Lord Lynke walked until they were out of hearing of the house. Then almost savagely he turned on her.

'How could you leave me like that? Did you not realise I should be worried, distraught for fear that something should have happened to you?'

'It was best that I should do it as I did,' Ventura answered in a low voice. 'I was afraid that you might come here or to my ... my grandmother's house in search of ... your page; that you might have revealed how I had managed to travel to Madrid. It would have done you immeasurable harm.'

'To hell with that!' Lord Lynke ejaculated. 'You had me nearly crazed with worry about you.'

'Were you? Were you really?' Ventura asked.

'Of course I was, you little idiot,' he replied. And then suddenly cut himself short. 'Dammit! But I suppose I should not speak to you like that. You are a lady now, and from what the *Marqués* has been telling me a lady of some considerable importance.'

'He told you that Doña Alcira is dead?' Ventura asked in a low voice.

'Yes, he told me,' Lord Lynke answered. 'And suggested that I should marry the new heir to the Carcastillo fortune. I refused.'

'You refused!'

There was a sudden note of joy in Ventura's voice.

'Yes, I refused,' Lord Lynke said savagely. 'What do they think I am? A mountebank, to be switched from one woman to another? Besides, I had already decided that I would not marry Doña Alcira.'

'You had decided that?'

Ventura stared at him with wide eyes.

They had reached a part of the garden that was out of sight of the house. There was a small goldfish pool enclosed by flowering shrubs, and a seat on which two people could sit and watch the fountain which played in the centre of the pool. As if they both felt their legs could carry them no farther, they sat down.

'So you did not mean to marry Doña Alcira after all,' Ventura said.

'Was it likely after she had tried to murder you?' Lord Lynke asked.

'All the same, it would have been hard for you to escape her,' Ventura suggested practically.

'That is true,' Lord Lynke said. 'I suppose it is a mercy that she was killed by the dwarf. Yet I cannot pretend to be sorry about it.'

'Nor I.' Ventura shivered. 'At the same time, it was a terrible death.'

Lord Lynke looked at her downcast face.

175

'How did you discover who you are?' he asked.

'I found a picture of my mother in the hidden chamber where I listened to the Duc de Montemar and the others plotting to capture Gibraltar.'

'Why did you not tell me?'

'Because, even though I had seen the picture and visited my grandmother upstairs,' Ventura replied, 'I realised that I could not prove it. It was only when I got back to the Palace that I found the letters which my mother had spoken about before she died.

'Where were they?'

'There was a secret drawer in the jewel-case. I had never parted with it because it was the one thing she treasured, the one thing she begged me always to keep. It was fortunate that I obeyed her.'

'Why did you not bring those letters to me?' Lord Lynke asked.

'Because I realised that, being who I am, having come to Madrid as I did under your protection, it would discredit you in every way were the truth to be discovered.'

Lord Lynke shrugged his shoulders.

'You may think it of no consequence,' Ventura said quickly. 'But think what they would say. They would have said that you actually brought the new heir to the Carcastillo home with you; that you made sure of her by contriving that she was in your employment in disguise.'

'I never thought of that,' Lord Lynke admitted.

'I did,' Ventura said simply.

'I cannot really credit it,' he said. 'That you, who have been with me so long, are really of such import.'

'I cannot quite believe it myself,' Ventura said a little wistfully. 'The *Marqués* made me stay here in his house last night. He gave me clothes and these pearls, and this afternoon I was to be presented to the King and Queen. Now that Doña Alcira is dead I think perhaps it would be gracious to wait until after the funeral.'

'Then, of course, you will take over your grandparents' palace, Lord Lynke said reflectively. 'Will you like living there alone?'

'My grandmother is there,' Ventura answered.

He bent towards her.

'Ventura! I discovered something last night,' he said.

'What was that?' she inquired.

'I discovered how much you mean to me; what the loss of you could mean in my life.'

Her whole face seemed to light up. Her eyes were shining as she said:

'You missed me, really missed me?'

'More than I could have believed it possible,' Lord Lynke said. 'I felt desperate, I did not know what to do. I thought you might be in danger and yet I was powerless to help you.'

'I thought perhaps you were sleeping peacefully, glad ... to be rid of someone who had been so much ... trouble,' Ventura said ingenuously.

Lord Lynke put out his hand and laid it on hers.

'I have never felt like this about a woman before,' he said, and his voice was full of sincerity. 'I have never wanted to protect someone, to look after her, to be with her not only at chosen times, but always, all day and every day, as we have been together this past month.'

Ventura gave a little sigh that was half a sob.

'Oh, but I am glad ... so glad, you feel like ... that,' she answered. 'That is what I have felt, too; and I was afraid ... terribly afraid that I was merely ... a nuisance to you.'

'You could never be that,' Lord Lynke replied. 'Ventura, I never thought to say this, but ... will you marry me?'

To his astonishment the delight went from her face. She stared at him, for a moment blindly, then turned her head away.

'No,' she whispered. 'No, do not say that.'

'Say what?' he asked bewildered.

'Do not ask me to ... marry you.'

'But, why not? 'Tis obvious, isn't it, if we love each other?'

'No! No! No!' Ventura replied. 'No, it is not obvious. You do not understand. You are asking me because I am who I am, because I have inherited Doña Alcira's place, because ...'

She had sprung to her feet, but now she stopped suddenly because Lord Lynke had put his hands on her shoulders and swung her round to face him.

'Stop!' he commanded. 'I am not asking you because of any of those things. I am asking you to marry me because I love you, because I want to be with you. I have only just discovered this and it is rather new to me, and I suppose I

177

am not expressing myself as well as I might. But I love you, Ventura. I am sure of it now. I love you.'

'If you knew what it meant to hear you say that ... but I cannot ... marry you.'

'Why not?'

'Because I cannot ... because I will not.... There are ... reasons, but those I cannot ... tell you.'

'Secrets! Secrets! Do you Spaniards ever think of anything but secrets and intrigue?' Lord Lynke asked savagely. He shook her in exasperation. Then pride made him drop his arms. 'Very well then,' he said stiffly, 'if you do not want me, I will not force myself upon you.'

He turned away irritably. Ventura put out her hand to stop him, opened her lips to speak, and then checked herself. Without saying a word she watched him walk back along the path down which they had come. His shoulders were very square, his whole back was eloquent of his anger.

And then, when at last he was out of sight, she sank down on the seat and started to cry, the tears very slowly running down her face and dripping through her fingers.

Lord Lynke walked through the house without seeing anyone of importance. He stepped into his coach and directed the coachman to drive to the British Embassy. He found Sir Benjamin Keene surrounded by papers and obviously none too pleased to see him.

'I am busy this morning, my lord,' he said a little coldly. 'You will forgive me if I ask you to be as brief as possible in anything you have to say.'

'I will be brief all right,' Lord Lynke replied. 'I am returning to England forthwith.'

Sir Benjamin's eyebrows went up.

'I have heard of Doña Alcira's death,' he said. 'It would, of course, be only courteous for you to attend the funeral.

'My reasons for leaving are of more importance,' Lord Lynke replied briefly.

'I have also heard,' Sir Benjamin went on, 'that Doña Anna Louisa's daughter is a very beautiful girl. I had thought perhaps ...'

'You need not waste your time or mine in saying it,' Lord Lynke said. 'As I have told you, I am returning to England.'

'Do you imagine that your uncle will be pleased to see you?' Sir Benjamin inquired.

'My uncle can go to the devil,' Lord Lynke retorted. 'He sent me here to marry a certain lady. She is dead. There is nothing more I can do. Besides, I consider it my duty to inform him of what was overheard in Doña Alcira's house. If you will not believe that Montemar and Montijo are ready to attack Gibraltar, perhaps he will.'

'Do not be quite so hasty,' Sir Benjamin pleaded in a conciliatory tone. 'I did not say I did not believe your story, I merely asked for proof. You would not bring me the boy who had overheard the conversation. Where is he, by the way?'

'He has had to leave Madrid unexpectedly,' Lord Lynke said a little uncomfortably.

'How unfortunate,' Sir Benjamin said.

'Very,' Lord Lynke replied. 'So in the circumstances you must take my word for it.'

'That I have done,' Sir Benjamin agreed. 'At the same time I have sought corroboration. I am waiting this very moment for a report from someone in the household of the *Duc*. One of my best and most trustworthy men is interviewing him. He should be here at any minute.'

'Very interesting I am sure, Lord Lynke said. 'But I am no longer concerned. I shall return to London. I shall inform my uncle of what is afoot, and doubtless he will receive your report in due course.'

'You are behaving in a very high-handed manner, my lord,' Sir Benjamin remarked.

'I feel that the time for talking pretty nothings is past,' Lord Lynke replied. 'If England is to act in this matter, she will have to act soon, otherwise it will be too late and the Spanish fleet will already be in the Mediterranean.'

Sir Benjamin tapped with his finger on the desk.

'I wish you had brought me the boy,' he reflected. 'I cannot understand your reluctance to do so.'

'As I have already told you, the boy has left Madrid. It is unfortunate, but I assure you that what he told me and what I have related to you is absolutely and completely true.'

'Will you wait for five minutes, my lord?' Sir Benjamin asked suddeny. 'My man should have returned by now and there may be news from other sources.'

'Do not make it any longer then,' Lord Lynke said. 'I have a great desire to be gone.'

Sir Benjamin left the room. Lord Lynke poured himself a glass of wine from a side-table and then, without drinking, set the glass down violently.

Why had Ventura behaved as she had? he asked himself. Gradually his anger was being replaced by a despondency and a depression such as he had never known before. She had refused to marry him, and yet he could be almost sure that she loved him. There had been that light in her eyes, that sudden quiver of her red lips which was unmistakable.

Was it his fault that she had said no? He realised suddenly that for perhaps the first time in his life he had been gauche and awkward in telling a woman of his love. It was because he felt it so intensely, he thought. It was because she meant so much to him that he could not speak to her in the flowery language the fulsome words of love which he had used to other women.

He loved her and it was something past words, something so deep, so fundamentally a part of him that he could hardly explain it in anything but action.

'I should have kissed her,' he thought, and felt himself thrill suddenly at the thought. He remembered how she had clung to him that night when she had fled from the dwarf and he had found that she was a girl and not a boy. He remembered the feeling of her soft body in his arms, the fragrance of her hair, the trembling of her hands as she clutched him.

'Dammit all! Why am I running away?' Lord Lynke asked himself aloud.

He would go back to her and tell her once again that he loved her whether she was rich or poor, important or of no consequence whatever. That must have been the real reason why she had refused him—because she thought that he wanted her money and her position; because, however much he had said to the contrary, she believed that he had merely turned his affections from Doña Alcira to the new heir to the Carcastillo fortunes.

'I will convince her,' Lord Lynke vowed, and he knew in that moment that nothing else mattered.

He had thought himself in love before, but this was something different. This was a glory and a joy such as he had never known. It was, too, an ache, an anxiety which made him suddenly afraid that after all he might fail to convince Ventura.

'She loves me. I am sure she loves me,' he tried to

reassure himself. And yet it was difficult to be convinced, for he remembered that she had run away from him without apparently another thought. She had not told him of her plans, she had just disappeared. Under those circumstances could she be as much in love as he wished to believe?

He found himself striding up and down the room as he had done in the night. He was so restless that he felt it would be impossible for him to sit down and relax. All he could see, all he could think of was Ventura's little face and big blue eyes.

He thought then that he must have loved her for a long time—perhaps from that very first moment when she had run to him for help and he had casually asked her to fill the place of Roderick Lane.

How strange life was! A chance meeting in the street of a Spanish port and he had found the one woman to whom he was ready to devote the whole of his life, for whom he would give up everything, even his hope of Heaven.

'I love her! I love her!'

He said the words aloud and went on walking the room. What a long time Sir Benjamin was. He thought of going away and not waiting for him; and then, even as his impatience seemed to get the upper hand, the door opened and the Minister returned.

His face looked grave. He shut the door carefully behind him and turned to Lord Lynke.

'I have news,' he said briefly.

'I was right?' Lord Lynke inquired.

'I think so,' Sir Benjamin replied. 'The man we have in the *Duc's* palace had heard very little, but it is enough to corroborate in some details your own story. But there is worse than that.'

'What is it?' Lord Lynke inquired.

'Our couriers!' Sir Benjamin groaned. 'The last one is dead—murdered by bandits so they say—just before he reached the frontier. The diplomatic bag has, of course, vanished. The other one, who was sent a few days earlier, is under suspicion. We think that he is in league with the Spanish authorities and is well paid for any information he can give them.'

'This is serious,' Lord Lynke said.

'Very serious,' Sir Benjamin answered. 'I am not suggesting for one moment that it is the Prime Minister who is instigating these crimes. But the Duc de Montemar will stop at nothing to get his own ends. It is undoubtedly his men who are interfering with my dispatches. The question is what am I to do about it?'

'Five minutes ago I could have given you the answer to that question,' Lord Lynke answered. 'I had told you that I was returning to England. I could have taken your reports with me. Now I have changed my mind.'

'You are staying?' Sir Benjamin asked.

'Shall I say that I am going to see Doña Ventura again?'

Sir Benjamin raised his eyebrows.

'Doña Ventura?' he questioned. 'Oh, the young woman who has inherited the Carcastillo fortune. I was not certain of her name. So you intend to marry her?'

Lord Lynke shook his head.

'No,' he answered. 'But I intend to beg her to marry me.'

Sir Benjamin did not smile, instead he said in a worried tone:

'But, instead, I would ask you to do something for me. I believe it is imperative that London should know what is happening here. I dare not put into writing what you have told me. It would be too dangerous. You must go yourself. You must tell Lord Liverpool the situation as you know it. If he considers that you have deserted your post or not carried out your instructions, I will take full responsibility.'

'I have told you that I wish to remain here,' Lord Lynke said.

Sir Benjamin looked him straight in the eye.

'The choice, my lord,' he said quietly, 'is not of your wishes or of mine, but of what is best for our country.'

Lord Lynke looked at him and almost instinctively he stiffened his shoulders.

'I will leave tonight.'

Sir Benjamin held out his hand.

'Thank you, my lord. And all other information that I can obtain will be in your hands by eight o'clock.'

Lord Lynke turned towards the door.

'Until then my time is my own,' he said.

He ran down the steps of the British Embassy and got into the carriage. He ordered it to return to the Chancellery and sat forward impatiently as the horses travelled slowly because of the crowded streets. When they reached the Ministry he jumped out before the footman could let down the steps and hurried to the front door.

'I wish to speak with Doña Ventura immediately,' he said.

The major-domo looked surprised at his impatience. He led him down the corridors he had travelled before to the private apartments.

'If you will wait here, my lord,' he said, opening the door of a room, 'I will find out if Doña Ventura will receive you.'

Lord Lynke walked into the room. For a moment he thought it was empty; then, with a sudden stab at his heart which made him feel as if he had been struck, he saw Ventura at the far end of the room.

She was standing in front of a chair as if she had suddenly sprung from it, her head was thrown back and her arms were round the neck of a young man who was holding her close against him and speaking softly against her cheek.

14

Lord Lynke stood transfixed, staring at Ventura and the unknown man. He felt as if a sudden darkness encompassed him while his whole world sank into a bottomless pit such as, until this moment, he had never believed.

He saw, in the flash of a second, as a drowning man sees his whole life pass before him, that the only thing of any importance in all he had ever attempted or done was his love for Ventura.

The love that he felt for her was, indeed, so overpowering that the emotions and passions he had felt in the past sank into their right perspective and he knew the utter anguish and loneliness of a man who has given his whole heart to a woman only to find that she does not want it.

Nothing he had ever experienced, nothing he had ever felt was such misery as this. To see her little face upturned towards another man, to see her arms around his neck, to know by the tiptoed eagerness of her that she was alight with happiness was sheer unmitigated torture.

Lord Lynke turned his eyes away. He could bear it no longer. Blindly he sought the door. He wanted only to escape. But as he turned the handle Ventura's voice arrested him.

'My lord! Oh, my lord! I did not see you.'

She was running across the room to him and with an agony that was almost a physical pain he watched her come. He had never believed before that any woman could be so lovely, so alive, so vivid in everything she said and did.

Ventura reached his side a little breathlessly.

'I am glad ... very glad you are ... here, my lord. I would have sent a note to you in a few minutes.'

Lord Lynke said nothing. Tense with his hurt, he watched the young man coming down the room towards them and hated him with a hatred so violent that he felt it hard to behave with dignity.

Ventura put her hand on his arm.

'Everything is all right now,' she said excitedly. 'I had not believed it was possible, but ... he is ... back. Yes ... he has come ... back.'

'So I perceive,' Lord Lynke said drily. 'And now, if you will permit me, I will make my farewell.'

He was about to bow when Ventura stopped him.

'You do not ... understand,' she said with a little catch in her breath. 'This is Alastair. We thought he was dead, but he is ... alive.'

'Very much so,' the young man said from behind her.

Lord Lynke looked closely at the stranger, then his eyes widened and he stared. Red hair and blue eyes. It was impossible! Quite impossible!

Ventura was watching him and now there was laughter on her lips.

'I told you that you do not understand, my lord. Will you permit me to present my brother, the Earl of Kinbrace?'

'Your brother!'

Lord Lynke heard himself repeat the words in a voice that seemed to belong to a stranger.

'My twin brother,' Ventura said. 'I thought he must be dead. Mamma and I had almost given up hope of Alastair and yet here he is alive and well.'

Lord Lynke sighed.

'Is there no end to your secrets?' he asked. 'Why did you not tell me?'

'For so many reasons,' Ventura answered. 'But mostly because, as I have already told you, I thought he must be dead. And Mamma ...' She stopped and looked towards her brother. 'Mamma had warned me so often, Alastair, not to speak of you while you were away.'

'She was wise,' her brother said. 'But now I suppose it will be hard to prove my identity.'

'There will be no difficulty in that,' Lord Lynke interposed. 'Anyone who had seen your father has only to look at you. You are, indeed, exactly like him.'

He smiled at the young man, feeling suddenly lighthearted with the happiness which only a few moments before he thought he had lost for ever.

'Tell us what happened,' Ventura begged her brother.

'It is a very long story,' Alastair Kinbrace replied. 'But I'll try to put it briefly. When I left you all in San Sebastian, I thought I was taking ship for England.'

'And didn't you?' Ventura questioned. She turned towards Lord Lynke. 'My father sent Alastair to England so that he might petition His Majesty the King to restore to him the castle and estates that had been forfeited when my father was exiled. I think my father knew that he had not *long to live.*'

'He was sure of it,' Alastair said quietly. 'That was why he sent me to England and also why he told me before I left who our mother was when he married her.'

'So you knew,' Ventura cried.

'Yes, I knew,' Alastair replied.

'But what happened in England?' Ventura asked.

'Well, to begin with, I did not get there,' Alastair answered. 'When we had sailed, the captain of the ship told us he had orders to proceed at once to the West Indies.'

'How terrible!' Ventura exclaimed. 'And there was nothing you could do about it?'

'No, there was nothing I could do,' Alastair replied, 'and to be truthful I rather enjoyed the voyage. It was an interesting experience to see the world. But my arrival in England was delayed for nearly two years.'

'Dear Alastair! And we wondered why we never heard, why you did not return.'

'I could not communicate with you although I often inquired amongst the ships in Panama and Havana whether there was one returning to San Sebastian. Once I missed a cargo boat by only a day. But otherwise there was no opportunity of telling you where I was.'

'Mamma worried,' Ventura said quietly.

'I was afraid she would,' Alastair said. 'And I tried by every possible means to find my way to England. Finally, after a series of adventures which I will tell you later, I managed to ship aboard an English privateer. They, of course, had no idea that I had any connexion with the Spaniards; and it was, indeed, only after we had taken a number of prisoners that I admitted to speaking the language.'

'Alastair! But was it not exceedingly dangerous?' Ventura asked.

'It was, uncomfortably so, at times, but the fighting did not worry me,' Alastair replied. 'Anyway, we eventually reached England with a cargo full of Spanish loot in which every member of the crew had his share. I was grateful for that, for it enabled me to get to London.'

'And you saw the King?'

'Yes, after hanging about Whitehall for nearly two months I was granted an audience with His Majesty.'

'And what happened?'

Ventura could hardly say the words.

'Our lands are restored!' Alastair cried triumphantly. 'Father would not have been allowed to return to England. But you and I, as English citizens, can go there whenever we wish.'

'How wonderful, Alastair, how wonderful!'

Ventura gave a sigh of ecstasy and turned toward Lord Lynke.

'Now do you understand?' she asked.

'I am beginning to,' he answered. 'Tell me, Kinbrace, how did you find out what had happened to your sister?'

'When I arrived in San Sebastian,' Alastair answered, 'I went at once to the house where I had left my family. The new occupants were full of news as to what had happened—how my father had died, my mother and sister had moved into one room in the town and how, after my mother's accident, my sister had disappeared.

'At first I was horrified, wondering how I could begin to look for her. But soon someone suggested that Señor Padilla might know something about her. They said it with a wink, a little nudge in the ribs, and after I had heard Señor Padilla's story I guessed that your disguise, Ventura, had not been as effective as you imagined.'

'I was quite convinced that nobody knew,' Ventura said sadly.

'In Spain everybody knows everything,' her brother smiled.

'So you went to Señor Padilla and he told you where I had gone,' Ventura prompted.

'He told me that you had set off for Madrid with an Englishman, disguised as his page. I thought then, of course, that you must have learned our mother's secret and were trying to get in touch with our grandparents.'

'I knew nothing of that until after we had been here some time when quite by chance I dropped Mamma's jewel-box,' Ventura said. 'Then the secret drawer opened and two letters fell out. One for me—the other for the *Marqués*.'

'And did you then tell the *Marqués* about your brother?' Lord Lynke inquired.

Ventura shook her head.

'In her letter to me Mamma said she was certain that Alastair was dead and therefore, knowing the difficulties of Spanish inheritance, she had made no mention of him in the letter I was to present to the *Marqués*. But in my letter, Alastair, she sent you many messages.'

As she spoke Ventura ran across the room and picked up a little reticule which lay beside the chair on which she had been sitting before her brother had entered the room.

'It is here,' she said. 'Since I found the letters, I have carried mine everywhere with me for fear the servants . . . or anyone else . . . should be prying.'

She saw her brother's surprised face and said:

'Do not look so astonished. If you knew what Lord Lynke and I have suffered since we have been in Madrid, you would understand why I find it difficult to trust . . . anybody.'

Alastair took the letter from her.

'I'll read this later,' he said. 'I suppose now I had better introduce myself to the *Marqués*.'

'Have you not yet seen him?' Lord Lynke inquired.

Alastair shook his head.

'I only arrived in this house a few moments before you came in,' he replied. 'I got to Madrid last night and I thought it wise, before I called on my grandparents, to find out if Ventura was really there. I anticipated that she had used you, my lord, merely as a convenience to enable her to reach the capital.'

'That is something Ventura must answer,' Lord Lynke said quietly, but with a question in his voice.

'No, no,' Ventura said quickly. 'It is not true. I liked being your page. I was proud to serve you. There were only a few moments when I was afraid. That time in the inn and when the dwarf came to my bedchamber. For the rest it was very exciting and I was happy.'

'Were you really?' Lord Lynke asked in a low voice.

She looked up at him, and then her eyes fell before him. Quite oblivious, Alastair went on:

'So I made a few inquiries and found out that Doña Alcira was dead, but that a young lady calling herself Lady Ventura Stuart was staying with the Marqués de Torre Nueva. Apparently the whole of Madrid already knew who she was and the Doña Alcira had died just in time to save herself from having to relinquish the Carcastillo fortunes.'

'But now they are all yours,' Ventura said.

'I have prepared myself for going back to Scotland,' Alastair replied. 'Now I am not certain what I should do.'

'You should make the best of both worlds,' Lord Lynke advised him. 'And if I have any knowledge of what has happened to your Scottish estates after having been confiscated nearly twenty years ago, you will find that you will need all the wealth of Spain to put them in order again!'

Alastair laughed. 'That, indeed, seems a perfect solution,' he said. 'What do you say, Ventura, to spending six months of the year in Spain and six months in Scotland?'

'It sounds ... delightful,' Ventura answered hesitatingly.

'Then I had best go and stake my claim,' Alastair said. He looked down at the letter in his hand, then bent forward to kiss his sister on the cheek. 'I am tremendously glad to see you again, Ventura.' he said. 'It has been lonely wandering the world without a family.'

'And here you will have not only me,' Ventura answered, 'but Grandmamma as well. She is a very sweet person and when you have talked with the *Marqués* we will go and see her together.'

'I should like that,' Alastair answered.

He bowed to Lord Lynke.

'I must thank you, my lord, for looking after my sister. If it had not been for you, she might never have been able to reach Madrid.'

'If I had known who she was, I might have been able to

do more,' Lord Lynke answered. 'As it is, it seems that I only forestalled you by a few weeks.'

'Nevertheless I am grateful,' Alastair smiled.

He bowed and went from the room, leaving a sudden silence behind him. Lord Lynke watched Ventura. It seemed as if she was determined not to meet his eyes. Talking a little quickly as if she was agitated, she said:

'He looks well, doesn't he? 'Tis hard for anyone to believe that we are twins. We are certainly not identical in any way. Alastair is exactly like my father, while I am like my mother, save for my eyes.'

'Yet being twins, you would be unhappy without him?' Lord Lynke asked.

'I am certainly happy to be with him,' Ventura answered. 'He had been away for so long that I had given him up for lost.'

'And now you will rule this little kingdom together,' Lord Lynke ruminated. 'Six months in Spain and six months in Scotland, I think your brother said.'

'It sounds an excellent idea,' Ventura agreed. 'But then, of course, Alastair may take a wife. And I might also . . .'

She stopped suddenly. It was as if lightheartedly she had stumbled into the very subject that she wished to avoid.

'And you also might get married was what you were about to say,' Lord Lynke prompted.

'I did . . . not . . . say that,' Ventura stammered.

He went a little nearer to her.

'Are there any more secrets?'

She shook her head.

'Then why are you playing with me?' he asked. 'Surely you know what I want to say.'

'I do not think you understand,' she answered. 'In Spanish law the eldest child inherits everything. Any provision for the other members of the family is made by the head of the family. The youngest members are entitled to nothing—what they possess depends entirely on their father or brother. I . . . I am penniless.'

'Do you think that matters to me?' Lord Lynke asked.

'I think it will matter very much to those who sent you here, my lord.'

'I am not concerned with their feelings,' Lord Lynke answered. 'Ventura, I love you!'

She stood very still. And then, as she did not move or speak, his arms went round her. He felt her tremble as she had trembled that night when she had fled to him for protection and lifting her in his arms he had discovered that he held not a boy but a woman.

At the thought of it he felt his breath come quickly and his hold on her tightened.

'I love you,' he said. 'I love you so much that I cannot live without you. Without you I do not want to go on living. Ventura, listen to me for a moment.'

She lifted her head towards him and he saw a sudden light in her eyes and her lips were parted.

'I want you to marry me,' Lord Lynke cried, 'as I have never wanted anything in my life before.'

He held her closer still; then suddenly, with a little sound that was half a groan, he sought her lips. For a moment he thought only how soft and sweet they were, and then his self-control broke. He kissed her wildly, passionately, possessively; and he knew with a thrill of joy that was beyond words that she did not resist him.

'I love you! Ventura, Ventura, how can I let you go?' he asked.

He held her closer and closer, murmuring wildly his love, his need, until he felt her stir against him.

Instantly she was free. He stepped back, ashamed of his passion, blaming himself for his lack of self-control.

'Forgive me, Ventura,' he said humbly. 'I love you too much to behave sanely, or, indeed, wisely.'

He saw then her face and almost gasped at the glory of it.

'Then you do ... love me—really love me?' she stammered.

'What more can I say?' he replied. 'Give me only a chance to prove it. Tell me that you will marry me and to hell with everybody and everything.

She put out her hands towards him and suddenly there were tears in her blue eyes.

'I can hardly ... believe it,' she said. 'I have longed above all things to hear you say that and to know that you ... meant it. Are you sure ... quite sure? Have you remembered that ... that it is Alastair ... and not ... I ... who owns the Carcastillo estates?'

'Damn the Carcastillo estates!' Lord Lynke said impatiently. 'If you want to know the truth, I am glad to be rid of them. I am homesick for England, for the green fields of Hatharton, for grey skies and mud in St. James's Street.'

He stopped suddenly.

'By God! I have it,' he exclaimed.

Ventura looked at him, her eyes wide.

'Have what?' she inquired.

'An idea,' Lord Lynke said tersely. 'Listen, Ventura, I have got to start for England this evening. I came here really to say good-bye.'

'You are going ... away?' she asked, the light vanishing from her little face, her eyes darkening.

'I have seen Keene again,' he told her. 'I almost persuaded him to believe our story—your story. He was about to send it to England by courier when he learned that the last two diplomatic bags have been tampered with Do you know what that means?'

Ventura shook her head.

'It means,' Lord Lynke said, 'that the Duc de Montemar, or maybe the Count, is determined that England shall not learn what is afoot. There is only one thing to be done. I must carry the news myself.'

'You?' Ventura ejaculated.

'Who else?' he inquired.

'But it would be dangerous,' Ventura cried. 'Far more dangerous than it was when we came here. Supposing they lie in wait for you? Supposing they try to murder you, as Don Carlos tried, and this time I shall not be there to save you?'

'But you will be,' Lord Lynke told her.

'But ... how?'

'You are coming with me,' he said masterfully. 'We are going to be married now, this afternoon. There is a private chapel in the Carcastillo Palace. There is also, I presume, a family chaplain. He must marry us immediately and you will come back to England with me as my wife.'

'But, I ... I cannot. I ... I mean it is ... too soon. I cannot ... think,' Ventura faltered.

Lord Lynke checked her by putting a hand under her chin and lifting her face up to his.

'I know, I know,' he said. 'Convention, tradition, people, gossip! Do any of them matter except us?'

She quivered for a moment beneath his touch and then was still. Her eyes looked up to his—eyes full of trust and love.

'No, they do not matter,' she whispered. 'I will ... come with ... you.'

He looked at her for a long moment and then he

dropped down on one knee before her and taking her hand in his, kissed it gently and tenderly.

'I will make you happy, Ventura,' he vowed, 'my most beloved, my last love.'

Just for a moment he knelt there, and then he rose again to his feet and swept her into his arms. They clung to each other. Lord Lynke looked down at the little pointed face raised to his.

'This is the biggest and sweetest adventure of all, my little love,' he said; and then his lips held her utterly captive.